Forever
at
Conwenna Cove

DARCIE BOLEYN

CANELO

First published in the United Kingdom in 2018 by Canelo

This edition published in the United Kingdom in 2019 by

Canelo Digital Publishing Limited
57 Shepherds Lane
Beaconsfield, Bucks HP9 2DU
United Kingdom

A CIP catalogue record for this book is available from the British Library.

Print ISBN 978 1 78863 415 1
Ebook ISBN 978 1 78863 050 4

Look for more great books at www.canelo.co

Printed and bound in Great Britain by Clays Ltd, Elcograf S.p.A.

Prologue

Zoe Russell's heart pounded as she waited. She was nervous, but she was always nervous in the water, especially when she knew he was watching. The sun was high in the blue sky and the clear water lapped at her surfboard. She pushed away all of her concerns and focused. Waited. Anticipating the perfect wave.

A seagull screeched overhead and her senses pinged, fully alert.

It was coming, the wave she wanted.

She braced herself…

Then she paddled hard through the sea using long, smooth, deep strokes and when the moment was right, she sprang to her feet, everything instinctive now. She'd practised hard for this, wanting to get it right so that he would be proud of her.

The board sliced through the water as she rode the wave, in perfect control of her movements. She was fluid, at one with the water, and joy filled her heart.

The sun was warm on her wet hair, the salt tangy in her nose and on her lips, and she felt as if she was flying. Zoe gained speed, the water sprayed into her face and she laughed as exhilaration consumed her. This was what she lived for; this was what she enjoyed… at least now. She had learnt to love it because of him.

A scream pierced her concentration and she looked up to see a dark object hurtling towards her across the curl of the wave. She tried to duck but it was coming too quickly. She froze, accepting in that moment that someone had bailed and it was too late for her to evade the board's path, and it smashed into her head, knocking her from her own board and into the depths.

One word shot through her head: *Wipeout*.

The full force of the wave she'd been riding ploughed down on top of her as the sea sucked her down. She was simultaneously pushed and pulled, a ragdoll subjected to the power of the ocean. She opened her mouth to scream and it filled with water as her vision clouded with red and her lungs burned.

This was it.

She was gone.

The sea had claimed her.

Chapter 1

Zoe jumped up in bed, gasping and waving her arms around.

It was okay. She was in bed, not in the water. She was alive. It had been a dream.

A nightmare. Another one. One that had made her cheeks wet with tears and left her heart thundering. Even though Zoe could suppress her memories during the day, at night, when she slept, they took advantage of her vulnerability and forced themselves into her mind. It was exhausting, this constant battle with the demons of her past, and she wondered if she would ever be free of it. But that would take some serious emotional progress and Zoe knew, though she hated to admit it, that she was guilty of burying her past rather than dealing with it.

She threw back the duvet and stood on trembling legs, then grabbed her dressing gown and pulled it on over her sweat-soaked cotton pyjamas. There was no point trying to sleep now, so she'd go downstairs and make a herbal tea.

Zoe padded down the stairs, not bothering to turn a light on because she could see perfectly in the moonlight that shone through the frosted glass pane in her front door. The door opened straight into her small lounge where Zoe's eyes were drawn to the sofa. Her stomach plummeted to the wooden floorboards and she bit her bottom lip hard.

The sofa shouldn't be empty. But it was. She was convinced that it was one reason why her nightmares had returned. Forgetting her tea, she went to the sofa and sat down, then pulled the soft fleecy blanket from the back of it and pressed it to her face. It still smelt of her.

'Raven,' she said as her vision blurred. 'My sweet black beauty.'

When she'd moved to Conwenna Cove, after buying the diner over two and a half years ago, she'd overheard a conversation in the Conwenna Cafe about the greyhound sanctuary up at Foxglove Farm. She'd vowed never to visit it for fear that she'd fall in love with one of the rescue hounds, but that hadn't stopped her seeing them just about everywhere she went. Then, one day, about seven months ago, she'd been walking along the cove enjoying the refreshing February air when she'd bumped into the owners of the sanctuary, Neil Burton and his wife, Elena. They'd been walking some of the greyhounds and when Zoe had stopped to talk to them, one dog had stepped forwards and leant against her leg. Before she'd realized what she was doing, she'd stroked the dog's soft black head then asked about her.

Neil had told her that the dog was called Raven. She was an older girl of about twelve years and her owner had been forced to go into a care home, which meant he couldn't look after Raven any more. Neil had agreed to take Raven at the sanctuary, although he'd been concerned as she was elderly and unlikely to find a home. He'd also expressed his concerns that at Raven's time of life, it was likely to be very hard on her as she'd lived in a home for the past eight years.

And like that, Zoe had known that she couldn't see Raven suffer. She'd offered to foster her and that, of course, had become what was known in the greyhound community as a failed foster. Raven had lived with her up until six weeks ago, when Zoe had come down in the morning to find that the greyhound had passed over the rainbow bridge. She still couldn't bear to think of it as dying, and instead, she liked to imagine Raven running around in sunny fields and on sandy beaches, her ebony fur shining and her pink tongue lolling from her mouth as she raced along with her friends.

Zoe hugged Raven's blanket hard. She'd called the local vet, Oli Davenport, that morning six weeks ago and he'd come to collect Raven. Zoe had asked to have Raven's ashes and Oli had brought them to her the following weekend. She'd taken Raven to her favourite field up behind the cottage and released her there early one morning, scattering her around in the pattern in which she liked to run. Even though she'd been older, Raven had loved to run. Not for long but as fast as she could before heading straight back to Zoe and causing her to scream in case the greyhound knocked her off her feet. But somehow, Raven never did; she always swerved just in time. Zoe found that she was smiling at the memory. And as much as she hoped she had given Raven some happiness towards the end of her days, she knew the greyhound had done the same for her.

Raven had been able to help keep the nightmares at bay. Not every night, but most, and when Zoe had a bad dream, she'd been able to hurry down the stairs and bury her face in the dog's soft fur then listen to her reassuring heartbeat. It had been comforting sharing her small cottage with another creature and she felt privileged to have been able to offer Raven a home, even if for such a short while.

But now she missed her canine companion so much it was like a physical pain. There was no way she could consider adopting another dog; the loss was too much to bear and she couldn't stand the thought that if Raven still existed in some form or other, she might feel she'd been replaced in some way.

And, of course, Zoe had been getting used to her solitary state before Raven had entered her life. In fact, she'd been managing quite well – apart from the nightmares – and even embraced solitude as something she could live with. Raven's presence had started to stir something inside her though, and to make her aware that perhaps she didn't really want to spend the rest of her life alone. Zoe spent most days at her diner, chatting to staff and customers, smiling and laughing with them and doing her best to ensure that they had as pleasant an experience at the diner as possible. She was good at being sociable, at playing the hostess, and during the daytime, her smile rarely slipped. But once she left work and headed home the shadows gathered and, as she walked the short distance through Conwenna to her cottage, her own sense of isolation wasn't helped by seeing other couples and families, by knowing that while she would spend the evening alone, they would be eating together, watching TV together and falling asleep together. Zoe had no one around to give her a hug or to bring her a cup of tea in the morning, no one to banish the nightmares by enveloping her in a strong embrace.

She hated admitting to being lonely, but she was. Raven had been a wonderful companion, easing the sense of isolation for a while, but now that she was gone, the empty space in Zoe's heart and in her life seemed even bigger, as if one day it would swallow her whole.

Zoe sighed then lay down on the sofa and wrapped Raven's blanket around her. It was the first Saturday of July and she needed to rest, because it was the busy season in Conwenna Cove and she'd have a hectic day at the diner ahead of her.

She thought she wouldn't sleep another wink, but soon she found her eyes were heavy and she drifted off once more.

–

Nate Bryson placed a large mug of coffee on the table then put a plate of toast next to it.

'Are you sure you wouldn't like anything else?' he asked Jack Adams.

'No, this is great, thanks. I only popped into town to pick up some groceries but I'm really tired and thought this would perk me up a bit.' Jack's dark hair was longer than usual and messy, as if he'd forgotten to comb it, and there were shadows under his brown eyes.

'Baby Iain keeping you up, is he?'

Jack smiled. 'He's a good baby but he still wakes once or twice a night. I got up at three to see to him and it took over an hour for him to settle again.'

'I don't know how you do it.' Nate shook his head. 'Rather you than me.'

7

'Well, you're still out partying until that time, aren't you?' Jack laughed. 'Probably roll straight on into work in the mornings, I bet.'

Nate nodded but inside he sighed. Ex-Marine and local artist Jack was a good friend of his but even so, it sometimes seemed that he had the same opinion of Nate that lots of the locals did. Nate didn't mind but sometimes he wished they could see beyond the cheery, surfer-dude appearance. He was, of course, cheery and a surfer, but there was more to him and he'd like to let people know but... he worried what they'd think if he tried to tell them. So he didn't. How would he go about starting a conversation like that?

'Yeah, that's me all right, Jack. Didn't get a wink of sleep. Enjoy your toast.'

'Before you go, how'd you fancy a pint tonight at the pub? Oli's coming. We'll only have one or two drinks but thought it'd be nice to catch up, seeing as how the three of us are so busy these days.'

'Yeah, I'd like that. What time?'

'Around seven?'

'Suits me.'

Nate returned to the counter and gave the surfaces a quick clean. It would be good to catch up with Oli and Jack. With Jack having the baby and his wife, Eve, to keep him busy, and Oli and Grace planning their engagement party, as well as being parents to Amy and Tom, they rarely had a chance to get together. But Nate was glad they were both settled and happy now. It suited them both, although he could never imagine doing it himself.

Jack had fallen in love with his landlady's niece, Eve, when she'd come to Conwenna Cove two years ago, and they'd been inseparable ever since. The village vet Oli had been widowed over two and a half years ago and with two young children, he'd found life tough. But then Grace Phillips had arrived in the village the previous Christmas, to help her parents settle into their new cottage, and she and Oli had been unable to fight their mutual feelings.

He heard giggling and glanced across the cafe. Two young women were sitting at the window table and as he looked over, they both smiled at him, flashing perfectly aligned white teeth that made Nate think they'd both probably worn braces at some point. The one with long blonde hair blushed when he returned her smile and her friend nudged her. He knew he could go over and ask for her number, probably get it too, but he didn't want to. She was pretty with her lovely sun-kissed hair and bright blue eyes, and she had long tanned legs displayed in cut-off denim shorts. Her top was a baggy transparent T-shirt that showed off a tiny string bikini underneath and he could see the shadow of a small tattoo just under her collarbone. She was the type of woman Nate had been dating for years and it had been fun. But…

He thought about last night and his date with Belle, a travel agent from Truro. They'd met at a bar the week before and she'd asked for his number then phoned him the following day to ask him to meet her. She was Cara Delevingne's doppelganger, with thick dark brows and a figure many women would kill for. They'd had a great night by Nate's previous standards. They'd drunk too much and danced at a club until gone two, then she had wrapped her arms around his neck, kissed him passion- ately and asked him to go home with her. He had to admit that he'd wavered. She was gorgeous, funny and smart. But two things had held him back. One: it wasn't the right time for him to get involved with someone because of his plans, and he suspected that Belle might want more than a fling, and two: he'd realized that he didn't want to wake up the next day with more than a hangover, and by that he was thinking of the strange, empty feeling that he'd experienced the last few times he'd spent the night with a woman. Perhaps it was his age, perhaps it was something else, but Nate knew that something in him was changing and he wasn't quite sure how to deal with it.

So he made an effort not to look over at the pretty blonde woman again and when she came to the counter with her friend and paid, then deliberately touched his hand as he passed her change, he didn't offer her any encouragement. He flashed her a brief smile then turned back to the coffee machine and made a point of frothing some milk, nice and noisy, and pretended he couldn't hear her disappointed sigh or her friend's tut of disapproval.

'Thanks for the coffee and toast.' Jack had come up to the counter. 'Could you wrap me up four of those cherry scones and make a latte to go. I'd better take something nice back for Eve to eat, and she could probably use the coffee, too.'

'No problem.'

'How much do I owe you?'

'It's on me.'

'No, let me pay.'

'Buy me a pint later.'

'Sure, okay then.' Jack stuffed his wallet back into his jeans.

'What's Eve up to this evening?'

'She's arranged a girls' night in with Grace and Amy at our cottage. Oli said Tom wasn't fussy on being with the women, so Edward and Mary said he can go round there and Edward will tell him some stories.'

'Stories?'

Jack nodded. 'Apparently Tom loves hearing about Edward's time on the water.'

'As a fisherman?'

'Yup.'

Mary Millar was Eve's aunt and Eve and Jack lived in the cottage next to hers. She'd married fisherman Edward two years ago and Nate knew the older couple both doted on baby Iain, and Oli's children. Even when people weren't blood relatives of Mary and Edward, they still had plenty of love and time to offer them. That was the good thing about Conwenna Cove; it was a small, close-knit community and there was always friendship and support on offer if you needed it.

'Good for him.'

Nate handed Jack a box with the scones in it, then a disposable coffee cup with a plastic lid.

'I've popped a carton of clotted cream in the box too, in case Eve fancies it.'

'Thanks, I'm sure she will. See you later.'

'Look forward to it.'

Jack left the cafe and Nate watched as he passed the window. Outside, the sky was clear and blue and the air was warm with the promise of a long, hot summer. Tourists were already traipsing up and down the main street in their sandals and flip-flops, their skin sticky with suncream. Nate knew they were in for a busy day at the Conwenna Cafe, which was fine. He liked working there and meeting new people, as well as seeing the cafe regulars. He was going to miss them when he left, but that was something he wouldn't allow himself to dwell on for now, because he had weeks until he was due to leave, and plenty could happen in that time. So he'd take life as he always did… one day at a time.

Chapter 2

Despite wearing her flat black pumps with the cushioned insoles, Zoe's feet were throbbing by four o'clock. She loved working at her diner but some days were really hard going, physically. The first Saturday of July had been busy, which was promising for the summer ahead. Good business was good for Zoe's bank balance. It was important to have savings and security, and she certainly had plenty of both. The diner had been very successful, which was a huge relief as she'd invested a significant portion of her inheritance in the business.

The bell over the door tinkled and Zoe suppressed a sigh. When the last customers had left, she'd hoped that she might have a quiet half hour, but she was well aware that was highly unlikely on a busy Saturday. She plastered on a smile and strode towards the family that had entered.

'Hello there! Welcome to Zoe's Diner. I'm Zoe, the owner.'

The tall man with wavy grey hair and small brown eyes behind silver-rimmed glasses smiled in return.

'Well, hello there, Zoe. Say hello, kids!' His American drawl was strong.

'Hello, Zoe!' The two girls and one boy at his side greeted her.

'Let me guess... New York?'

'New Jersey.' The man smiled, flashing perfectly white teeth.

'I'm from New York but I moved to New Jersey to be with Ted, many moons ago.' The woman at Ted's side offered Zoe a smile as dazzling as her husband's. 'Isn't this a quaint little place!' She waved her hands at the interior and Zoe looked around, as if remembering what she'd done to make the diner as pleasant a place to eat as possible.

The floor-to-ceiling windows offered a wonderful view of the harbour and, if diners sat at the front tables, they could feel as though they were actually on the water. The lighting was low, to create a relaxed atmosphere. The seats were red and chrome, and there was a black and white checked floor. The jukebox played a stream of Fifties hits, and right then Sinatra was crooning rather appropriately about New York.

'Well, thank you for choosing to eat at Zoe's today. Let me show you to a booth.'

When Ted and his family had settled, Zoe took their drinks order and then handed them menus. 'I'll be back with your drinks shortly.'

She went behind the counter, which had an open window to the kitchen, and made a start on the drinks order. Conwenna Cove attracted people from all over the world, and she wasn't at all surprised. It was such a beautiful location and although small, it offered tourists the opportunity to soak up the wonderful Cornish experience. Zoe knew she was lucky to live in the village and to have a business there. After what had happened, she'd needed a safe place to flee to and Conwenna had been that haven. Now she never wanted to leave. It was as if she could escape the real world and harsh reality if she just stayed at the cove.

She carried the tray of drinks back to the booth and handed them to the family.

'Are you ready to order yet?'

She wrote the orders in her notebook, looking at each family member in turn. When she got to the older girl, she couldn't help noticing how she played with a stud in her tongue as she spoke, and the eternity symbol tattoo under the girl's right ear.

'And Zoe, we'll have an extra side of fries with that, please.' Ted tapped his menu.

'Sure thing. Anything else?' Zoe scanned the family again and when she met the older girl's eyes, she caught her knowing smile then followed the girl's gaze down to her left arm that was exposed as she held the notebook up. The girl had spotted her own tattoo – that of a rolling wave that she'd had etched on the inside of her wrist. Zoe returned the girl's smile, but as she walked away, her hand crept to her fringe and she patted it across her forehead to check that it was still in place. There were some marks from her past that she wouldn't try to hide but there were others that she didn't want anyone else to see, because she didn't even want to see them herself.

-

'So what do you think, Oli?' Nate sipped his pint of lager as he waited for the vet to reply.

Oli nodded. 'I think it would be a great idea to have another Surf for Sighthounds this summer, but have you got time to organize it?'

'I think so.' Nate nodded. 'I'd like to do something to help the dogs out.'

Before I go away.

'We could always do it a bit later on,' Jack suggested. 'Perhaps September time.'

Nate shook his head. 'It has to be August.'

Jack and Oli stared at him and he realized he needed to say something.

'Look, uh, don't say anything about this to anyone yet, as I haven't told my aunt and uncle, but I've decided to go away soon. Probably the second week of August.'

Guilt flashed through him as he thought about how good his aunt and uncle had been to him. He probably should stay until the summer was over to help out at the cafe but he was worried that if he didn't go soon, he wouldn't go at all.

Jack frowned. 'Is this your bucket list trip?'

'I told you about it before, huh?' Nate asked.

'One night when we'd had a few, yes. But I thought it was just one of those things.'

'Well, I've been thinking about it quite a lot lately and I'm not getting any younger. Plus I'm single, footloose and fancy-free as they say, so I figured why not this year? I've saved enough to go, so why not now?'

'What's this?' Oli asked. 'I must've missed that night out.'

'I've always wanted to travel a bit, for six months, possibly longer. You know, buy the plane tickets but wing the rest. I didn't know if I'd ever do it but it feels like the time is right.'

'Good for you.' Oli raised his glass. 'To foreign adventures.'

The three men clinked their glasses then drank.

Nate glanced around the Conwenna Arms, the pub where he'd spent so many nights and eaten so many meals with friends, in particular female friends. With its cosy corners and circular bar, as well as a separate dining area, it was perfect for the small village, and Nate knew it did a roaring trade in home-cooked pub meals during peak season.

'Where are you thinking of heading?'

'Well, I always wanted to catch the surf in Australia.'

He caught the knowing look that passed between Jack and Oli.

'I'd also like to visit Hawaii and California. It doesn't have to be just a surf trip but I do want it to be the main focus. Obviously, I need to plan it a bit better but I've only recently decided that this is the year I'll do it. I'm thirty-four now so perhaps I could spend my thirty-fifth birthday on an Australian beach.'

'Sounds amazing.' Jack smiled. 'But you'd like to run Surf for Sighthounds before you go?'

'Definitely.'

'Well, I'm happy to help with the planning.'

'Me, too.' Oli drained his glass. 'As long as you're happy to help with my engagement party.'

Nate laughed. 'Exactly how big is this party going to be?'

'Not that big. But if you could help with the food, then that would be fabulous.'

'No problem at all.'

'You could get some of the local businesses involved in Surf for Sighthounds,' Jack said. 'I'm sure they'd be happy to help.'

'There's Catch of the Day, Sugar and Spice, A Pretty Picture, Pebbles and, of course, the Conwenna Cafe.' Oli ticked the names off on his fingers.

'There's also Riding the Wave.' Jack referred to the local surf shop.

'Lucinda was a great help last time.' Nate referred to the owner of the surf shop. 'She put up a board and a wetsuit, as well as a course of lessons.'

'What about Zoe's Diner, too?' Oli asked. 'I'm sure Zoe will sponsor the event. She lost her own greyhound, Raven, not that long ago, but she loved that dog.'

Nate nodded, although the thought of approaching Zoe made him slightly apprehensive. Zoe Russell was a quiet woman who kept very much to herself. Whenever he'd seen her she was polite enough, but he sensed that she was holding something back, almost as if she didn't trust people and didn't want them to get to know her properly. He'd been his usual self with her whenever she came into the cafe, teasing and joking and flirting a bit, but she had a veneer that he'd been unable to penetrate. It was as if she didn't approve of his openness for some reason, and because of that he'd felt awkward around her, and a bit foolish.

Not that it mattered, of course. He couldn't be friends with everyone and Zoe was not his type at all; she was far too quiet, reserved and aloof. Although, having said that, the fact that she was so seemingly unreachable did make him curious about her. Why was she so quiet? Why didn't she ever seem to go on dates? She was certainly quite attractive, so he was sure she could have had plenty of attention, but then not everyone liked to play the field.

After all, even Nate was getting tired of it. Perhaps Zoe had tired of dating a long time ago and…

He shook his head. Why was he thinking about her at all? It was none of his business.

'I'll go round the village next week and start asking people if they'll help out.' Nate finished his drink. 'Right, who wants another one?'

'Go on then, one more, seeing as how I just got a text from Grace saying she's looking at bridal magazines with Eve now.'

'Bridal magazines?' Nate chuckled.

'Yeah, well, we're thinking about next summer or possibly the Christmas. We might go away somewhere with the children and our parents and get married there.'

'If you went to Hawaii you could get married on the beach and have a swim in the sea afterwards.' Nate had always thought this would be a lovely way to celebrate getting married.

'Sounds amazing.' Oli nodded. 'I'll suggest it to Grace. Although how her father will get the huge cake he's talked about making onto a plane will be something we need to consider. Make sure you stay in touch while you're away so that I can keep you posted. After all, if we decide to get married here in Conwenna, you could come back for the wedding. Or if we hop on a plane… which I doubt, but I can dream, right… then you could meet up with us somewhere.'

'I don't want to miss your wedding, Oli, that's for sure.'

'Are you definitely going to come back then? Once you've travelled?' Jack asked, as he stood up and picked up their glasses.

'I think so. I mean, I love Conwenna. My aunt and uncle live here and my mother isn't far away, so I don't want to go for good. However, if I meet a beautiful Australian woman then I can't promise to return.'

'You have to see where life takes you,' Jack said. 'I really believe that.'

'I know.' Nate nodded, but he wondered if it was easier for Jack to say that because he was in love. Oli was also at a different stage in his life to Nate, but after all Oli had been through – losing his first wife to cancer – Nate was delighted to see him and Grace so happy.

Nate hadn't ever been in love and he didn't think he ever would be. He couldn't imagine giving his heart to someone, because he didn't know how. However, he was happy to do as Jack had suggested. He would enjoy the summer, then head off into the world and see what happened.

Chapter 3

Nate walked along the main street early on Monday morning with a smile on his face. It was going to be a beautiful day. The air was warm and a gentle breeze blew in from the sea, gently caressing the bright pink and purple geraniums growing in the window boxes outside the cafe and toying with the lavender stems, causing their sharp, sweet scent to rise. He loved this time of year. It always made him feel as if anything was possible, which was probably a good thing this morning, seeing as how he was going to be asking local business people to help fund Surf for Sighthounds. He decided to go down to the harbour first, then work his way back up the main street.

When he reached the harbour, he took a few moments to stand in front of the rail to savour the beautiful view. The tide was in and small white boats bobbed on the water, their windows glinting in the sunlight. From further out at sea, he could hear the whine of an engine, presumably someone either heading out or returning from a fishing trip. He rested his hand on the railing; the metal was cold and damp with dew as the sun hadn't yet had time to warm it.

Nate loved the sea. He was more at home on the water than he was on solid ground. When he was swimming or on a surfboard, he experienced a freedom that he didn't feel on land. He'd been that way for as long as he could remember. As a child, he'd been quiet and reserved; in high school he was teased for his shyness and even beaten up a few times when he refused to get involved with some of the shenanigans that other teenage boys thought made them appear daring and brave. But he had always loved to swim. His father took him when he was very young then, when he was old enough, he'd go to the local leisure centre in Newquay to swim early in the morning before it became busy. In the water, as he swam, he was alone with his thoughts and his breathing, able to escape from other people and their demands and assumptions. He could just be himself. All the swimming paid off and he grew strong and fit and, coupled with a growth spurt, he was soon tall and stocky enough to take care of himself. When he tried body boarding, then surfing, in his early teens, it became an obsession for him. Days, weeks and months spent in the surf made his skin tanned and bleached his hair. Before he knew it, Nate was one of the guys and the shy, quiet boy he'd been was replaced with a popular, outgoing young man.

Nate might not have been the brightest in his school year – he was never going to be a doctor or an accountant – but he passed his exams and left school as soon as he was old enough. He spent two years at college studying for A levels but his lack of dedication and interest, combined with his desire to spend all his free time at the beach, meant that he hadn't achieved pleasing grades in further education. But he hadn't minded. He'd worked at different jobs, from helping out at a garage to teaching surfing to holidaymakers and pouring pints at several different pubs, as well as working as a lifeguard. He had got by over the years, and he'd been content.

It was just that now he was starting to wonder if he'd actually done anything worthwhile with his life. He didn't have a career – he enjoyed surfing and had entered competitions but had never made it as a professional (the competition was fierce) – and he had never been in love. He'd thought that it was okay to drift along during his twenties but at six years off forty, he needed to do something meaningful at some point soon. He had organized Surf for Sighthounds two years ago but it had been a relatively small affair, and he was hoping that this time it would be bigger and raise more money.

The clinking of glass dragged him from his thoughts and he glanced over at the wine bar on the edge of the harbour. One of the employees was putting out the recycling. That was one thing with busy summers: there was far more recycling to be sorted then, than in the winter months.

He checked his mobile and was surprised to see that it was eight-thirty. He must have been day dreaming for over twenty minutes. It was so easy to lose time when he got lost in his thoughts. He turned around and spotted Zoe Russell in the window of her diner, wiping the glass with a yellow cloth. Seeing that she was there, he thought he might as well go and speak to her first.

Nate ran a hand through his hair then made his way over to the diner, a strange fluttering in his belly making him take a few deep breaths.

As he walked towards her, Nate saw Zoe stop cleaning and looked beyond whatever it was that she could see on the glass. She frowned, it seemed, when she realized he was approaching the diner. He took another deep breath before knocking on the door, suddenly worried that this wasn't going to be easy at all.

'Hello.' Zoe stepped into view, the frown replaced by an expression of interest.

'Morning, Zoe. I was wondering… could I come in and talk to you for five minutes?'

'Oh!' She folded the yellow cloth several times before replying. 'I guess so. But I don't have long. This place needs a blitz before I open today, and I have to pop up to Foxglove Farm to collect my ice cream order.'

'I thought they delivered.'

'They do, but… I like to make an effort to visit the greyhounds.'

Her cheeks flushed slightly, as if she was a bit embarrassed about admitting this to him and revealing her softer side.

'I do the same.' He smiled. 'I always offer to go and get the order for the cafe.'

Zoe nodded. 'You walk the dogs too, don't you?'

'How d'you know that?'

'I've seen you.' Her blush deepened. 'I mean… I saw you… When I was up there last week. You had two of the dogs and were taking them to the field.'

'Ah, right. Yes, I took them for a run around. I like to help out when I can. Actually, that's why I'm here.'

'About the dogs?' She smiled briefly and Nate saw something in her expression – a softening that made her prettier. Not that she wasn't pretty, because he could see that she was, but with her brown bob and willowy figure, she wasn't as in-your-face attractive as the women Nate usually dated.

'That's right.'

'Come on in, then.'

Nate followed her into the diner, taking in the Fifties decor and the scent of lemon that he suspected came from whatever cleaning products she'd used that morning.

'Would you like a drink?'

'That would be great, thanks.'

'Milkshake or coffee?'

'Ooh! I'll have a milkshake, please.'

'Flavour?'

'Surprise me.'

A flicker of something crossed Zoe's face and he wondered if she ever surprised anyone with anything. She seemed so... quiet and serious. He couldn't imagine her laughing, and didn't recall ever seeing her smile until today.

Nate took a seat at the counter, fighting the temptation to spin around on the high circular stool to see how fast he could go. There was something about the stools that made him want to do that, but he didn't think it would go down well with Zoe. He could imagine her frown of disapproval and he shivered. Instead, he rested his feet on the floor then leaned forwards so his elbows were on the counter. He watched Zoe as she moved around; everything she did was purposeful and efficient. Soon she placed a frothy banana milkshake in front of him.

'The ice cream from Foxglove makes for extra-special milkshakes.'

Nate drew on the straw she'd tucked in the glass, and creamy banana milk filled his mouth.

'This is amazing.'

Zoe nodded, clearly accustomed to receiving compliments about her milkshakes all the time.

'So, you wanted to talk about the dogs?'

'That's right. Well, the thing is, I'm hoping to run a Surf for Sighthounds event in a few weeks, but I need the support of local businesses.'

He sipped his milkshake again, almost draining the glass. When he glanced up, Zoe was staring at him with what seemed like a look of utter horror. She'd gone as white as the counter and was repeatedly flattening one side of her fringe with her palm.

'Zoe? Are you all right?'

'What?'

'You don't look well. I asked if you're okay.'

'Yes. I'm fine.' She pulled her hand away from her hair and tucked it into her apron pocket, next to her other one.

'If you don't want to help, there's no pressure. I'm going around asking people this morning, so I have an idea of who'll be interested and what we can raise.'

Zoe finally met his gaze and he did a double take. Her eyes were the darkest brown he had ever seen, surrounded by thick black lashes. Perhaps it was because he'd never been so close to her before, or he'd only seen her with sunglasses on, but he'd never noticed how pretty they were, how warm and soft they could be if only she'd let down her guard and relax.

'It's not that. Of course I'd like to help.'

'You would?'

'Yes. I love the dogs. But... will I... will I need to be on the beach during the competition?'

26

'That's entirely up to you. You can be as involved as you'd like. Again, no pressure. We'll have the main part of the event at the cove and the surfing will take place over in Luna Bay, because there's more space there, obviously. You can head over there, stay at the cove or stay in the village.'

'Right. Okay. Thanks.'

Her eyes roamed the diner as if she was searching for something.

'You can even take part if you like,' he added, jokingly.

'Absolutely not!' she snapped.

Nate had hit a nerve, and the last thing he wanted to do was to upset her when he was hoping she'd agree to help. 'Uh… Shall I leave you to have a think about it?'

'No. It's fine. I'll sponsor the event and I'll be happy to come to the cove, but I don't have to go in the water, do I?'

She started toying with her fringe again, and Nate experienced an urge to gently take her hand and stop her. It seemed to be a nervous habit, as if she reached for her hair when she was agitated, and he wondered if she did it a lot.

'Only if you want to take part in the surfing, which you're welcome to do. But I'm guessing that you don't. I'm hoping we can get some big names here… you know, possibly professional surfers, but there'll be room for everyone else to show off their board skills, too.'

'I'm not getting in the water.'

'No problem.'

She really didn't want to go in the sea and he wanted to ask why, but sensed that this wasn't the time.

Nate nodded then finished his milkshake, slurping the dregs through the straw.

'Didn't want to waste a drop, it was so good,' he explained.

'Good. I'm glad you liked it.'

'Right, well, I'll be off then. But let me give you my number and you can let me know what you want to contribute.'

He read out his number and Zoe saved it in her mobile contacts, then sent him a text so he had hers.

'When will it be?'

'First weekend in August, probably.'

'Gosh, that's soon.'

'That's what I thought, but I wanted to get it done before I... well, when there are plenty of tourists around to make the most of it.'

'I'd like it if we could do something to remember all the hounds we've lost.'

'Of course... you fostered one for a while, didn't you?'

Zoe nodded. 'Raven.'

'Sorry for your loss.' Nate grimaced as he recalled that it hadn't been long ago and Zoe was probably still grieving.

'She was a failed foster. I knew once she came to live with me that I'd never be able to let her go. I was going to adopt her properly but she...' Zoe bit her lip and blinked hard. Droplets clung to her long lashes like diamonds, and Nate's breath caught in his throat. He reached out automatically and took her hand. Her skin was warm and soft, and he could feel her pulse beneath the surface, fast, powerful, enticing.

Zoe's eyes widened at his touch and something passed between them, akin to an electric shock. Nate released her then stared at his hand as if it had acted without his approval. But he knew it hadn't; he'd done what came naturally to him, trying to comfort Zoe when she was clearly distressed.

'She passed away one night. My sweet girl. So...' In front of his eyes, Zoe straightened her back and lifted her chin in a way that suggested she was used to putting on a brave front. 'As I was saying, I'd like to have something to honour the lost dogs, too.'

'Like a plaque, or a bench, or—'

'Why not both?' She clapped her hands.

'A bench with a plaque on it?'

'Yes. Somewhere that people can use it, people like me who loved and lost their dogs.'

'We could ask about having it on the cliff overlooking the cove, or perhaps out by the harbour.'

'Overlooking the cove,' she said softly. 'I'd like that, Nate.'

The way she said his name made his heart skip a beat. It sounded different somehow, as if he'd never heard it said that way before.

'Nate?'

'Yes?'

'Are you okay? You seemed a bit far away then.'

'I'm fine, thanks.' He forced a laugh to prove it. 'I was fantasizing about drinking that milkshake again.'

'I can make you another—?'

He shook his head. 'Not now, but I'll be back for one another time. If that's okay?'

She smiled then and this time it brought dimples to her cheeks; it was a warm, natural smile and Nate felt a bit strange, as if he'd never seen this woman properly before. He knew, in that moment, that he wanted to know more about her. Why did she play with her fringe when she was nervous, and why was she afraid of the water? He couldn't imagine being afraid to go in the sea, and knew that it must be a terrible fear to have.

'Next time, try a different flavour.'

'Next time, you can surprise me again.'

And, as he left the diner, he had a feeling she would.

–

Zoe closed the door behind Nate, then locked it. She pressed her forehead to the cool glass and closed her eyes. Her neck and shoulders were stiff with tension and she knew she'd suffer later if she didn't try to relax now.

She went back to the counter and got a bottle of water from the fridge, then opened it and took a long drink. This was silly, getting so worked up, and all because Nate had mentioned surfing and professional surfers, but it still had such an effect on her. She'd been trying to act nonchalantly but she knew she hadn't pulled it off. For one, Nate had noticed her tugging at her fringe, which must have looked quite strange and two, he might not have realized it but he'd pulled a face when she'd asked for reassurance that she wouldn't need to go in the water. Of course, she had reacted quite sharply when he'd mentioned her surfing but for some reason she couldn't fathom, she'd felt a bit unsteady when he'd come in to speak to her, and that had let her guard down, which in turn had made her jumpy.

She swallowed some more water then put the top back on the bottle and placed her hands on the counter. She took a few slow deep breaths and tried to imagine the tension leaving her body, travelling like smoke from her neck and shoulders, down her hands and out of her fingertips. The technique worked and she was soon able to function normally again.

Zoe had to finish setting up for the day, then head up to the farm to get her ice cream. She knew that seeing the dogs would help her too; it always did.

Nate Bryson was not who he seemed to be, though. Not at all. Zoe didn't know him very well but had never thought he'd be the type to arrange a charity event. She'd heard about the first one but assumed he'd helped with it rather than been responsible for it, and she had to admit that she was impressed. He looked like a typical chilled-out surfer. Zoe knew she could be accused of stereotyping but she'd known a lot of surfers in her time, and Nate had seemed to fit the mould perfectly. She'd seen him around the village and in the cafe, always the centre of female attention. It was hardly surprising as he was undeniably gorgeous, and he oozed that happy-go-lucky confidence that some women adored.

But not Zoe.

She didn't like that in a man at all.

Not after what she'd been through.

However, Nate did seem like a decent guy and he was doing something good for the hounds at the sanctuary, so Zoe would try not to judge him. Whatever he got up to in his own time was his choice, but if he wanted her help with Surf for Sighthounds, then she would gladly give it. She just hoped that when he'd mentioned professional surfers, he'd been thinking of ones she didn't know personally. But the chances of it being the one she did know, the one she knew very well indeed, were slim, so she'd try not to worry about that for now. After all, it was a big world and there were plenty of people out there who liked to surf.

She smiled as she realized that she had regained her composure, so she went through to the back and got her bag, then let herself out of the back door into the sunny Cornish morning. It was a brand-new week and Zoe was actually looking forward to seeing what it would bring, and she was particularly uplifted by the thought that ice cream and greyhounds were at the top of the agenda.

Chapter 4

Zoe enjoyed an hour at Foxglove Farm, during which time she took one of the greyhounds on a walk around the nearby fields and then purchased her ice cream order for the diner. When she returned to work she felt completely ready for whatever the week would bring. She also knew that Neil had dropped a few hints about her considering adopting another hound, but she wasn't ready yet. It wouldn't be fair on the dog or on her.

The morning at the diner was busy but not unbearably so, and it quietened down after one-thirty. When the door next opened, she was happy to see that it was Grace and Eve. She liked the two women, even though she didn't know them very well; they were the type of women she had imagined she could be friends with when she was growing up.

'Hello, Zoe.' Grace gave her a warm smile as they reached the counter. 'Are we in time for some lunch?'

'Of course you are. Take a table and I'll bring some menus over. What would you like to drink?'

'Eve?' Grace asked.

'A lemonade, please.'

'I'll have the same, thank you.'

Zoe took their drinks over with the menus.

'No children today?'

'Amy and Tom are at school,' Grace explained. 'I'm meant to be writing, but I've taken an hour off for lunch. An author's got to eat, right?'

Zoe nodded. 'Definitely.'

'And my aunt is watching Iain. He had me up and down last night, so she told me to take a break, then have a nap this afternoon.' Eve smiled, even though she was quite pale. 'Trouble is, I miss him when I'm away from him for just an hour.'

'He's a gorgeous baby,' Zoe said. 'But your Aunt Mary is right, you do need a breather now and then.' She handed them the menus. 'Let me know when you're ready to order.'

As the chef, Alistair, made the food in the kitchen, Zoe pottered about behind the counter. She was so glad she'd employed him: when she'd first opened, she'd tried to do it all herself and soon discovered how difficult it was trying to manage the business and cook all the food. She now employed two chefs: Alistair worked through the week and Kierney covered the weekends and any extra opening hours in peak season. Both had proved to be talented and adept in the kitchen, which left Zoe able to cater to her customers and to enjoy owning the diner.

At the table near the window, Grace and Eve chatted away and occasionally a peal of laughter drifted over. Zoe wished she knew what it was that made them laugh, and she experienced a stab of nostalgia for her past. Growing up, she'd always been extremely close to her own best friend, Amelia; in fact, they'd been inseparable. They'd gone through primary school, high school and college together, then it had all changed a few years ago...

She shivered. And that was why it was better not to let anyone into your heart and your mind. People couldn't be trusted, however long you'd known them. At least keeping them at arm's length meant that they couldn't hurt you.

When the food was ready, Zoe carried it to the table.

'Here you go, ladies. Hope you enjoy!'

'Ooh, thanks, Zoe, this looks wonderful.' Grace smiled. 'Things going well this summer?'

Zoe slid her hands into her apron pocket.

'Yes, thank you. Conwenna Cove certainly brings the tourists in and business has been steady since that gorgeous sunny weekend we had back in May. If it carries on like this, I might need to employ more waiting staff. I have two already, but it's nice to be able to offer local people work, too.'

'That's wonderful, Zoe,' Eve said, before biting into her veggie burger.

'Do you want to join us?' Grace asked. 'Have you eaten lunch yet?'

'No, but I had a snack up at the farm when I went to get my ice cream order. You know what Elena's like – she always has fresh scones available to tempt you, and the kettle on the boil. I'll eat a proper meal later.'

'Elena makes the best scones, doesn't she?' Eve nodded. 'Whenever I head up there, she always offers me a cuppa and cake.'

'Sounds like my father.' Grace smiled. 'I can't visit Mum and Dad without putting on half a stone.'

'I wonder if your father will want to help out with the surfing event.' The words escaped Zoe's mouth before she even realized she'd thought them.

'The one Nate's arranging?' Grace tucked her wavy red hair over her shoulder.

'He came in to ask me if I was interested in being a sponsor.'

'Jack said Nate really wants this to be a success, to give something back to the greyhounds before he leaves.' Eve smiled. 'He's a good one is Nate.'

Zoe's heart fluttered. 'Leaves?'

Eve grimaced. 'I don't think I was meant to say anything about that. Not sure he's told his aunt and uncle yet.'

'He's leaving?' Zoe tried to maintain an even tone to her voice, but she was suddenly and inexplicably quite disappointed.

'Apparently he's going travelling for a while. He wants to see some of the world.'

'Will he… uh… come back, or is it permanent?' Zoe tried to keep her hands still in her apron pocket.

'Oli said Nate told him he'd probably be back, but then Oli also said Nate could well fall in love with someone while he's away and that could be that. I suppose he could meet a beautiful Australian surfer, and we know how much Nate loves to surf!' Grace shrugged. 'I'd be sad to see him go, though. He's been a good friend.'

Zoe bit the inside of her cheek to stop herself asking any more questions. Why should she care? Nate was everything she despised in men, with his devil-may-care attitude, sun-bronzed skin and easy smile. He reminded her far too much of things in her past that she'd prefer not to think about. If he was going away following Surf for Sighthounds, then that was a good thing and she couldn't give a damn what he did.

'When I arrived in Conwenna Cove, he made me feel so welcome. He was convinced that I'd stay, even though I only came to help Mum and Dad settle in. And when I first met Oli, Nate tried to reassure me that he was a good person, although initially he seemed a bit… standoffish.' Grace's eyes glazed over as she remembered.

'Oli gave you the cold shoulder?' Eve asked.

'Kind of. But he was wary of women after what he'd been through.'

'And now you're living happily ever after!' Eve winked at Grace and they both giggled.

Zoe smiled at their happiness. She knew enough about them to realize that life hadn't been easy for either of them, and she'd never begrudge someone their happy moments. Zoe had once been happy too, in spite of some ups and downs along the way. At one point, years ago, she'd believed that she had it all. Then she'd had her accident and it had all seemed to fall apart.

But that was life and there was no point crying over spilt milk, a broken surfboard or the fact that people often let down those they claimed to care about. She simply had to make the most of what she had now and ensure that she never ended up in a position where she could be hurt again: not by a surfboard, a best friend and definitely not by a man.

–

Nate poured the wine he'd opened into three glasses, then checked the table again. He'd invited his aunt and uncle up to the flat for dinner so he could speak to them about his plans. The week had flown and it was Thursday evening already. He'd been meaning to break the news to them for days but just hadn't had the chance, and it wasn't something he wanted to blurt out in the cafe when surrounded by customers. His aunt and uncle had been so good to him since he'd come to the cove and he owed them a proper explanation, so that was what he was going to do.

It was ridiculous feeling nervous but, nevertheless, his stomach was churning, and he kept repeating the words he wanted to say over and over in his mind. He was thirty-four, and doing nothing wrong, but he'd become close to them in the five years he'd been in Conwenna and he didn't want to hurt them or make them feel that his life there was lacking in any way. Because it wasn't, not really. But he wanted to travel and he needed to let them know that without making them feel he wanted to get away from them.

Once he'd told them, he would speak to his mother and then he'd be ready to face the world, after he'd ensured that the greyhound sanctuary had the proceeds from the surfing event, of course.

'Nate?'

'In here, Auntie June.'

Nate smiled as his aunt entered his open plan lounge-diner through the door at the top of the steps at the rear of the cafe building.

'Something smells good,' June said, as she ambled over to Nate and gave him the hug she always did, even if she'd only said goodbye to him five minutes earlier.

'I've gone for a very simple roast chicken with rustic dauphinoise potatoes. I hope that's okay? It was something I threw together earlier, knowing I could leave it in the oven to cook.'

'That sounds wonderful.' June plonked herself down on his sofa. 'Your uncle will be up shortly. He was locking up the cafe, then thought he'd left his wallet in the kitchen.'

'Do you want a drink?' Nate asked, gesturing at the table where beads of condensation now coated the bottle of white wine.

'Twist my arm.' June laughed, the familiar throaty noise that always made Nate feel happy and secure. June was like that; she was such a warm and happy person that she lifted his spirits whenever he was in the same room as her. When Nate had come to Conwenna Cove following the death of his father, he'd been sad, confused and angry. All he'd known was that he needed to get away from Newquay, away from the places where he'd grown up and the places that reminded him constantly of his father. His father's death had been sudden. He was apparently a fit and healthy fifty-five year old, but it turned out that he'd had heart disease, the silent killer. Nate had been broken when his father passed so suddenly, but being in Conwenna had helped, as had his loving aunt and his Uncle Kevin, who happened to be the image of his father. This could have made Nate's grief harder to deal with, but Nate actually found it comforting to be around his uncle. It was as if, in some way, his father was still there.

Nate poured two glasses of wine then handed one to June and sat next to her.

'Oooh! This is delicious, Nate.' June nodded her approval of the wine. 'I could get squiffy drinking this stuff. Now, do you want to tell me what's going on?'

'Can't I invite my wonderful aunt and uncle to dinner?'

June smiled. 'You know I like my food, Nate' – she patted her ample belly – 'but since you've been in this flat, you've cooked for us about… three times. If that.'

'Sorry.'

'No, love, don't be! I'm not. We love having you round to ours and wouldn't expect to be invited here. You have your own life and are entitled to your privacy. My point was basically that something must be up. So do you want to tell me now, or wait until Kevin gets here?'

'We can wait until he arrives but before I forget, you haven't heard anything of my mum, have you?'

June shook her head. 'Not this week. We usually chat once a week but sometimes if we're particularly busy in the cafe, like in the summer months, it can lapse to once a fortnight. Why, love, are you worried about something?'

Nate shook his head. 'Not really worried, but I tried her at the weekend, then yesterday, and couldn't get through. She sent a text message to say everything was fine but I don't know… I like to hear her voice, too. But that's probably because I miss her.'

'I'm sure she's fine, Nate. Probably just busy. I'll try to ring her tomorrow.'

'I'm here!' Kevin said, as he entered the flat, his huge frame filling the doorway. 'Found my damned wallet in the fridge.' He scratched his thinning blond hair. 'Have no idea how it got in there, but it's been one of those days.'

'Wine?' Nate asked.

'Please.'

Nate fetched the wine bottle and the third glass, then filled it before giving it to Kevin.

'I was just saying to Nate that we know he has something to tell us.'

'Yes, son. Everything all right, is it?' Kevin sat in the armchair and Nate sat next to June again. He glanced around the small flat he'd called home for the past few years, then shook his head.

'Nothing's wrong. In fact, everything is right and that's why it's a good time for me to do this.'

'Do what, love?' June asked.

'Well, you know I always said that one day I wanted to travel around? To see more of the world when I had the chance?'

Nate met his aunt's hazel eyes and saw understanding fill them.

'Nate, we knew this day would come and I'm surprised it hasn't come before. So you've decided to head off on your travels, have you?'

He nodded. 'Probably the second weekend in August. I'm going to ensure that Surf for Sighthounds goes with a bang, then jet off.'

'Well, good for you, Nate, though we will miss you.' June patted his arm.

'Do you have enough money saved, Nate?' Kevin asked.

'I have some, yes. I've been putting most of my wages into an account, as obviously expenses have been minimal here. You've been so good to me.' Nate looked at his aunt and uncle in turn.

'It's been our pleasure, son.' Kevin shrugged off the praise from his nephew. He had such a kind heart but emotion and gratitude always embarrassed him. That was another way that he reminded Nate of his father. The two brothers had been similar in appearance and personality and Nate knew that losing his brother, Kyle, had hit Kevin hard too. With only two years between them, they'd been the best of friends throughout their lives, and Kyle had always looked out for his younger brother... sort of how Kevin looked out for Nate now.

'Well, love, we have a little something put aside for you that we saved for a time like this. It would have been there for you if you'd needed to put a down payment on a mortgage or towards a wedding, but this is just as good a cause.'

'I don't want your money. Really, there's no need—'

Kevin cleared his throat. 'June is right. We've saved money for you, Nate. It might be enough for you to travel *and* put money on a mortgage when... if... you return. I'm not saying you have to come back and live in Conwenna, but the money's there for you to use wherever you want to settle.'

'I will come back. I don't like the thought of being gone forever, but I thought that if I don't do this soon then I probably never will.'

'Well, this bit of cash will help you along then.'

'I don't know what to say, other than... thank you so much.'

'Who else would we give the money to, Nate? We don't have any children of our own and we don't want for anything at all. You're as good as a son to us and we love you.' June raised her glass. 'So here's to you and your travels, and to the future. May you always be happy and loved.'

Nate clinked his glass against his aunt and uncle's, then swallowed the cold fruity wine. Kevin and June had always been kind to him but this showed exactly how much they thought of him. They'd actually been saving money for him, as if he was their own son. He wondered how long they'd been putting cash away, how long they'd been planning for him, possibly hoping that he'd marry or buy a house in Conwenna. He hoped that they weren't disappointed that this was his chosen path. Their act of selflessness further confirmed to him that, although he was looking forward to broadening his horizons, he would return to the cove; he couldn't imagine life any other way.

'Anyway, Nate, is dinner ready? I'm famished and it smells incredible.'

'It is. Bring your wine to the table and I'll dish up.'

Nate went through to the kitchen area and lifted the chicken onto a serving plate, then got the potatoes from the oven. As he scooped creamy, garlicky potatoes from the ovenproof dish, he had a flashback to Zoe telling him she was going to the farm to get her ice cream order. He'd got the cream for this dish from there too. He wondered what Zoe was doing that night for dinner and whether she ate alone every night. As far as he knew, she didn't have anyone in her life; he'd never seen her with anyone, at least.

And he realized that if he did return to Conwenna Cove, he'd be able to see Zoe again too, and that thought warmed him. It was probably foolish but the idea of leaving and never seeing her again suddenly seemed unpleasant. How hadn't he noticed her all this time with her soft brown hair and warm brown eyes? He'd barely even looked her way and yet there she was, the opposite of everything Nate had ever looked for in a woman. She was beautiful, yes, but it was her manner and her aloofness that had made him discount her as a possible date, or more. And yet… she intrigued him, which was something he'd suppressed in the past, and he'd been unable to get her out of his mind since he'd spoken to her on Monday. What was with that? What was up with him?

He shook his head. Perhaps it was just because he'd made the decision to go and, possibly, his subconscious was trying to find a reason to stay. Perhaps he was secretly scared about leaving and Zoe seemed like someone worth sticking around for. Nate was tired of the women who simply wanted to fool around and tired of the lifestyle he'd been living. He'd never felt a true connection to a woman and something about Zoe's quiet, serious nature made him think that she was a woman with whom he could develop a connection, if he put in the effort to get to know her, to penetrate that veneer he suspected she had created to protect herself from others. In terms of timing, it was a damned nuisance that this had happened now, that he'd spoken to her and seen more to her than ever before. But Nate knew from experience that life often threw curveballs, sometimes ones that cut you to the core – like losing his dad – and sometimes ones that made you see people in a whole new light. Perhaps he hadn't seen Zoe in this way before because he wasn't in the right place mentally or emotionally; perhaps he was finally growing up…

Whatever it was, he knew he had to get his head sorted, and soon. He had mere weeks until he left and no woman, however smart, sweet and fascinating, was going to put a halt to his plans. Not that he thought Zoe Russell would have any intention of doing that. She'd barely shown a flicker of interest in him.

And that could be why she suddenly intrigued him. Zoe appeared to be completely oblivious to the fact that he was even a man. He smiled as he carried the plates to the table. He was looking forward to seeing her again, purely to assess his own feeling towards her, of course, and to try to work out what the hell had changed to spark his attraction to her now.

Chapter 5

The next day, Zoe walked through the village enjoying the late afternoon breeze. It was just gone four pm and the sun's heat had waned with the day. The diner was in the capable hands of her employees, so she'd decided to take an hour to stretch her legs and enjoy a coffee.

The sweet scents of flowers in pots, window boxes and hanging baskets teased her nostrils and she experienced that glimmer of hope that summer always roused in her. Everything was in bloom and there were weeks of sunshine and busy days ahead, which meant less time alone at home. It wasn't that she didn't enjoy her own company, because to a certain extent she did, but winter evenings in front of the fire weren't as much fun without someone to snuggle with, and this year she wouldn't even have Raven to hug.

She took a deep breath. She had to be more positive. Raven had been happy in the short time she'd been with her and, when she was ready, Zoe would open her home to another dog. But the time had to be right. As for opening her heart to anything else, well... she doubted that was going to happen.

She found herself outside the Conwenna Cafe, and peered through the glass. Inside, Nate was behind the counter, his cheeks flushed with the heat and his blond hair so messy it looked as if he'd just fallen out of bed. *Or from the sky…* She grimaced. Where on earth had that cheesy thought come from? Zoe was not one to lapse into soppy daydreams about men, no matter how blue their eyes or broad their shoulders. It simply wasn't her style. Not that she'd never allowed herself to indulge in a fantasy or two, but she didn't any more. Not since what had happened. She self-consciously touched her fringe and fluffed it up a bit, then ran her hands through the rest of her bob. Of course, it didn't matter what she looked like because Nate certainly wouldn't look at her in that way. She was as far removed from the type of woman Nate fancied as she was from being the next prime minister. Which was fine, good even, because Nate was never going to be Zoe's type…

Nate looked up and caught her staring. Heat filled her cheeks and she turned quickly, her instincts telling her to run away, but she'd forgotten about the hanging basket under the cafe sign and she smacked her head on it. As she wobbled, she reached out and her hands clawed at the air until they found something solid, but that gave way under her touch and she found herself face down on the pavement.

'Zoe!' Nate was at her side. 'Bloody hell, are you all right? Are you hurt?'

He gently helped her up and scanned her from the top of her head to the tips of her toes then back again, until he met her eyes. She was conscious of his roaming gaze and felt it like the heat of a torch.

'I'm fine.' She tried to laugh but it came out as a croak, and she wished the ground would swallow her whole.

'You should put that hanging basket up higher, though. It's a hazard there.'

'My uncle was in the process of watering the flowers but went inside to refill the watering can. See, it does go up higher.' He pointed at a hook higher up the cafe wall. 'He just hung it on there for a moment. God, Zoe, you could have been really hurt.'

Zoe rubbed her eyes then her face. Everything seemed fine.

'And now you need a wash.'

'What?'

Nate took her hands in his and heat shot through her at the tenderness of his touch.

'See.'

Zoe met his eyes and felt as if she could tumble into their azure depths.

'Mmmm?'

'Your hands.'

'Oh!'

She looked down and found that her hands were caked in mud from the window box she'd grabbed at as she went down – and had unfortunately emptied over the ground.

'I'm so sorry. I'm not usually this accident prone.'

'No?'

He reached out and ran his finger over the scar on her forehead. She winced then pushed his hand away and tried to brush her fringe back into place with her fingers.

'How'd you get that?'

'I fell.'

'So, you are accident prone, then?'

Zoe shrugged. 'Not all the time. Anyway, that's from a long time ago.'

'Perhaps you'll feel like telling me about it some time.'

'Perhaps,' she replied, although she doubted it.

'Come inside and let me get you something so you can clean yourself up, then make you a cuppa. You look like you need it.'

'I think I'd better try to tidy up that window box first. The poor flowers.' Zoe stared in dismay at the scattered pansies and geraniums that had been uprooted by her fall.

'It's okay, I'll help my uncle to sort it out in a moment. I want to make sure you're okay first.'

Zoe allowed him to guide her into the cafe, then she went through to the customer toilets. In the artificial light of the small space, she washed her hands thoroughly with liquid soap that smelt of violets, then faced herself in the mirror. She had streaks of mud up her cheeks and crumbs of dirt in her hair. She rubbed at the mud with her wet hands then grabbed a paper towel and dried them, before getting her brush from her small handbag and using it to clear the compost debris from her hair. What must Nate think of her? Let alone the customers in the cafe who'd watched the whole debacle, then eyed her from behind their mugs as she'd entered the cafe. She'd been so distracted by gazing at Nate, then horrified when he caught her staring, that she'd forgotten to look where she was going and had ended up walking into the hanging basket then face planted into the contents of the window box. Luckily, little more than her pride was hurt but then, in comparison to what she'd been through in the past, what was a little hurt pride?

Zoe dried her hands then checked her fringe one last time. She gave it a squirt of the mini hairspray she kept in her bag. Nate had actually touched her scar – the ugly, silver-red mark that dominated one side of her forehead – as if it was something to admire. And it wasn't. Zoe hated it because of all it represented about how life had been, and because of all it reminded her of: her failure to keep her friend and the man she loved close.

Pain pierced her heart like a dagger and she sucked in a breath.

Zoe knew the fault lay with them for what they'd done but, no matter how hard she tried, she couldn't believe that she was blameless in it all. If she'd been prettier, thinner, funnier, more alluring. If she'd been a better surfer, earned more money, been more exciting in bed… so many things she could have done and been for *him* – but would it really have made a difference? She had to admit that she didn't know, and she suspected that she never would. People would do what they wanted to do and sometimes nothing could stop them or change their minds, not even love and friendship. Sometimes they counted for nothing at all.

Caring about people was dangerous.

–

Nate carried a mug of tea over to the table in the corner, sitting down to wait for Zoe. She'd given him a fright when she'd bumped into the hanging basket then fallen over. He'd been busy making a ham and cheese ciabatta when he'd sensed that someone was watching him. Looking up, he'd spotted Zoe outside and been about to wave when she'd turned on her heel and gone face first into the flowers. It had been like slow motion as she'd bounced off the hanging basket then grappled for something to stop herself falling and managed to drag the window box down with her. The window boxes were secured in wooden frames that his uncle had constructed but, somehow, the very slender Zoe had managed to pull the one box out of its frame.

Right now, Kevin was outside repairing the damage. He'd agreed with Nate that he needed to ensure that he never left the hanging baskets unattended again when they were lowered for watering, and said he'd buy a bigger watering can or a sturdy ladder so he wouldn't need to bring the baskets to head height.

Zoe could have been seriously injured.

Nate swallowed. That thought was awful. The idea of anyone being injured was terrible but thinking of Zoe being hurt made his gut churn. He had an urge to protect her and that was not something Nate was accustomed to feeling. The women he dated were strong and independent, and so was Zoe as far as he knew, but there was also something about her that was… vulnerable. Soft. Gentle.

He shook himself. Her big brown eyes were playing havoc with his sensibilities and that was all it was. She reminded him of a taller Natalie Portman with her slim frame and fathomless eyes, and although he'd always made a point of dating blondes, he had nursed a secret crush on the beautiful actress for a while. In fact, it was probably why he was drawn to Zoe. She resembled his crush and nothing more, and it was highly likely that he was imagining things, possibly projecting his ideal onto her. And yet…

'Nate?'

He looked up to find Zoe standing next to him. He got to his feet.

'How are you?'

She'd washed her face and brushed her hair and, apart from a fleck of mud on the shoulder of her cream blouse, there was no evidence that she'd been lying in compost at all.

'I'm okay, thanks. My pride is bruised, or should I say muddied, but that's all.'

She was making a joke of it? He smiled in response.

'Here, have a seat.'

She sat down and he gestured at the tea. 'I don't know if you take sugar but I put some in it anyway.'

'For the shock?'

'Yeah…'

'Thank you.' She peered over his shoulder. 'Oh no… is your uncle out there tidying up my mess?'

'He's almost done. I would've helped but I wanted to check you were all right.'

'I should help him.' She went to get up but he put out a hand.

'You're going nowhere until you've drunk your tea and I'm certain that you are fit enough to leave.'

Her dark eyebrows rose slightly but she picked up the mug and drank.

Nate wanted to ask about her scar again but he didn't want to scare her away, so instead he went for what he thought would be a safer topic.

'I noticed that you have tattoos.'

She lowered the mug and nodded.

'One on your wrist and one on the back of your neck.'

'All down to my foolish and misspent youth.' She gave a wry smile.

'I like them. The one on your wrist is very cool.'

Zoe turned her hand over and they both gazed at the wave on her wrist.

'You like the sea?' After her reaction – when he'd gone to the diner – to his suggestion that she could surf during the greyhound event, Nate thought he knew the answer to this one, but then who had a tattoo of a wave if they didn't like the water?

'I did.'

'Not any more?'

She shook her head. 'I wasn't confident about swimming as a child but when I got older, I quite liked being out in the sea. Well… I got used to it, at least.'

'Swimming?'

'Surfing.'

'You surfed?'

'Don't look so surprised. We don't all need to be blonde and tanned.'

'That's such a stereotype, and it wasn't what I meant at all.'

She pressed her lips together and Nate watched as they blanched.

'Sorry, Zoe. Sometimes, when I'm around you, I don't quite say what I mean. I'm not sure why… What I meant was that I'm surprised that you surfed. Only because I didn't know anything about it, not because of what you look like or because I think there's a *type*.'

'You have a type though, right?' As the blood rushed back into her lips, it filled her cheeks too. 'Sorry. Now it's me being hasty with my words.'

'Are you trying to say that you only ever see me with a certain kind of woman, Zoe?'

'Well… yes. I guess so. When was the last time you dated a redhead or a brunette? Not that it's any of my business who you date or why. You obviously only fancy women with blonde hair.'

'That's not true, actually.'

Zoe shrugged. 'As I said, none of my business. Anyway, thanks for the tea. I'd better be getting back to work.'

'Don't go yet. I wanted to talk to you and I feel like this has gone all wrong. Like we've both been a bit… prickly… for want of a better word, and I don't know why.'

'Prickly?' Her eyes widened.

'Well, yes. I'm not like this, Zoe. I'm usually calm and able to hold a decent conversation with people… women… but with you, I'm like an awkward teenager again.'

'You were once awkward?'

He nodded.

'I can't imagine that.'

'I have photos to prove it.'

Her lips turned upwards and some of his tension slipped away. He didn't know why it mattered but he wanted to make her smile, to see laughter dance in those soft brown eyes.

'What about the other tattoo?'

'This one?' Zoe touched the back of her neck.

'Yes.'

'It's an eternity symbol.'

'Because?'

'You don't want to know.'

'I do.'

'Okay then, but it makes me sound a bit... harsh, I guess. I had it done to remind me not to trust a man ever again.'

'Oh.' Now things became a little clearer. Zoe had been hurt in the past. 'I see.'

'You asked.' She sighed. 'Sorry. I just had a bad experience and I wanted something to remind me not to put myself at risk again.'

'But you can't see it. Doesn't it need to be where you can see it to remind you?'

'I know it's there. Besides, I had it put on the back of my neck to symbolize how it's behind me now. The whole foolish and naive believing in love and happy-ever-after nonsense.'

Nate nodded. What had she been through to make her so against the idea of falling in love?

'I have some tattoos too.'

'What've you got?'

'This one here.' He lifted the sleeve of his T-shirt slightly to reveal a skull on the underside of his left arm. Either side of the skull were surfboards, and behind those towering waves. 'It's about—'

'Respecting the power of the sea.'

'That's right.'

'One false move and it can crush you.'

'Is that what happened to you?'

'I thought we were looking at your tattoos.'

'Of course. Well, there's one here.' He lifted the hem of his T-shirt to reveal the one on his right side that covered his ribs and disappeared beneath his jeans and over his hip.

'It's a tree.'

'*Yggdrasil*. The tree from Norse mythology.'

'It must have taken hours.'

'Three sittings.'

'How…'

'How what?'

'How far down does it go?' she asked him, and he watched as her cheeks darkened.

'You want to see?'

She glanced around her. 'Uh…'

'Not here… but I could show you sometime.'

Was he flirting with her now? He believed he was and he was enjoying himself.

'Ha!' She shook her head. 'If I did want to see it, it would be purely because I like tattoos.'

'Of course. Do you have more?'

She pursed her lips. 'Perhaps.'

'Well, one day I'll show you mine if you show me yours.'

'You really have the cheek of the devil, don't you?'

He laughed and she joined him.

'In answer to your question, Zoe, it runs down over my hip. The roots tail off at the top of my upper thigh.'

'Gorgeous.'

'Thank you.'

'I meant the tattoo.'

'I know you did.'

'I should be going.'

Nate pulled his mobile from his pocket and checked the time. He didn't want her to go now that the ice between them seemed to have thawed. He wanted to keep talking, to find out more about her and to show her the rest of his tattoos, as well as to see hers. If she actually had more, that was, and wasn't trying to wind him up. But boy, was he curious now…

'Zoe, would you like to grab a drink sometime?'

'A drink?'

'Yes. You know, at the pub or the wine bar.'

'Oh… uh…'

'Just as friends. No expectations, no pressure, no worrying. I'd like to talk to you more.'

'I guess I could join you for a drink.'

'Great. Shall we meet at eight at the wine bar on Saturday?'

'Make it nine, as I keep the diner open a bit later in the summer.'

'Nine it is, then.'

Zoe stood up and slid her bag over her shoulder.

'Now, look out for low-flying plant pots, Zoe.'

'Ha ha!' She shook her head, but just before she went through the door and into the summer afternoon, she flashed him a warm smile, and something inside him fluttered, as if she'd fanned the flames of the spark she'd already lit inside him.

Chapter 6

'There's a good girl, Monica.'

Nate smoothed the soft head of the black and white greyhound. 'Let's go for a good long walk, shall we?'

Monica dropped into a bow, her long tail curving upwards and wagging with delight. Nate clipped the lead onto her collar then waved at Neil as they left the sanctuary and headed off across the fields.

It was early Saturday morning and the grass was wet with dew. Birds were singing in the hedgerows and everything had that flawless aura that exists first thing in the morning before the day really gets underway. The air smelt of earth, grass and flowers and Nate sucked in deep breaths, enjoying the beauty of the location. That was one of the great things about Conwenna Cove; it was on the coast yet also so rural. You could walk up from the cove and be in the countryside in no time at all.

Once they reached the main road that led down into Conwenna, all Nate could hear apart from the birds' morning chorus were his footsteps on the tarmac, the pattering of Monica's claws and the tinkling of the clasp against the ring on Monica's collar. They walked briskly, warming their muscles as the sun began to heat the earth, and Monica trotted effortlessly at his side.

They soon reached the fork in the road that led off to the main street with the shops and the harbour and, in the other direction, to the cove. Nate took a right and followed the route along the cliffs until they got to the path that led down to the beach.

'Let's be careful going down here, Monica,' he said, as much for himself as for the greyhound.

At the bottom, Nate looked around. The beach appeared to be deserted, so he unclipped Monica from the lead then patted her gently.

'Go on, girl. You can have a run!'

Monica smiled for a moment, her brown eyes assessing him, then gave a skip and raced away, curving in a great arc until she came heading back to him. He laughed as she swerved at the last minute to avoid him, then bolted along the beach in the other direction.

Monica had only been at the sanctuary for a few weeks but she was proving to be a very sweet and friendly greyhound. At four years old, she had been raced but after winning her first few races, she'd apparently proved to be nothing spectacular on the track, so the owner had passed her on to the rehoming charity. As Nate watched her run, he knew that she did it for the sheer joy of running and not because she was being forced into it. And that was why he knew that he wanted to help the sanctuary financially. It was so important. He would have homed Monica in a second if he'd been staying around, but knowing that he was soon leaving meant that he had to distance himself from falling for her, a bit like he'd always distanced himself from the women in his life. A bit like he knew he should be distancing himself from Zoe, and certainly not taking her out for a drink that evening.

The pounding of small feet on the sand dragged him back to the present and soon Monica was at his side, leaning against him.

'Come on, let's have a wander together, shall we?'

He clipped her lead back on now that she'd had a chance to stretch her legs and they ambled down to the sea that was on its way out. In the morning light, the water appeared dark, deep and vast. There was a haze hanging over the sea that made the horizon blurry, as if a low-lying cloud of smoke was drifting across the water, and he watched as seagulls swooped and soared, apparently oblivious to the fact that they were being watched.

'Hello!'

Nate turned at the greeting and waved in return. He didn't recognise the couple approaching him with a fawn greyhound in tow. Greyhound owners tended to be pretty friendly on the whole and, in his experience, they were always keen to talk about their dogs.

'Hi there.' Nate smiled as the couple neared him.

'You here on holiday?' the man asked, and Nate noted the musical Welsh accent.

'No, I'm a local. This here's Monica from the sanctuary up at Foxglove Farm.'

'Not yours, then?'

'No, I exercise the dogs for the sanctuary manager when I can.'

The man smiled. 'I'm Nigel Maggs and this is my wife, Gaynor.' He held out his hand and Nate shook it. 'And this here's our boy, Ash.'

'Pleased to meet you.'

'We're on holiday in Cornwall and thought we'd visit Conwenna Cove today. Got an early start as Ash wanted sausages for breakfast.'

Nigel leant over and stroked Ash's head and the greyhound responded by leaning against his legs.

'Sausages, eh?' Nate laughed when Ash's ears pricked up.

'He does love his sausages,' Gaynor said. 'And he loves cake.'

At this, Nigel's grin grew bigger. 'Oh, we have some stories about this one, believe me.'

'I think most greyhound owners do.'

'Proper food thief he is. Good job we love him so much.'

'I don't know if you'll still be around but on the first Saturday of August, we're having an event to raise money for the charity. It's called Surf for Sighthounds.'

'We'd have loved that, but we'll be back home by then and back in work.'

'That's a shame.' Nate nodded. 'But I hope you enjoy your holiday.'

'I'm sure we will. We've travelled quite a lot over recent years, but we were just saying that we've never been anywhere quite as lovely as Conwenna Cove.'

'It is a beautiful location. Also, if it's sausages you're wanting, there's the cafe on the main street, or you could try the diner down by the harbour. You can get a good meal at both places.'

'Fabulous, thanks.' Nigel smiled. 'We're going to have a long walk now to work up an appetite, then head into the village for a well-earned breakfast.'

'Good for you. Bye!'

Nate gave a wave then headed back to the path with Monica.

Nigel and Gaynor had been very friendly and their dog looked so happy and well cared for. Ash was clearly adored, especially if they were laughing at his food-stealing antics. Nate hoped Monica would find a good home too. It was what he wanted for all the hounds that came to the sanctuary.

As they climbed the path to the cliffs, Nate spoke softly to Monica about the home she would find and the family who would love her, about the happy days she had ahead of her and the good walks she would enjoy. And all the time, she seemed to be listening, because when they reached the top, he sat down on the grass and she came and stood close to him, then licked his cheek. She clearly liked the dream he'd described to her and now he hoped it would come true.

And as he sat there, gazing at the sea, something inside him lurched. Something Nigel had said was playing on his mind. Conwenna Cove *was* a beautiful location and Nate lived there, yet he was thinking of leaving it all. He had all this on his doorstep and he realized in that moment exactly how much he was going to miss it.

Was he doing the right thing after all?

–

Zoe placed the diner phone back behind the counter and hugged herself. This was brilliant news! Grace Phillips had just phoned and asked if she and Oli could hold their engagement party at the diner the following Saturday. It didn't give her much time, but Grace had told Zoe what she wanted and it wasn't too ambitious, and Zoe could certainly manage it. With both her chefs on board, the diner could easily cater for around thirty guests. Grace had told Zoe that they'd decided to bring the engagement party forward because Oli wanted Nate to be there, so they'd decided to do it before he went away and before the Surf for Sighthounds event, when the village was likely to become really busy indeed.

She jotted a few notes down on her pad then checked her watch. It was four-thirty, which meant that she was meeting Nate in four and a half hours. Her stomach did a loop-the-loop and she rolled her eyes. Why was she getting nervous? She was simply meeting a nice local guy for a drink and a chat. And yet... the thought of what they'd discussed the day before was lingering at the back of her mind. He'd said that he'd show her the rest of his tattoo and it led down under his jeans...

She shook herself. This was silly. Yes, he was an attractive man but Zoe had no intention of getting involved with anyone. Nate represented everything she'd sworn she'd stay away from in life and she wasn't going to go back on her word, however nice he seemed. Besides, he was leaving at the end of the summer and that was probably a good thing because then Zoe could go back to her normal existence and focus on the diner and...

And what, exactly?

What, or who, was waiting for Zoe when she got home at night?

Who was there to run her a bath or make her a cup of tea or to hold her when she woke from one of her nightmares?

There was no one.

Zoe was alone.

She gripped the edge of the counter and waited for the dark cloud to pass. It would move on, she knew this from experience, but when it loomed, it was as horrid as always. All she needed to do was to remind herself how lucky she was to have her own business; to live in a beautiful seaside village; and to have a lovely Cornish cottage where she could walk around in her pyjamas all day and eat ice cream straight from the tub if she wanted. She could watch reality TV shows all evening without having to compromise on sharing the remote. She could stretch out in the bed and not worry about elbowing someone else in the face or whether she'd shaved her legs in weeks.

Yes, she was fine. Zoe was just fine... she was more than fine.

She released her grip on the counter and forced her face into a smile. She had several hours of work left so she would focus on that, on giving her customers the best experience they could have at her diner, then she would go and meet Nate for a drink. And she would not think about his tattoos: the ones she had seen... and the ones she hadn't.

–

Nate arrived at the wine bar twenty minutes early. He'd been pacing his small flat, watching the hands of the clock ticking slowly round, and it had been too much for him so he'd decided to take a gentle stroll down to the wine bar, thinking he'd get there about nine if he took his time. Of course, he'd got there in five minutes flat with his long strides, so he decided to go inside and get a drink.

At the bar, he ordered a glass of house red then he looked around, wondering if Zoe was early too, but apart from three couples and an older man reading a book, there was no one else there. The couples weren't familiar, so must be tourists on holiday or people from outside the village.

The interior of the wine bar was cool with the breeze that entered through the open windows, causing the sheer white curtains to billow against their tiebacks; along with the soft harp music that floated from speakers, there was a delightful ambience about the place. He could easily have sat inside, but as the evening was so pleasant, he decided to take a table outside overlooking the harbour.

Nate went back through the door and into the warm evening air then sat at a table for two opposite the harbour rail. He sipped his wine and gazed across the water. People strolled along the walkway that wound on past the harbour and along the coastal path, heading in both directions. The first building on the harbour was the lifeboat house with its stone jetty that led straight into the sea. Thankfully, there hadn't been many callouts this year so far, but when there were, everyone in the village held their breath, hoping that the outcome would be good and that no tragedy would darken their village.

Along from the lifeboat house was Sugar and Spice, the sweetshop that sold locally sourced sweets, like the clotted cream fudge from Foxglove Farm. Outside the shop was a bench and as Nate peered across, he thought he recognized the couple sitting on it eating ice creams. When a fawn greyhound emerged from behind the bench to snatch the ice cream cone from its male owner's hands, Nate snorted. It was Ash, with Nigel and Gaynor. Nate saw Nigel shaking his head at the dog then laughing as he hugged his wife.

They looked like a perfectly happy trio and something in Nate's chest ached. Whether it was seeing such a happy couple, the fact that the greyhound had its forever family, or just the beauty of the Conwenna evening, he wasn't sure, but suddenly he realized he'd never felt more alone than he did right now.

'How's the wine?'

Nate turned in his chair to find Zoe standing there. His breath caught as he gazed at her cream silk dress with a pattern of tiny black hearts. The dress fell to mid-calf where it seemed to float against her skin. She'd paired it with flat, black thong sandals that revealed perfectly straight toes and scarlet-painted toenails. And her hair… softly waved and shiny, it fell around her face. As she stood there smiling at him, he caught her scent on the breeze and it roused something deep inside him. She smelt of strawberries and vanilla and he had an urge to stand up and scoop her into his arms so that he could see if she tasted as good as she smelt.

'Oh…' His voice caught so he cleared his throat. 'The wine's good. House red. Want a glass?'

He stood up and leant forwards to kiss her cheeks. Her skin was soft and warm and her hair tickled his skin.

'I'd love one, please.'

'Do you want to stay out here… or to sit inside?'

'Shall we sit out here? It's a glorious evening.'

'Of course. Back in a moment.'

Nate pulled out a chair for her to sit down then went back into the wine bar. He was glad of the opportunity to collect himself, because seeing Zoe in that pretty dress that caressed her perfect curves and moved gently in the breeze, along with smelling her delicious scent, had proved to be a bit much for him. And to think he'd barely known the woman existed a week ago. It just showed that sometimes he walked around in his own little bubble, not noticing what was right in front of him. Perhaps deliberately so, because now that he was getting to know Zoe, Nate knew that he was starting to want more.

He was glad he had the chance to spend more time with Zoe, more time to gaze into her soft brown eyes and to get to know if there was something beneath that veneer of hers that made her even more enticing than she already was. Because Nate was certain that there was far more to Zoe, and that he had only scratched the surface of who she really was and what secrets she had to hide. That this growing attraction towards her was something he should suppress, whilst knowing it was something he wanted to put to the test, because it was making him feel as if there was a whole other side to himself and to life, that he had, as yet, failed to explore.

–

Zoe tried to relax on the wicker chair outside the wine bar, but her stomach was a boiling pot of nerves. When she'd arrived, she'd spotted Nate straight away and had used the time that he was unaware of her approaching to enjoy looking at him. Nate's blond hair was in its usual messy style, some of it gelled up and back while some fell carelessly over his smooth forehead. His faded jeans and white linen shirt set off his golden tan. The cuffs of the shirt were loosely rolled up, showing off his strong toned forearms with their dusting of white-blond hairs and his lovely strong hands, hands that Zoe had watched create coffees and teas, as well as sandwiches and crepes, along with many other meals. She couldn't help but wonder what it might be like to feel those long lean fingers on her skin and that hard male body against her own.

When she had spoken to Nate to let him know she'd arrived, she'd liked the way his eyes had lit up as he'd looked at her. He'd clearly approved of her choice of dress and she'd felt at once feminine and empowered by the soft light silk. She had purchased it last summer although it was the first time she'd worn it, not having found a suitable occasion until this point.

When Nate returned with a glass of wine and placed it in front of her she thanked him, then waited for him to sit back down before taking a sip.

'Is it okay?' he asked.

'It's lovely.'

'Good. How was your day?'

'Great, thank you.' She took another sip of wine, enjoying the sensation as it slid down her throat and warmed her tummy from the inside. It was strong too, she could already feel it filtering into her bloodstream, relaxing her and soothing her nerves. 'Grace rang and asked if they could hold their engagement party at the diner next Saturday.'

'Oh, that's great news! Good for you and the business.'

Zoe nodded. 'It is wonderful. They want a buffet and champagne for about thirty guests.'

'Oli did mention they'd have one soon, but they've must've decided to do it right away.'

'And, why not? Life is for living right?' Zoe winced inwardly. Why had she used that line? She didn't want to tell him that Grace had said it was so Nate could be there; it wasn't her place to do so.

'It is for living. That's why I thought I'd better go away soon, or I'll never go. I'm so comfortable in Conwenna Cove that it's made me a bit complacent.'

'Is that wrong, then?'

'Being complacent is, if sometimes…' He worried his full bottom lip and Zoe had to look away because all she could think about was kissing him. 'I mean… I sometimes I feel as if there's something missing.'

'There's something missing from your life?'

He nodded. 'I'm not quite sure what, but lately I've been feeling that there must be more to life than what I have. Perhaps it's down to my age, and don't get me wrong, I do love my life, but…'

'There's an emptiness. Behind everything.'

'Yes! A sense that time is slipping away and although I've had a ball, I haven't really achieved anything.'

'But you have, Nate. You make people happy.'

'Like who?'

'Your aunt and uncle, the customers who come into the cafe, and your friends.'

'But, no one special.'

'You have your fair share of special *someones*, don't you?' She drank more wine to suppress the pang of jealousy she experienced as she acknowledged the fact that Nate dated a lot of women.

'I guess I deserved that.'

'No, I didn't aim to be mean. I just… I know you date from time to time.'

Nate laughed. 'So I do, but none of them are special to me, Zoe. Perhaps that's wrong of me but I've never fallen in love. It's more a mutual agreement to have some fun but I always, always make it clear from the start that there's nothing ahead for us. I never lead my dates on.'

'Some women see that as a challenge, you know.'

'Really?'

'They think they can be the one to change your mind.'

Nate shook his head. 'My mind won't be changed.'

Zoe nodded. 'It's good that you're honest. Some men… and women… aren't, and that can lead to other people getting hurt. Far better to say you want some fun and nothing else than to lead people on or to deceive them by marrying them and making them feel secure while you…' She sighed as she realized what she'd said. 'Sorry. I sound so bitter sometimes, and I hate it. This isn't who I am and I won't be defined by anger and pain.'

'Zoe, it's fine. I guessed someone let you down in the past, and he's an idiot. I'm a good listener if you want to talk about it.'

'Thank you.'

'And you're a good listener too, you know.'

'I am?'

'You are.' He drained his wine. 'Now, how about I get us another glass of red and we put the world to rights?'

'Why not?'

'Yes, let's celebrate.'

'Celebrate?'

'It's a gorgeous evening and I'm here with a gorgeous woman, so I think that's a reason to celebrate.'

'Okay then!' Zoe finished her wine, flushing at his compliment. 'Let's celebrate.'

And as she watched Nate head back into the wine bar, she meant what she'd said. At least, right now, anyway. Her idiot of an ex might have hurt her, lied to her and broken her heart but that was in the past. She had a new life and a future in Conwenna Cove, and the chance to spend some time with a lovely man. Celebrating that seemed like a very good plan indeed.

Chapter 7

Zoe's face was aching from smiling. For over an hour, Nate had regaled her with stories about his time at the Conwenna Cafe and up at the sanctuary. He knew so many people and had such great relationships with others, as if being friendly was effortless. He was clearly one of life's likeable characters and she marvelled again at how he was single. He was the type of man that a woman would want to spend time with. And women did, clearly, want to spend time with him, but he'd already told her that it never became anything long term.

Not that she'd forgotten her previous reservations about him; she hadn't at all. She'd merely tucked them to one side in order to enjoy their evening and she was glad she had made the effort, because Nate wasn't the shallow, narcissistic surfer dude that Zoe had suspected him of being. This, in turn, made her question why she had made up her mind about him so soon after arriving in Conwenna. Yet she knew why: Zoe did not want to like anyone who could be similar to her ex in any way, shape or form. Even the fact that Nate surfed had made her determined to dislike him.

Now she'd spent some time with him, she knew that she couldn't help but like him.

However, Nate wasn't looking for commitment, and neither was Zoe.

So where did that leave them?

She shivered and Nate's expression changed.

'Are you cold?'

'No... not really. Just the breeze has cooled down a bit.'

'And when did it get dark?'

Zoe looked around them. 'About twenty minutes ago, I think.'

The street lamps had come on as they chatted and a waitress had come out and lit the candles in the yellow glass holders on the outside tables. The moon was visible now, a silver crescent high above the sea, casting its glow over the surface of the water that was otherwise black, mysterious, wonderful and intimidating.

'Perfect time for a swim.' Nate gently touched her arm, and goosebumps rose on her skin.

'Maybe. At least if you can't see, you can't be afraid, I suppose.'

'Afraid? The water should be respected, not feared.'

'It depends what it's done to you.'

'I agree.' He nodded thoughtfully. 'Shall we go inside now?'

'Okay.'

He stood up then held out a hand. Zoe hesitated for a moment; she was not used to holding men's hands, but Nate's smile was so warm and kind that she linked her fingers in his and they walked into the wine bar together.

It was quite busy and all the tables had been taken except for one in the far corner, near the open fireplace. No fire burned there, as it was July, but there were logs and bunches of dried lavender in the grate and when they sat down, Zoe could smell the sharpness of the lavender and the faint aroma of smoke from old fires. It was comforting and homely, reminding her of the open fireplace at her cottage.

'More wine?' Nate asked, as he lifted his empty glass.

'I'll get it. It must be my round now.'

Zoe went to the bar and ordered a bottle. The barman gave her fresh glasses and as she waited for him to uncork the wine, she thought about what a good time she was having. Nate had turned all her assumptions about him on their head and she was enjoying his company immensely. It had been a long time since Zoe had gone out on a date and a long time since she'd been able to relax in a man's company. Did that mean Nate was special, or that she was finally ready to move on from her past? Was this the start of her new life? Were there possibilities ahead for her that involved a man and companionship? So many thoughts whirled around in her head that she felt almost dizzy.

Best to focus on the evening for now and on getting to know Nate better. Sure, he didn't want a relationship or anything serious – he was going away soon – but he'd definitely made Zoe start to think about a life that wasn't shut off from the possibilities of love and romance.

She carried the bottle and glasses back to the table, where Nate was gazing up at the drawings above the fireplace.

'Are they Jack's?' she asked.

Jack Adams drew some amazing pictures of greyhounds and local scenery that he sold at the Conwenna art gallery; many of the local businesses displayed his work for him for a small fee. Zoe had some at the diner too, although she always refused to accept anything from him in exchange.

She was happy to have the artwork on her walls as she enjoyed looking at it, and the continuous sales meant that there was always something new to admire.

'Yes, I think so. That looks like Gabe.' He pointed at the sketch of a beautiful big black greyhound.

'He's a gorgeous dog, isn't he?'

'He is, and he adores Eve and his family.'

'Would you like to adopt a dog?'

'I would love to, but not until I return. What about you?'

'After losing Raven, I'm not ready. But I like to think that I will in the future.'

'What else do you see in your future?'

Zoe poured wine into their glasses. 'Ooh, I don't know. Perhaps I'll open another diner in another village and create a chain of Zoe's Diners. You know, sell the franchise.' She smiled, knowing that while it was something she believed she could do if she put her mind to it, it would mean a hell of a lot of work and she liked the pace of her life right now. She wanted time to do normal things like read a book, watch TV and walk. Life wasn't all about the buzz of business, much as she loved owning the diner. She wanted to be able to enjoy life too.

Possibly even go on a few dates... She swallowed a smile as the thought popped into her head.

'Would you do that, then? Open a whole chain?'

'No. I like the personal touch and I'm happy enough here. Sometimes, though, I think...' She paused and met his gaze.

'What do you think?'

'That I'd like to see a bit of the world. That it would be nice to travel, but then I remember that I have the diner and I'm all set up here. I couldn't leave it all, so it is a tie, I suppose, but it's one that I love.'

'You could always get someone to run it for you if you did go away.'

'Perhaps for a week or two, but not for anything long term. I mean… who'd run a business for someone else for six months, or more?'

Nate nodded, and Zoe's heart sank a little. What if her comment about travelling had made him think that they could have travelled together? This was so premature of her to consider and yet, something about Nate and getting to know him made her feel that she'd like to think there could be adventures ahead for them. After all, if she was going to have adventures in her life then Nate would be a good person to have them with, wouldn't he? Did he like her too? Or was the wine affecting her common sense? It was, most probably, dulling her inhibitions and bringing out her romantic side. And that side of her had been locked away for a long, long time.

'Zoe… I'm having a great time.'

'Me, too.'

They clinked glasses.

'I wish we'd met sooner.' He smiled at her. His cheeks were slightly flushed and he seemed very relaxed.

'We met ages ago, didn't we? We've both been in Conwenna for quite a while.'

'Well, we met, but we didn't meet properly. You've been here all this time, walking the same streets and the same beach, breathing the same air and all those type of things… but it's only now that I feel like I'm getting to know you properly.'

She swallowed hard as her thoughts struggled to escape as words. Just because Nate was being nice didn't mean she could dump the contents of her head in his lap, or unburden herself about her past and why she was so terrified of being hurt again. There was no point in letting her mouth run away with her.

'I understand what you mean.'

And she did. And it was too late. Nothing could happen between them now. Perhaps this was because he was leaving anyway. Perhaps Nate would have ended up marrying one of those beautiful dates sooner or later, if he hadn't been going away, and Zoe would never have got to know him like this. Perhaps, but who knew? Nothing was certain in life; nothing was guaranteed.

Especially not finding the one person you could love and rely on, the one person who would love you unconditionally and keep you safe from harm. A person you could trust.

–

Nate picked up the wine bottle.

'Looks like we drank it all.'

'It's a very easy-drinking red.'

'What shall we do now? Do you want another?'

Zoe shook her head. 'Better not.'

'Shall we make a move, then?'

Zoe nodded, even though leaving was the last thing she wanted to do.

She stood up and slipped her bag over her shoulder, then followed Nate into the evening air. They stood outside the wine bar and gazed at the dark expanse of the sea.

'It's exciting, isn't it?' Nate said, as he leant his arms on the rail.

'What is?'

'The sheer size of the sea. It goes on and on, and makes me feel that anything is possible. I could go anywhere if I got into the water and let it take me.'

Zoe shuddered. 'Let it take you?'

He turned to face her and straightened up. 'Yes. Well, it's far more powerful than I'll ever be. Yet I've always felt that it empowered me. Until I discovered my love of surfing, I was a very different person.'

'How so?'

He glanced at his shoes then met her eyes.

'I was a very quiet and shy young man. I always tried to avoid people, growing up.'

'You? Really?'

'I believed I was… insignificant. I didn't like to impose my company on anyone.'

'Of course you aren't… weren't. No one is insignificant, and that's a very sad way to feel.'

Zoe's heart squeezed as she stared into the depths of Nate's eyes and saw the vulnerable boy he'd once been. Why had he felt that way when he had so much to offer the world?

'I did as a boy. Then I found the water and I changed, almost overnight. Not wanting to sound cheesy but it's as if I found *me*… out there.' He swept his arm across the harbour.

'Well, that's a very positive thing… in that you became more confident. Life changes us all. Some for the better, but some not.'

'Hey.' He reached out and gently cupped her cheeks, smoothing his thumbs over her cheekbones. 'Whatever happened to you, Zoe, it wasn't your fault. You're a good person, I can tell.'

Zoe couldn't reply. She was struck mute by the sensations his touch had aroused in her, and by the deep blue of his eyes that shone in the light from the wine bar. It was as if he glowed from within and his warmth could envelope her and keep her safe and warm.

Nate moved closer and she could feel the heat of his breath on her lips, smell the berry flavours of the wine they'd drunk. His hands slid round her so that one entwined in her hair at her nape and the other rested on her back. He was so close that the heat of his body warmed her and her heart pounded as he lowered his lips to meet hers.

The sea lapped at the harbour wall and voices carried through the open windows of the wine bar as they kissed. Zoe was frozen in time, held firmly by Nate, knowing that she should stop this, prevent this, but though a part of her mind tried to fight, the rest of her surrendered. She shouldn't want this, but she did.

When Nate finally released her, Zoe was breathless. She hadn't been kissed like that her whole life: every nerve ending was on fire, burning with need and desire and threatening to make her fall completely and irrevocably in love with this man.

She took a step backwards and grabbed the handrail for support.

'Zoe...' Nate touched her arm. 'I... I hope that was okay.'

She nodded. 'It was more than okay but—'

'No buts. Not for tonight.' He sighed. 'Tonight was perfect.'

'It was.'

He wrapped his arm around her shoulder and they stayed that way for some time, gazing at the horizon, unable to tell where the sea ended and the sky began. And Zoe, in that moment, Zoe didn't know where she ended and Nate began, because the kiss they'd shared had been so intense, so wonderful, so emotional, that she'd become one with him in a way that she'd never experienced before. It was terrifying, exhilarating and it shouldn't have happened. But she didn't regret it for a second.

'Nate!'

Zoe and Nate turned to the direction of the shout that was quickly followed by peals of laughter. Two young women were staggering around the harbour, clinging to each other as they wobbled on very high heels. As they got closer, one pointed at him.

'I thought it wash you! Nate, I lovesh you.'

She released her friend and lunged at Nate, causing Zoe to quickly sidestep to avoid being knocked over.

'Oh… uh… come on now… You look like you need to get home.' Nate held the girl away from him by her arms.

'My name is Calishta! Kish me, Nate!' She windmilled her arms as she tried to get closer to him but he'd locked his wrists and she couldn't get close enough.

Nate glanced at Zoe and grimaced.

'Calista, I think you and your friend had better go home,' Zoe said.

The young woman turned to Zoe and glared at her. 'And who the hell are you? What kind of frump tellsh me what to do?'

'Yeah!' Calista's friend put her hands on her hips and squinted at Zoe. 'Calista, don't take no shit off…' She eyed Zoe up and down. 'Frumps!'

Both women cackled then, and Zoe's contentment crumbled as the warmth from Nate's kiss ebbed away. Calista was right, even in her inebriated state. Zoe wasn't the type of woman Nate went for; she wasn't a good match for him, and she never would be. She'd let herself be fooled for a moment, for an evening, and enjoyed spending time with him. She'd actually allowed herself to hope that this evening signalled the start of something more for her, that her future didn't have to be lonely. Perhaps that was true, but it was also clear that there couldn't be a future for her and Nate.

Nate would be better matched with Calista in her short denim skirt and pink crop-top, with her beautiful, long wind-ruffled hair and her flawless golden tan.

'I'll see you,' Zoe said, giving Nate a quick wave before walking away.

She hurried along the harbour, glad she'd worn flats, trying to think of nothing at all except for getting home and crawling into bed then pulling the covers over her head.

Behind her, she heard a few shouts then a squeal of fury, but she kept her head down and kept moving. She passed her diner, the deli and the art gallery, then marched up the main street of the village, all the while taking deep, cleansing breaths and shutting out the sounds around her, behind her, and especially the voice in her head that told her to go back and fight for her man. There was no way she was going to be humiliated again, no way on this earth! Better to be alone than to risk the pain of heartbreak. And Nate was not her man…

She took a left at Riding the Wave, then turned right onto the road that would take her to her cottage. She breathed quickly as she tried to fill her lungs with enough air to keep her going until she got home.

When a hand landed on her arm, she screamed and instinctively swung her bag at her assailant.

'Argh!'

Nate held his cheek as he looked down at her, his chest rising and falling rapidly.

'What are you doing? Why have you followed me?' Zoe glared at him. 'And… oh… did I hurt you?'

'I think the zip caught me.'

'Let me see.'

Zoe gently pulled his hand away and a droplet of blood trickled down his cheek.

'Oh, Nate, I'm so sorry. I just… you scared me and I reacted. I wouldn't have done it if I'd known it was you.'

'I was calling you, Zoe. How didn't you hear me?'

She opened her bag and pulled out a tissue, then pressed it to his face.

'I didn't, I'm sorry. I was lost in my thoughts.'

'Why did you leave?'

'Why d'you think?'

'Because those two idiots were babbling nonsense?'

'Nate… they were just being honest. Saying what they saw.'

'What they saw?' His voice broke. 'That was utter crap, Zoe. You're not frumpy. They're jealous. You're beautiful, classy… you have substance they could only dream of.'

'They're young, Nate, and Calista clearly has a huge crush on you.'

'I barely know her. She's here on holiday and has come into the cafe a few times.'

'It doesn't matter.'

'What?' His eyes were dark hollows now in the moonlight, and Zoe saw the blood seeping through the tissue.

'We should get that cleaned up. I think you need a plaster.'

'Okay.'

'Come on.'

They walked the rest of the way to her cottage in silence. Zoe unlocked the front door and they went inside. She turned on the two lamps in the lounge.

'Sit on the sofa and I'll find my first aid kit.'

Five minutes later, she'd cleaned his cheek and was relieved to see that it was just a scratch. Nate had sat there silently, watching her as she tended to him. When she'd finished and stuck a small plaster on his cheek, he took her hand.

'Zoe, please. I'm a bit confused. I thought we had a good time.'

'We did. It was lovely.'

'So what's going on here… now?'

She leant forwards and rested her forehead against his, breathing him in for a moment and savouring his gorgeous scent, knowing that tonight had been like a lovely dream and that tomorrow it would be replaced by cold reality.

'Nothing's going on, Nate. I got carried away on too much wine and a very pleasant kiss. But thank you. It was lovely to imagine how different life could be, if just for an evening.'

'Zoe?' He stood up and tried to take her hands but she folded her arms across her chest.

'I'm tired, Nate.'

'Right, but…'

His face was so handsome in the lamplight and his eyes so full of questions and confusion that Zoe almost weakened. Almost. Then she remembered the look in Calista's eyes and the feelings she'd tried to bury for so long. And she knew that she couldn't go through all that again; she'd left that life behind her.

'Good night, Nate.'

His expression changed, and it was as if a shutter had come down in his eyes to hide his emotions.

'Good night, Zoe.'

He opened the front door and stepped out, then closed it behind him, leaving nothing in his wake other than a waft of his sandalwood aftershave and the heat of his kiss that still lingered on Zoe's lips.

Chapter 8

Nate rubbed a hand over his stubble and sighed. He needed to have a shave but he'd been struggling to muster the energy or inclination to do much at all since Sunday. He still couldn't understand how Saturday evening had gone so terribly wrong. At the wine bar, he'd had such a great time with Zoe and then that kiss they'd shared outside… He'd kissed a few women in his time but never like that. It was as if Zoe was the one he'd been waiting for all his life, and now that he'd finally found her, she didn't want to know.

Or was it that her reluctance to take things any further between them was making her a more attractive prospect? Nate had never had to work for a woman's affections, and part of him wondered if he liked the challenge that Zoe presented. Yet the other part whispered to him that it was because Zoe Russell was special, that she was right for him on so many levels, even those there was no logical explanation for.

Nate's decision to go away now had been, in part, because he'd thought it was now or never, but it was also because his life – as pleasant as it was – had stagnated. While those around him like Jack and Oli fell in love, got married and had children, Nate was in the same situation as he had been in his twenties. He could continue to live like that, he knew he could, but recently he'd realized that he didn't want to. He'd also been thinking more and more about his dad and how his life had been cut short. It could happen to anyone at any time. But at least his dad had loved his wife and his family; he'd had a deep connection with other people. Nate had friends and acquaintances but no one special. He'd spent years with beautiful, funny, successful women but not one of them had been someone he'd thought he could settle down with, and looking back at his behaviour now, it was obvious that he'd chosen those women deliberately. Nate might come across as the gregarious party animal, but inside he was more than that. Inside, he was still the quiet, serious boy he'd been growing up. Whatever he did and wherever he went, he would always carry that person with him. That side of him wanted more from a woman than the likes of Calista had to offer – they didn't want the real Nate, the gentle, serious man underneath the flamboyant exterior, and as a result, he knew he could never reveal that side of himself to them. But something told him that he could share that part of him with Zoe. Of course he could, and she would never judge him for being that way because she was so similar.

They were alike.

Nate could be himself with Zoe, and that was something special.

But then he sighed. Zoe had pushed him away and closed herself down to him following their date, so even if he was aware of all this, it wouldn't do him any good.

It was Wednesday evening, and he was sitting in the cafe alone after closing, trying to get his head around the plans for Surf for Sighthounds. It would have been great if he could have invited Zoe round to help him with them.

He rubbed his eyes then lowered his forehead to the table where he had his notebook open. He'd been trying to focus on the things he'd written, to push the pretty diner owner from his mind, but without much success. Zoe Russell had got under his skin and it was ridiculous. Nate was about to embark upon the trip of a lifetime, and he'd have plenty of opportunities to get to know beautiful women on his travels, but for some reason that thought did not appeal at all. Panic fluttered in his chest. What if he never felt like being with another woman again? What if he couldn't think about any woman other than Zoe? How the hell would he manage if he went away for six months or more, knowing that Zoe was here in Conwenna and that she wasn't thinking about him? At all. Ever.

He groaned and rubbed the back of his head. What was he going to do?

Focus! That's what he was going to do. Time was flying past and he needed to get his plans for Surf for Sighthounds up and running.

A noise from outside the cafe caught his attention and he turned to look out of the window. A couple walked past, holding hands and laughing as if they hadn't a care in the world. They were dressed up, presumably heading out for dinner or drinks, like he'd been on Saturday with Zoe. He'd felt lighter being with Zoe than he had done in ages, and although it seemed impossible, he actually missed her already. And Nate didn't do this: he didn't care about women, it just wasn't his style at all.

But Zoe…

He shook his head then took a deep breath. He was going round in circles, getting nowhere.

Right, where was he?

His mobile buzzed on the table next to him and he picked it up, briefly hoping it might be Zoe, but it was a text from his mum inviting him for dinner on Sunday. He thanked her and said he'd be there, then released a slow breath. He'd been a bit worried about his mother recently because she hadn't been as responsive to his text messages, and when he had managed to get through to her on the phone, she'd been a bit quiet and not her usual upbeat self. Nate knew people went through ups and downs, and his mother had been through some tough times – such as the loss of his father – but she always seemed to be so stoic that he was able to avoid worrying about her. He needed to see her, so lunch gave him a perfect excuse to go and check how she was getting on.

He scanned the page in front of him where he'd written a list of local businesses that had agreed to help, and in what ways. The shops in the main street were involved, the Conwenna Arms, the deli, the art gallery and the wine bar, and Zoe had agreed to help out too. He ticked off the last few on his list, then smiled. It should be a good day and, more importantly, it would hopefully raise money for the greyhounds that would keep them going for a while.

He stood up and stretched. He needed to burn off some energy, and a run or surf would be a good way to do that. His muscles were tight and his shoulders tense; he clearly needed to exercise. He'd head down to the cove and clear his head before it got dark, and try not to think about the engagement party on Saturday. The party that he couldn't avoid because Oli was one of his best friends, so he couldn't exactly decline the invitation to attend his engagement celebrations, even though the party was at the diner and that meant that Nate would be in the same room as Zoe for a whole evening. She hadn't sent him so much as a text since Saturday, and he hadn't liked to contact her in case she got mad, because she'd seemed pretty certain that she didn't want to pursue their friendship when she'd basically kicked him out of her cottage.

Yes, Nate needed to face facts: Zoe Russell was off limits and there wasn't a thing he could do to change her mind.

-

Zoe walked along the cliff top enjoying the way the wind lifted her hair from her face and cooled her heated skin. Usually, she hated when the wind blew her fringe from her forehead in case anyone saw her scar, but the path was deserted and she could enjoy the freedom of being alone and unseen.

It had been a busy day at the diner and she was aching all over with tiredness, but she was glad of the exhaustion. Being so busy slowed her mind down and helped her to fall asleep, without going over the same old things hour after hour.

And there were so many things competing for space in her mind right now. The dominant thought was of Nate and how sad she was that she'd had to push him away on Saturday evening. It had been one of the hardest things she'd ever done because it had meant going against her desire to fall into his arms and forget about everything else for a few blissful hours. Zoe could have asked him to stay at her cottage after their date, and she knew it would have been good, but she also knew she'd have been terrified afterwards. For Zoe, giving her body meant giving her heart too, and what if Nate hadn't wanted that? What if he'd woken the next morning, still intent on leaving Conwenna? Zoe couldn't have borne that. At least by not making love to him, she'd preserved something of herself, kept a part of her heart protected, and would hopefully be able to treat him kindly and respectfully when she next saw him.

She sat on a grassy verge that gave her a panoramic view of the cove. It was still light enough to see the beach and the sea, and she watched the waves crashing onto the shore for a while as the tide came in. The push and pull of the water was calming from her vantage point because she was far enough away to be out of danger. She wished she could love the water as she used to but after she'd almost drowned, it was difficult to rekindle the love she'd developed for it. The sea could hurt her and falling in love could hurt her; this was why she'd had no intention of getting close to doing either again. Yet Nate was different to her ex in many ways; she was sure of it. He loved the sea and surfing, but he didn't have the same, almost blasé attitude towards the water that Finn had shown. Finn was arrogantly convinced that he was in charge of the water, almost as if it was there for him, but Nate clearly respected the power of the sea. Nate had also admitted to her that he'd been a quiet and shy child; something which Zoe could empathize with, because she'd been the same growing up. This made her feel that she didn't need to put on an act with Nate, whereas with Finn she'd been under pressure to be the woman she thought he wanted her to be, whether it was surfing, having a hairless body and a perfect tan, or just being perpetually cheerful, upbeat and nonchalant about everything. She couldn't count the number of times he'd told her to 'Be chill, babe', whereas she couldn't imagine Nate saying anything so damned insulting.

A movement on the beach over to the right caught her eye and she watched as a figure ran towards the water, surfboard under arm. Her breath caught in her throat as she recognized the messy blond hair and broad shoulders encased in a black wetsuit. Soon, Nate was out beyond the smaller breakers, confident and calm as he waited for a good wave.

Zoe wanted to get up and walk away because she didn't want to watch him out on the water, but she couldn't tear her eyes away from him as he spring into action, catching a wave then riding it expertly to the shore.

She stayed where she was, her eyes glued to him as he repeated the process several times, his wetsuit shining with water and his hair flat to his head. If only she could run down there and join him, throw herself and all her cares and worries behind her and surf at his side. But the thought of being in the water, at the mercy of the sea, turned her cold inside.

As Nate caught a large wave, Zoe got to her knees and her hands curled into fists that she pressed into her legs. It was so dangerous and she knew that even the most capable surfers could be thrown from their boards and into the depths.

As the wave curled, Nate suddenly disappeared. His board bobbed up without him and Zoe heard a cry, which she realized had come from her own lips. Was he all right?

She scanned the water, willing the waves to subside, but they kept rising and falling then crashing forwards. She held her breath as panic filled her and she pulled her mobile from her bag. Should she phone the coastguard? The lifeboat house? Nate's aunt and uncle? What if he was gone and she never saw him again?

Her heart fluttered at the thought and dread spread through her veins. She'd only just started to get to know him; if she lost him now it would be a cruel twist of fate, far too cruel for a man as lovely as him to be torn from life in his prime.

She hurried across the cliff top, heading for the path. She paused for a second at the top to scroll through her contacts to find the number for the coastguard, then scanned the water one last time before calling for help.

And there he was!

She could see his head bobbing in between waves, his blond hair slick with water, then he had his arms around his board and he hauled himself out of the water and sat on the board while he caught his breath.

'Thank goodness for that!' Zoe muttered from between trembling lips.

She stepped slowly backwards as Nate rode his surfboard to the shore, then hopped off and ran along the beach to his belongings.

When she was certain that he was safe and not going back into the water that evening, she turned around and headed for home. But she left a piece of her heart behind, right there on the cliff top, watching over Nate.

Chapter 9

It was all well and good for Nate to tell himself he couldn't have Zoe when he wasn't around her, but when he arrived at the diner on Saturday evening, his palms were sweating and he was more agitated than he'd been in years.

He'd taken ages to decide what to wear, which wasn't like him, because he usually threw on whatever he thought would suffice, but this evening he wanted Zoe to think he looked good. Why, he had no idea, because she clearly wasn't interested in him, but it was something he had to do.

Strangely, on Wednesday evening, when he'd gone for a surf, he'd thought he'd seen Zoe on the cliff top watching him in the water, but he couldn't be certain. The slim figure and brown hair blowing in the breeze made him think of her but when he'd been thrown from his board, then looked up again, the figure had disappeared. He'd hoped it had been Zoe and he'd even shown off a bit. But when he'd been thrown from him board, he'd felt like a bit of an idiot for behaving like that. That was what he got for trying to impress a woman, although he wasn't sure if surfing would impress Zoe, as she had her reservations about the water.

He entered the diner and found Oli and Grace just inside the doorway.

'Nate, thanks for coming!' Oli shook his hand.

'Wouldn't miss this for the world, man. Hi, Grace.' Nate leant in and kissed Grace's cheek.

'Thanks for coming, lovely.' She offered him a warm smile. 'And don't you look all dressed up.'

'Do I?' Nate frowned. 'Too much?'

'No, I love it!' Grace touched the sleeve of his blue shirt. 'It's a fabulous colour and it matches your eyes.'

'Don't tell him that. He thinks he's chocolate as it is.' Oli laughed. 'Just kidding, Nate. We're simply not used to seeing you in anything other than jeans or shorts.'

Nate nodded. He'd bought the beige chinos from Riding the Wave the previous day, not knowing if he'd wear them or not, but he'd decided that the occasion warranted something a bit smarter than his usual attire.

'Have you done something with your hair, too?' Grace asked, as she tilted her head to peer at him.

Nate ran a hand over his head. 'Had a trim, that's all.'

'Gosh, it's much shorter, isn't it? And you've shaved.'

'Am I usually that scruffy, Grace?'

'Not at all. You look nice that's all… very nice.'

'Thank you. I think…' Suddenly, Nate delved a hand into his back pocket. 'Ooh! Before I forget.' He handed Grace the card he'd bought. 'I didn't know what you'd want or need, so I put some money in the card. Thought you could get what you wanted then.'

'You didn't need to get us anything, Nate.' Oli shook his head. 'We're just glad you came. That's what tonight is all about – celebrating with our friends and family.'

'It's not much and you can spend it on Amy and Tom if you like.'

Nate pressed the card into Grace's hand.

'Nate!'

Tom ran towards Nate and grabbed his leg. 'You came to the party.'

'Of course I came. Where else would I be?'

Tom peered up at him. 'Well, Daddy and Grace wanted to move the party sooner so you could come before you go on your big, long holiday and then Grace said to Daddy that she wasn't sure you'd come after Saturday and what happened with Zoe.'

Nate met Grace's eyes and she blushed.

'Tom! What have we told you about eavesdropping?' She took Tom's hand and crouched down close to him. 'Do you remember?'

The little boy chewed his bottom lip. 'You said I mustn't tell what I hear when I'm in bed.'

'Well, words to that effect.' Oli shook his head.

'Yes… like when I hear you and Grace cuddling.'

'What?' Grace glanced up at Oli, and it was his turn to blush.

'Tom… you don't hear us cuddling.'

'Sometimes I do and Grace giggles a lot when you're cuddling.' Tom looked back to Nate. 'They don't always hear me when I'm on my way to the toilet. And one time when I went to Daddy's room—'

'Tom! That's enough.' Oli ruffled his son's hair. 'Nothing's sacred when you have kids, Nate. Honestly.'

Grace stroked Tom's cheek. 'Tom, you must call in the night if you need us.'

'I know. I'm teasing because it makes you and Daddy go red like tomatoes.'

Oli grabbed his son under the arms and swung him up onto his shoulders. 'Right, that's it, I'm going to throw you into the sea.'

'No, Daddy!' Tom squealed with delight. 'Not tonight! I have my very best clothes on that Louise and Simon bought for me. I can't ruin them in the water.'

'No excuses. You need to be dunked!'

'No, Daddy! Noooo!'

As Oli carried Tom to the door, Grace smiled at Nate. 'Come on, there's plenty of champagne. If I drink enough I can forget about how Tom just mortified me and Oli.'

They went to the counter, where a young woman in a white blouse, checked red scarf and flared red skirt poured them two glasses of champagne.

Nate glanced around but he couldn't see Zoe anywhere.

'Do you want to talk about it?' Grace asked.

'About you and Oli having noisy cuddles?'

'God, no! Anyway, I'm sure Tom is winding us up. He's only young but he has a wicked sense of humour and you don't know what he picks up from the TV or from his friends at school. Probably heard a friend talking about catching his parents… you know… in the act, then decided it would make a good joke to use on me and Oli.'

Nate nodded. 'He's precocious, that one.'

'He's bright and funny and sensitive, and I love him to bits, you know? I'm certain I couldn't love him more if he was my own child. Amy, too.'

'Where's she this evening?'

'Coming down soon with Mum and Dad. She was helping Dad with a surprise.' Grace waggled her eyebrows then patted her red hair.

'You were on about my hair, but that's quite an "up do", Grace.'

'I know, right?' Grace giggled. 'Not my usual style, and I keep wondering where my hair is, but I thought I'd have something special done for this evening. I just have so much hair that it took about a million clips and two cans of hairspray to hold it in place.'

'It looks lovely.'

'Thank you.' She smiled, then held up her champagne. 'Cheers, Nate.'

'Cheers.'

'Now, do you want to tell me what happened on Saturday?'

'What do you mean?'

'Well, you took Zoe out, didn't you?'

'How'd you know that?'

'Oh, come on, love. It's a small village. People talk. You were seen having a fabulous time at the wine bar... by more than one person. And I swear I haven't been gossiping. Mum overheard some woman talking about it in the grocer's. Apparently, they thought you and Zoe were getting on very well until some drunken woman turned up and created a scene at the harbour.'

Nate sipped his drink then sighed.

'Oh, Nate, I'm sorry. Was it one of your exes?'

'No.' He shook his head. 'Not at all. I'd never had anything to do with her, barely know her, in fact. She turned up out of the blue, drunk... extremely drunk... and threw herself at me. Before that, I did have a lovely time with Zoe. She's—'

Grace put her hand on Nate's arm. 'Bloody hell, Nate! You've fallen for her, haven't you?'

'What?'

'You have, I can see it. You've got that look.'

'What look?'

'It's not just the chinos and the hair, or the fact that you've shaved. There's something different in your eyes.'

Grace was beaming at him now, her eyes shining.

'Are you getting emotional?'

'Well, yes. I'm so happy for you.'

'Look… don't be. It's nothing. Nothing's happened. We kissed and it was… very nice, but then there was that scene and Zoe left. I went after her but she didn't want to know.'

He rubbed the small mark on his cheek left from where Zoe's bag had caught him.

'What's that?'

'She hit me with her bag.'

'She didn't!' Grace raised her eyebrows.

'Not deliberately. When I chased her, I startled her and she reacted. The zip on her bag scratched me.'

'So you tried to talk to her?'

'To be honest, Grace, I think I did. But we'd had wine and a kiss that… made me feel feelings…' He flashed her a rueful smile. 'Then that horrible Calista turned up and ruined it all. I went after Zoe but she was… different. I think I tried to explain my feelings but I can't be sure that I articulated my thoughts clearly enough.'

'What happened then?'

'I left. Or she threw me out. I'm not quite sure how it went to be honest, because I was a bit… dazed.'

'Have you seen her since?'

'No.'

'And how does that feel?'

He shook his head. 'Pretty awful.'

Just then, Nate looked up and it was as if he'd been struck by lightning. Because Zoe was standing at the entrance to the kitchen, staring at him. He stared back, taking in how good she looked in a short-sleeved, black lace dress with a black satin slip underneath, black wedge sandals and with a sparkly clip in her hair holding the one side back from her cheek. Her hair shone and her eyes were dark and deep. Drawing him in. Making him long to hold her again.

Nate was frozen to the spot, unable to speak or move.

Then Zoe walked towards him and he thought his heart was going to burst out of his chest.

Chapter 10

'Hello, Nate.'

Zoe thought it would be better to get this over and done with. After all, the party was in her diner and she could hardly avoid Nate all evening, as she'd need to mix with the guests and to be the perfect host.

'Evening.'

'Excuse me,' Grace said, 'I need to check where Oli and Tom have gone.'

Zoe saw Grace flash Nate a look of encouragement before she walked away.

'You look incredible, Zoe.' Nate smiled at her but his eyes were wary.

'Thank you. So do you.'

'What, in these old things?' He did a jokey swagger and her heart went out to him. He seemed nervous, wounded almost, as if their last exchange had left him bruised. His face did bear the mark of the zip from her bag.

'Is your cheek okay?'

He nodded. 'It's fine. I'll never be as handsome as I once was, but I can live with that.'

In spite of her own nerves, Zoe smiled. 'Always joking.'

'It's my way of dealing with difficult situations.'

'Is this difficult then, Nate?'

'How're you finding it?'

She sighed. 'It's a bit awkward.'

A bit?

'Can we start over?'

She gazed into his azure eyes and tried to settle her heart beat by slowing her breathing. She was inexplicably drawn to him and it was more than a physical attraction. For the past few days she'd tried to forget him, to remind herself that he was representative of everything she couldn't deal with in a man, but her foolish heart had refused to be swayed. Seeing him surfing, then being thrown from his board, had made her fear for him but also for herself. If there was something special about him, as she thought there was, then she wanted to get to know him better and find out if there was the possibility of anything ever happening between them. Yet she knew he was going away and that she couldn't take things further between them, because it would break her when he left.

But she did want the chance to be his friend. There was no point fostering animosity between them as an alternative to romance, as a way to drown out her desire for him, when they knew the same people and would undoubtedly be thrown together in a few situations over the coming weeks, so it would be better for both of them if they could agree to get on.

'I'd like that.'

She held out her hand and he shook it.

'Friends.'

The next hour of the party passed in an enjoyable haze of greeting guests, serving drinks and socializing. Zoe found herself smiling as she circulated; she really did live in a lovely village with a lot of lovely people. She knew she didn't always appreciate exactly how friendly the locals were, but perhaps it was time to get to know everyone better and to integrate more into the village. If she was going to move on from her past and allow herself to heal properly, then she'd have to let her guard down and learn to trust people. She wasn't sure how easy that would be, but she hoped she'd be able to try. Perhaps then the nightmares would vanish completely and she would find peace of mind. Well, one step at a time was the way to begin...

At just gone eight, the door opened and Amy sashayed in, followed by Louise and Simon – Grace's parents – who were carrying a large white box between them.

'Make way! Make way!' Amy called.

Zoe directed them to a centre table and they placed the box on it.

'If you could get Oli and Grace to look away for a moment,' Simon said to Zoe, 'I'll get this all set up.

'Of course.'

Zoe went to Grace and Oli and told them to look out through the window. The newly engaged couple held hands and giggled excitedly as they waited.

'Oooh! Daddy and Grace, you are going to like this surprise!' Tom announced, as he rocked on the balls of his feet, his small hands scrunched up with excitement.

Zoe waited until Simon waved her over.

'Can we check everyone's glasses are full, please, Zoe?'

'Of course!'

Along with her two waiting staff, she nipped around and filled adult glasses with champagne, and the children's with non-alcoholic fizz.

'Ready?' Simon asked.

'Ready!' Zoe replied.

'Come on over to the surprise!' Tom said, as he grabbed Grace and his father's hands and tugged them towards the cake.

'Oh!' Grace squeaked, as she gazed at her father's amazing creation.

'I helped with it, Grace.' Amy smiled proudly from beside the cake.

'Actually, Grace, Amy did most of the work. She was fantastic with ideas as well as practically in the kitchen. I just supervised.' Simon smiled proudly at Amy.

The girl's cheeks glowed at her adopted grandfather's praise.

'It's wonderful, Amy.' Oli's face lit up as he stood in front of the cake, with his fiancée.

'Right then.' Simon waved his hands for everyone to be quiet. 'I'd like to say a few words.'

The diner fell silent and Simon took his wife's hand as they stood close to Grace and Oli.

'When we first came to Conwenna Cove, it was to follow our dream. Louise and I fell in love with this beautiful village many years ago on our honeymoon, but never in our wildest imaginings did we think that our daughter would fall in love here, too. But she did! With Oli and with Amy and Tom, and Hope the greyhound, of course!'

Laughter rippled around the room.

'I'm going to use the cliché now because it sums up my thoughts and feelings, and I know I speak for Louise, too... We are not losing a daughter but gaining a whole family. We never thought we'd be grandparents...' He paused, and it was evident that he was fighting his emotions.

Louise patted his arm. 'I'll take over, shall I, darling?'

He nodded.

'As my husband was saying, we never thought we'd be grandparents... for various sad reasons that life had thrown our way... but Grace has given us the most wonderful grandchildren we could wish for, in Amy and Tom.' There was a gasp as Amy rushed towards Louise and wrapped her arms around her waist. Louise hugged the girl with one arm while she held on tight to her husband with the other hand. 'Yes, Grace brought Oli, Amy and Tom into our lives and Simon and I couldn't have asked for more. We're here in this beautiful village surrounded by wonderful people and now we have an extended family.'

Simon coughed, then raised his glass. 'Now I can speak again... I'd like to toast Grace, Oli, Amy and Tom. May you be happy and healthy and enjoy many, many years together. Congratulations to you all as you embark upon what will no doubt be a wonderful future!'

Everyone in the diner raised their glasses and toasted the happy couple.

Zoe had to blink hard as she watched; it was such an emotional moment, and the air in the room was suffused with joy. She looked around, enjoying seeing so many smiling faces – then her eyes met Nate's and she gasped. He was staring right at her, his beautiful blue eyes shining with emotion. It was all she could do not to rush over to him and throw herself into his strong arms.

She forced herself to look away and focused on the cake instead.

'Thank you so much,' Oli said. 'We are extremely grateful to you, Simon and Louise, for coming here to Conwenna and for bringing Grace with you. Until I met Grace, I...' He shook his head. 'Excuse me. I'm afraid this is all rather moving.' He paused for a few moments and the guests waited quietly. He cleared his throat. 'Anyway… as I was saying, I thought I'd never fall in love again, but Grace proved me wrong. And she brought us new family, too. Amy and Tom are as delighted as I am and I'm a true believer that children cannot ever have too much love. Now they have an abundance of it and life is so much better again.' He gazed around the room. 'So… to Grace, who has brought such love with her, to our beautiful children, and to Louise and Simon, as well as to my dad and Maxine, my mum and stepdad, and to you all. Thank you for sharing in our celebrations this evening!'

'CONGRATULATIONS!' resounded through the diner.

'And as for this cake, Amy and Simon… Wow!'

Oli grinned as he and Grace posed for photographs with the cake, the children and with everyone in turn. Zoe circulated, filling glasses again before going to have a good look at the cake herself.

The dark chocolate sponge was covered in white chocolate frosting. Simon and Amy had decorated the outside with fondant hearts and roses in red and silver, and at the centre was an icing photograph of Grace, Oli, Amy, Tom, Hope their greyhound and Katy Purry, their cat. It was a beautiful creation and must have taken Simon and Amy hours to decorate.

'Is it time for dancing now, Daddy?' Tom asked, as he tugged at Oli's hand.

'You'll have to ask Zoe.'

Zoe nodded. 'I'll turn the music up.'

Tom followed her to the counter and when Elvis filled the room, crooning 'Have I Told You Lately', Tom began to sway around the space that served as a dance floor whenever the diner was used for functions and parties.

Soon, others joined in and Zoe was able to move around the room and collect used glasses and plates.

One song led into another and when she felt a tap on her arm, she turned to find Nate with his hands raised in front of his face.

'Just in case, you know. I can see you're not carrying a bag but I didn't want to risk getting another wallop.'

'Nate, that was an accident.'

'I know. So… would you dance with me?'

Zoe paused. This probably wasn't a good idea at all.

'Come on, Zoe. As friends?' He held out his hand.

Zoe looked at his hand, then at his face and, before she could overthink it, she took his hand and allowed him to lead her to the dance floor.

Nate slid his arms around her waist and she automatically entwined hers around his neck, as 'Always On My Mind' drifted from the speakers. They moved in time, eyes locked, and emotion bubbled in Zoe again. Life could be so good but it could also be so unfair. If things had been different, if she hadn't been hurt in the past and Nate hadn't been about to go away, if there hadn't been things about him that reminded her so much of her old life and if… She sighed inwardly. What was the point in wishing that things had ended up differently? Life was what it was and people were who they were. Part of her believed, deep down, that she could have had something good with Nate but it just wasn't meant to be.

Nate leant forwards and she thought he was about to kiss her but he moved to the side slightly and his warm breath tickled her ear.

'Zoe?'

'Yes.'

'I really like you. A lot. But I understand that, for whatever reasons, we can't be more than friends.'

She swallowed hard against the ache in her throat.

'Okay.'

'But I do want to be your friend and to work with you for Surf for Sighthounds. I'd also like to stay in touch while I'm away, if that's all right with you?'

'You would?'

'Yes. The thought of not being able to hear from you is proving to be tougher than I'd anticipated.'

Zoe leant backwards and met his gaze. His cheeks were slightly flushed and his eyes shone. He was the most beautiful thing she had ever seen and her heart swelled. He was also really honest and open about his feelings and that was something Zoe wasn't used to, either. It unnerved her at times, as if he might be mocking her and toying with her feelings, but whenever she met his eyes, she was certain that he was being genuine and upfront with her. That was another difference between him and Finn; Nate didn't seem to be playing any games with her.

'I'd like to stay in touch, too.'

'Good…' He smiled. 'Good.'

His arms tightened around her waist and he rested his head against hers, and they stayed that way for some time as the music flowed and the party guests danced, and the evening wore on. And Zoe absorbed every detail of being held in Nate's arms, savouring the way his body felt against hers, the way his breath gently moved her hair and how good he smelt. In spite of all her thoughts about not allowing it to happen, Nate had something that Zoe had never thought anyone would ever have again.

Nate had her heart, and she was beginning to trust him.

–

Nate made his way home after the party with an aura of sadness and a strange sense of loss shadowing him. It was like being followed by a storm cloud, wondering when the storm would break and he'd be soaked to the skin.

He'd left the party before Grace and Oli, not wanting to be the last one there, alone with Zoe. Simon and Louise had taken Amy and Tom home an hour before, as Tom had danced his socks off and was yawning constantly. Amy had been happy to go with Louise, encouraged by the offer of a hot chocolate in front of the TV. Grace and Oli had been finishing off a bottle of champagne with Zoe, Jack and Eve, and Nate had thought it would be a good time to slip away.

He'd enjoyed the evening and it had been lovely to see Grace and Oli so happy. They had the perfect life now and Nate believed that they fully deserved it. They'd been through so much in the past and seemed aware of how precious their current happiness was; they clearly treasured every moment together with family and friends.

Nate reached the cafe and went around the back to the stairs that led to his flat. Once inside, he kicked off his shoes and went to the front windows to pull the curtains, but he paused. It was such a beautiful evening. The moon was shining over the village, bathing everything in a silvery light. If he leant forwards, he could see down the main street and out to sea. The moon cast a shimmering pathway along the surface of the water and Nate imagined walking along that pathway, heading towards his future. He intended on going away from the cove for a while, but he knew now that his journey wouldn't be as straight-forward as it had initially seemed. His pathway into the future and into the world wasn't clear, and neither was it set in stone; it could waver like the pathway of moonlight did right now on the sea. And that was okay. Nate had the luxury of being able to make his own decisions and to change his mind if he wanted to. But he knew he couldn't change his mind about going away; it was something he had to do. Wasn't it?

The more he thought about it, going away had repre-sented a rite of passage for him, a way of breaking away from his bad habits and moving towards the grown-up version of himself. It was as much a symbolic journey, a figurative stepping stone away from his past, as it was a literal desire to travel and surf in foreign waters.

He closed the curtains and sank onto the sofa. Zoe evidently had some issues linked to her past that were holding her back. He had a basic idea of what they were but she hadn't told him the gritty details and he hadn't wanted to pry. He was going away and he sensed that that could be a stumbling block for him and Zoe, and that she wouldn't entertain the thought of allowing anything to happen between them if they were going to be separated. Nate also thought it wasn't a good idea to try to have a long-distance relationship: it would be far too painful and stressful and completely work against his reasons for going away in the first place. Nate didn't want to cause Zoe any hurt or sadness at all, so he wouldn't ask her to do anything that would be difficult for her.

Yet the thought of never being with her was becoming a bigger deal for him by the hour. Holding her as they danced and breathing her in, being aware of how perfectly she fit in his arms and wanting her more than he'd ever wanted a woman was making this a big deal for him. Zoe was special and Nate wanted her. He'd spent the past few years so close to Zoe yet unaware of her. How conceited he had been, dismissing her as cold and aloof whenever he saw her. He hadn't tried to get to know her before and he deeply regretted that now. Life could have been very different if he'd just gone into the diner for a milkshake sooner. But if he had, would it have been the right time for Zoe? Or did things happen when they did for a reason? Nate wasn't a big believer in a divine force that set out human paths but he did find comfort in the idea that things happened for a reason. It was something his mother had always said to him when he was growing up. Perhaps the time hadn't been right for him and Zoe before, and they'd needed the pressure of him leaving to make them see each other clearly.

If only there was a way forward for them, a way that they could work through things to be together. He rubbed his eyes then ran his hands through his short hair. There had to be a way, surely? They were both adults, both free and single. What if there was a way to convince Zoe that he wasn't going to hurt her, that he was a good guy and that he could make her happy? A way to manage his trip away while making her his…

But, right then, with so much raw emotion filling his chest and so many thoughts racing around his head, he couldn't plan clearly. Hopefully, if he slept on it, an idea would come to him. And with that reassurance, he got up and went to bed, hoping that the morning would bring him some clarity.

Chapter 11

The next day, Nate was on the road by eight-thirty as he was going to his mother's house for lunch. The drive to Penzance would take about fifty minutes, as long as the roads weren't too busy.

He drove with the radio up loud, singing along to the eclectic mix that the DJ played on the request show. His mother still lived in Penzance where he had grown up. After his father had died, she'd been on her own for over two years, then she'd fallen in love with a local businessman, Richard Cooper, and within six months they were married. Nate had been a bit surprised at their whirlwind romance, but not begrudged his mother her happiness at all. He'd known that even though she kept busy with her social circle, she must still get a bit lonely. The fact that she had Richard made him feel less guilty about leaving Penzance and settling in Conwenna Cove, but he still liked to know that she was all right. Her quietness of late had set some alarm bells ringing, so he was keen to see her today to check that she was okay.

When he reached the cul-de-sac of detached bunga-lows where his mother had moved with her new husband, Nate followed the road to the end then turned around before parking outside the long driveway of the first one on his left. It was a white, four-bedroom bungalow with a spacious garden that ran right around the house, and it had a huge conservatory on the back. Richard owned a tile warehouse on one of the local industrial estates and he'd done very well for himself. That was another thing that Nate was glad about; his mother didn't need to worry about money.

Nate cut the engine of his uncle's Ford Focus, which he borrowed whenever he needed a car – Kevin and June rarely went far and had told him the car was his as much as it was theirs – and climbed out. He paused, to see if he'd experience a wave of nostalgia, but nothing came. It was probably because the house he'd grown up in was some distance from there and he hadn't needed to drive past it, so he hadn't seen many of his childhood haunts during the drive. Which was a good thing, really. Nate didn't like to come back very often because he still found it difficult. His grief for his father was a strange thing and although it was always there, it didn't often rise to the surface. Most of the time he was able to suppress it and he could live with that.

He locked the car then opened the gate and headed along the curved drive that was hidden from the street by the well-established trees of the front garden. As he rounded the corner, the nostalgia he'd waited for earlier hit him like a blow to the gut and he froze.

There it was. His red and white VW campervan, the one his father had bought him for his twenty-fifth birthday. It was parked on the driveway, gleaming in the sunshine, and looking as good as it had the day his father had proudly handed him the keys.

Nate approached the campervan and ran a hand over the bonnet, appreciating how clean it had been kept. The hours he'd spent in this van, driving to different beaches with groups of his friends before heading into the surf for more adventures. He'd loved this van, and it had been a part of him for so long. He knew his mother had kept it after he'd left but he didn't come back very often and, somehow, he'd managed to forget that it was there, almost waiting for him.

Seeing it was bittersweet, an onslaught of good and bad memories. After his father had bought him the campervan, he'd told Nate he had just one condition: they were to spend a fortnight together, driving around the Cornish coast and surfing at all the best beaches. It had been one of his father's lifelong dreams and Nate had loved the idea of spending that time with him. However, they'd both been busy and the trip had been delayed and then his father had died so suddenly. Nate had been consumed with grief at the thought that they'd never have that trip, that his father had missed out. Even now he couldn't shake the guilt, which lingered like a bad smell, whenever he thought about the unimportant things he could easily have put off in order to spend those precious few weeks with his dad.

What made it more poignant still was the fact that Nate suspected his father had always wanted to see more of the world but sacrificed his own desire to travel to be a good provider for his family. His dad had never told him that he had any regrets, but things like the maps on his study wall and the photographs of different locations that he had on his pin boards made it obvious. If Nate's father hadn't got married and had Nate, he might have led a very different life. These thoughts had stayed with Nate while he was growing up and played on his mind after his father's death. Marriage and children could mean surrendering your freedom and your dreams, and Nate wasn't sure that he'd ever want to do that.

And yet, here he was, in his thirties and he still hadn't travelled extensively. So what was holding Nate back? The past, the present or the fact that he had been so contented living in Conwenna Cove?

Or even the fact that he was just a different man to his father…

'Hello, darling.'

He turned to find his mother standing in the doorway, smiling at him.

'Hi, Mum.'

'I told you I'd keep her until you decide you want her back.'

He smiled. 'Thanks, but I'm not certain that I ever will.'

'You never know, Nate. I'd hate to get rid of the campervan then for you to regret it.'

His mother walked towards him and opened her arms. 'Gosh, you look good, Nate. So much like your father it takes my breath away.'

His mother embraced him on her tiptoes, and he had to lean forwards so she could kiss him. When she pulled away, she rubbed at his cheek.

'Lipstick.' She smiled. 'When did you start wearing chinos?'

He shrugged. 'Just getting older, I guess.'

'Well, they suit you, Nate. Very smart.'

'Thanks, Mum. Are you still driving the van around?'

'Oh, yes, darling. The girls love going to bingo in it. They all get quite excited when I pick them up and I have to play all the old hits nice and loud so they can sing along. You'd think I was driving a bunch of teenagers around, not women in their fifties and sixties.'

'I'm glad you're keeping it going.'

'And I will, until you decide to take it.'

Nate sighed – there was no point debating this with his mother again. They talked about it every time he visited and, every time, he'd say he didn't want the van and she could sell it. Secretly, he knew that if she sold it he'd be devastated, but he still couldn't use the van, so he was glad his mother kept it going. One day, he hoped, he'd be able to drive the campervan again and to feel happy about it, not overshadowed by guilt. One day… perhaps.

'Come on inside and have a drink. You must be parched after that drive.'

She took his arm and led him into the bungalow where it was cool. The scent of roses emanated from a plug-in air freshener in the hallway, not quite hiding the smell of roast dinner.

'Richard's cooking pork, so I hope you're hungry. He's done that fancy apple sauce he makes, and the crackling will be divine.'

Nate smiled. He wasn't a big fan of pork but didn't want to offend his mother or his stepfather after they'd clearly made such an effort. Nate had always been welcomed into their bungalow but it was strange for him, because it didn't feel like home. He couldn't imagine staying there or running there if he had any trouble. He knew his mother loved him but Richard, nice as he was, would always be someone his mother met after his father. He was a kind man with a good sense of humour, but Nate always felt that he had to be slightly formal around him, that he couldn't fully be himself in case he caused offence or shocked Richard and disappointed his mother.

In the kitchen, his mother opened the fridge and brought out a bottle of white wine.

'Nate?'

'Oh, no, thanks, Mum. I'll have a coke if you've got one.'

She nodded, then opened the fridge again and brought out a bottle of Madagascan vanilla cola. Nate hid his smile; it couldn't be plain old cola, it had to have something fancy in the title. That was how his mother had changed. When she was with his father, she was down to earth and happy to buy supermarket budget products, but Richard had money and he liked to live the highlife, so it had become the same for his mother too.

She pressed a glass into the ice dispenser on the front of the fridge, then filled it with coke.

'Let's take these into the conservatory, shall we?'

They sat on the plump cushioned wicker furniture that smelt of fabric softener, and Nate placed his glass onto a coaster on the small glass table.

'Everything's all right, isn't it, Mum?' He'd just as well find out now and check if his suspicions were right or if he was worrying unnecessarily.

'Well...' She bit her lip.

'Are you okay? Mum? Where is Richard anyway? I thought you said he's cooking lunch.'

Paula glanced around.

'Look... I can't say much, love, but things haven't been going too well with the business. What with the recession and some... unpaid taxes that Richard had forgotten about, our financial situation isn't looking too good.'

'Bloody hell, Mum, I'm sorry to hear that.'

She sighed, and Nate realized that although she'd initially seemed as flawless as ever in her purple silk blouse and black, wide-leg trousers, she actually appeared quite tired. In the bright sunshine that warmed the conservatory, he could see that she was wearing quite a lot of foundation and that it was blusher making her cheeks appear rosy, not healthy as he'd first thought when she'd greeted him. She'd also seemed rather thin when she'd hugged him. She'd always been fit and toned because she did Pilates and yoga six days out of seven, but she'd been rather angular in his embrace.

'What about your job, Mum?'

She lifted her glass of wine to her lips and sipped it before replying. 'I was made redundant. Four months ago.'

'What? You didn't say anything.'

'Oh, well… you know, Nate, you've got your life and I didn't think it was a *biggee*.'

'A biggee?'

'A big problem. I thought we'd be fine as Richard still had the warehouse, and we had savings.'

'And do you still have those savings?'

She shook her head. 'Back taxes.'

'Shit. I can't believe you didn't say anything.'

She stood up. 'Richard's probably in the shed getting more tonic water. I'll go and call him to let him know you're here.'

'Hold on a minute, Mum. Is there anything I can do to help?'

'No, darling. We'll be fine, I'm sure. It's simply a blip.'

'Well, if I can help, let me know.'

'I'm a caterer, Nate. I've worked in the hospitality industry for years but I'm fast heading towards sixty. I could probably get a job if I looked, I just didn't expect to be looking at my time of life.'

'You have a pension though, right?'

She nodded. 'But I don't want to draw on it until I'm sixty-five, if possible. I had a redundancy payout but it wasn't that big, and certainly won't pay the mortgage on this place for long. Besides, I like to think of the redundancy money as a buffer in case of emergencies.'

Nate moved to the edge of his seat. 'I assumed the mortgage was paid off a long time ago.'

His mother's dark green eyes flitted nervously around the conservatory.

'Don't tell me he remortgaged it?'

'Please don't say a word about any of this, darling. There he is!' Her voice became shrill as she waved at her husband.

She rushed towards the double glass doors that opened onto the flawless lawn.

'Richard! Nate has arrived.'

Richard entered the conservatory and Nate stood up to shake his hand.

'Good to see you, Nate. How the devil are you?'

Nate smiled at his stepfather and suppressed the urge to say, *Far better than you it seems.*

–

Zoe entered the Conwenna Arms and went to the bar. She didn't normally go out for Sunday lunch but today she couldn't face cooking for one in her cottage. The diner was closed on Sundays, except for special occasions, and she was glad because she was tired after the engagement party last night.

Oh, but it had been lovely! Such a fabulous occasion with Grace, Oli and their families and friends, all together in Zoe's lovely diner. The champagne had flowed and the cake that Simon and Amy made had been delicious. It had taken over an hour to tidy up after everyone had gone, but Zoe had been in a daze, so she'd barely noticed what she was doing.

And the daze had been down to dancing with Nate at the party. She could still feel his hands on her, his warmth against her, and the scent of his aftershave lingered on her hair. She'd tossed and turned all night, waking from sensual dreams thinking he was there with her, but it had been her imagination toying with her, her long-latent desire increasing her longing for him. She'd given in at five am and gone downstairs to snuggle with a mug of tea and Raven's soft blanket, then she'd reclined on the sofa, day dreaming about the handsome man she knew was falling for. All the while cursing herself for allowing it to happen.

But Zoe's practical side had forced her into action by ten o'clock and she'd made herself clean the house thoroughly before taking a long, hot shower. She couldn't spend all day moping around like a love-sick teenager, so she'd decided to go for a walk then to eat out, and the pub had seemed like the obvious choice.

She paid for her glass of lemonade then went around the bar to find a seat.

'Zoe!'

She spotted Grace, Oli, Amy and Tom at a corner table. Grace was waving her over.

'Well, I didn't expect to see you two out and about today after all that champ—' Zoe glanced at Tom and found his brown eyes glued to her face. 'I mean, after all that celebrating.'

'Oh, we're fine!' Grace smiled. 'Probably still *celebrating* a bit now, you know. That's why we walked here.'

'I like celebrating,' Tom said, as he picked up his glass of orange juice. 'Cheers!' He tapped his glass against Amy's just as she was taking a sip, causing her juice to slosh over the side and over her cheeks.

'Tom!' Amy scowled at her brother.

'Here, let me get that.' Grace used a napkin to dry Amy's face. 'Tom, we've told you not to do cheers when someone is already drinking.'

Grace shook her head at Zoe.

'Thanks again for last night, Zoe. It was a fantastic party and we all had a great time.'

'You're welcome. I was delighted to host you.' Zoe sipped her lemonade.

'Are you meeting anyone?' Oli asked, peering behind Zoe as if searching for her companions.

'No. No. I'm here for some lunch.'

'Then you must join us.' Grace patted the seat next to her.

'I couldn't do that. I don't want to impose.'

'It's not imposing at all. We're friends, aren't we?' Grace smiled up at Zoe, her bright blue eyes suffused with warmth.

'Yes, have lunch with us, Zoe, and I can tell you all about my new makeover plans.' Amy smiled at Zoe and held up her red handbag. 'I have my kit with me so I could always help you with your make-up if you like.'

Zoe glanced at Grace and found her eyes wide in warning, but what could she do? If Amy wanted to help her, then who was she to refuse?

'That's very kind of you, Amy, thank you.'

Zoe sat next to Grace and allowed Amy to make her look *pretty for dinner*, which turned out to be quite an ordeal as the girl spread foundation over her skin with a sponge then topped it up with powder before starting on her eyes. Zoe's skin tightened with the weight of the make-up and she tried to keep her face still to avoid cracking the layers.

'Ha ha!' Fifteen minutes later, Tom was pointing at Zoe, his little face scrunched up with amusement.

Zoe had been chatting away to Grace about books, movies, wine and summer plans, so she'd let Amy carry on with her makeover. Now, though, she was a bit worried.

'Oh, it's lovely, Amy, well done.' Grace winked at Zoe. 'Perhaps you should let Zoe check it out in the toilet mirror.'

'Not yet,' Amy said, leaning closer to Zoe again, her tongue poking out of the corner of her mouth. 'I've a bit more to do first.' She turned to Grace and whispered, 'Her eyebrows are a bit bushy.'

Zoe winced as Amy attacked her with tweezers, pulling and plucking and making her eyes water.

'Ouch! I wasn't aware that I had hairs between my eyebrows.'

'Your monobrow more like.' Amy tutted, and Zoe bit her lip. Nothing like a pre-teen to put you in your place.

'Would you like to go through to the dining room now?' It was one of the bar staff.

'Yes, thanks, I'm ravenous.' Oli helped Tom from his seat and Grace got up.

'Come on then, Amy. Let Zoe come and have some lunch.'

Amy leaned backwards and admired her work.

'I'm done now anyway, and you look beautiful, Zoe. So much better than when you got here.'

'Thanks so much,' Zoe said, her tongue firmly planted inside her cheek. She picked up her bag and her drink and followed the family through to the dining room.

As she walked, she was conscious of a few nods and some people smiling, but she suspected it was because she rarely wore much make-up and now her face felt as if she'd donned a mask. Hopefully, Amy had given her a beautiful, airbrushed appearance to rival the Kardashians, and not a face that would make a clown pale in comparison.

'While we wait for lunch shall I do yours too, Grace?' Amy asked, getting her make-up purse out in readiness.

'Oh, not today, thanks, Amy. I'm having a day off to let my skin breathe.' Grace lifted her menu and Zoe saw that it was shaking as Grace laughed.

'Okay, fine. Well, I'll just do Louise's later when we go round for tea.'

'Yes, Mum will love that.' Grace's menu shook even harder.

They perused the menus and when the waitress arrived to take a drinks order, Oli asked if Zoe and Grace would like some wine. They agreed, so he ordered a bottle of house white.

When it arrived, Zoe sipped hers and began to relax. She loved the dynamics of this little family. Before Grace had arrived in Conwenna Cove, Zoe hadn't known Oli very well. She'd dealt with him when she'd taken Raven in and done a few trips for the sanctuary dogs, but he'd been shut down after his first wife's death and, at times, Zoe had found him cold. But now… he was a different man. He'd been through such a lot of pain and sadness and Grace coming to Conwenna had been wonderful for him and his children, because she'd helped them all to heal. None of them would ever forget his first wife, Linda – Zoe knew this because she'd heard him talk about her with Grace and the children – but falling in love again had given him a second chance at life. And people did deserve second chances. The same could be said of her, couldn't it? Both Oli and Grace had been afraid to love – for different reasons – but they'd seen something in each other that had made the risk worth it. Sometimes, taking a chance on someone and moving on had to be worth a go…

She was dragged from her musings by the arrival of the waitress who'd come to take their orders.

'And what's it going to be for you, Tom?' Grace asked.

'Garlic bread.'

Oli rubbed his eyes. 'Don't start that again, Tom.'

'When I first went out with Oli and the children, Tom always wanted garlic bread,' Grace explained. 'We thought we'd weaned him off it but…' She shrugged.

'Tom, it's Sunday, you can't have garlic bread.' Oli pointed at the Sunday lunch menu.

'Okay then, can I have…' Tom tapped his small fingers on his cheek. 'Steak with that sauce.'

'Steak?' Oli's eyebrows shot up.

'What sauce?' Grace asked.

'The leprechaun one.' Tom clapped his hands. 'Yes, I want steak with leprechaun sauce.'

Zoe leant closer to Grace. 'Leprechaun sauce?'

'I have no idea,' Grace replied.

'It's brown and it makes your tongue go...' Tom opened his mouth and waved a hand in front of it.

'Do you mean peppercorn sauce?' Oli asked.

'Yes!' Tom's eyes lit up. 'That's the one. Simon always has it and I tried some and it made my eyes sting.'

Grace and Zoe started giggling.

'Look, Tom, you can have peppercorn sauce next time we come here, but today you'll have to have beef and gravy. Is that okay?'

Tom nodded.

'The smiles never end with this lot,' Grace said to Zoe. 'I never know what Amy's going to do to my hair or face or what Tom's going to say next.'

'You have a lovely family.'

Grace glanced around her and, when she met Zoe's gaze again, her eyes shone. 'I do and I know I'm very lucky indeed.'

After they'd eaten, and there hadn't been a leprechaun in sight, Amy and Tom went off to play in the park at the back of the pub, and Oli followed them to keep an eye on Tom. Amy had, of course, insisted that she wouldn't be playing but would be entertaining her brother, and Zoe and Grace had nodded along, but when she'd gone, Grace told Zoe that Amy still liked to race Tom on the swings.

'She's so grown up in many ways but part of her still wants to be a little girl. It's as if she lost part of her childhood when her mum died, and she's trying to cling to that time because when she's all grown up, she'll be letting go.'

'Is she doing all right, though?'

Grace nodded. 'She's an absolute sweetheart and we get on so well. More and more, she'll come up to me just to hug me. If I'm editing on the sofa, I usually have Hope on one side and Amy on the other. That's if Tom doesn't beat one of them to it. And there's Katy Purry, of course. Amy takes that cat everywhere, and would have brought it out for lunch if we'd let her.'

Zoe smiled, imagining how warm and lovely it would be to have people and dogs wanting to snuggle up to her. Amy's cat had been a rescue that she had found at Simon and Louise's cottage before they'd moved in.

'Are you missing Raven?' Grace asked.

'Very much.'

'I don't know how you cope. It would break my heart if I lost Hope now. Although I do know that one day I will.'

'One day a long, long time from now,' Zoe said. 'She'll be here for ages. The thing with Raven was that she was already getting on in years.'

'But you made her happy, didn't you? After her owner couldn't keep her any more.'

'I really hope so, Grace. I loved her, that's for sure.'

'And she loved you, but loss does come part and parcel when you love people and animals.'

Zoe nodded. Grace was so right; love was accompanied by loss but the alternative of never loving and enjoying being with others, was a dreadful one.

They drank their wine and when the waitress came to clear the table, they went back through to sit in the bar.

'How are things with Nate?' Grace asked.

'With Nate?' Zoe acted surprised to hear his name, even though she had been picturing him throughout dinner, wondering where he was and what he was doing.

'Well, yes. I saw the way he looked at you last night and how he held you when you danced.'

'What?' Zoe's cheeks warmed as Grace's bright eyes assessed her.

'It's all right, Zoe, I'm not prying. But I wanted you to know that you can talk to me if you need to.'

'Thank you.'

Zoe finished her wine then sat back on the bench with its plump red cushions. She ran her fingers over the worn studs that pinned the cushion to the bench and wondered how many people had sat there over the years feeling a variety of emotions. Perhaps Nate had sat in that exact spot, thinking about his life and his plans to travel the world.

Suddenly, she experienced an overwhelming urge to share her feelings about him with someone and when she looked up, she found Grace watching her, waiting.

'You're right, Grace. I do like Nate. I like him a lot.'

Grace nodded.

'I barely knew him before we went out for a drink, even though we've both lived in Conwenna for a while. But I avoided him because he was everything I never wanted to like in a man.'

'What do you mean?' Grace prodded.

'He's handsome, confident, funny, popular and...' Zoe took a deep breath. 'He's a surfer.'

'Oh.' Grace frowned. 'Is that a bad thing, then? In fact, aren't all those things you listed rather positive?'

Zoe gave a wry laugh. 'I guess they are but I'm just wary.'

'Aren't we all?'

'Yes. When we've been hurt.'

'So, there was someone else? Before you came to Conwenna?'

Zoe nodded.

'He hurt you and you're scared of being hurt again?'

'Yes.' Zoe's answer was barely a whisper.

'We all get scared, Zoe. I was terrified of getting involved when I met Oli, and so was he. But when you find that someone who you share a spark with… then you have to take a chance.'

'Do you?'

'Well, I think so. Nate helped me to work through some of my initial fears about getting involved with Oli. He was, and is, a good friend.'

'You won't tell him—'

'What you've said?' Grace shook her head. 'Of course not. I see you as a friend too, Zoe, and I wouldn't do that. This isn't high school and I'm not going to ask him out for you, or vice versa.' She smiled.

'Thank goodness for that.'

Grace placed her hand over Zoe's and squeezed her fingers gently.

'Look, I like you and I like Nate. You're good people. It's obvious to everyone around you that you have some… electricity between you.'

'It is?'

'Yes. Eve mentioned it to me last night, too. But, whether or not you to choose to pursue those feelings is up to you and Nate. No one can tell you what to do.'

'You're right. Though I wish sometimes someone could tell me what to do and I could just nod along and do it. Being a responsible adult is hard going when the stakes are so high. I mean… Nate is going away soon. I have commitments here. I also have some issues because of what happened in the past and I don't want to bring those issues with me and to hurt anyone with them, especially not Nate. He's such a nice guy.'

'He's a gorgeous guy and he has a massive heart. Okay, so sometimes he's a bit soft with some of the women who trail around after him, but I think that's mainly because he doesn't have a significant other. If he did… then I bet he'd be different.'

'In what way?'

'He'd be firmer with the women who chase him and I'm certain that he's as loyal as they come. Nate wouldn't hurt you, Zoe, if you gave him a chance.'

Zoe worried her bottom lip as she let Grace's words soak in. If only it was all that easy, if only she could let go and fall in love with Nate, then life might be full of joy and excitement again. But it wasn't that simple and there were things that she needed closure with.

'I know it's hard to let go of the past, Zoe, but it's the only way to move forwards. Never forget, but forgive and move on… if you can.'

'Thank you.'

'What for?'

'For listening and for helping me to work out what I need to do.'

'My absolute pleasure, Zoe. Now, how'd you fancy a spin on the roundabout?'

'After that enormous meal?'

Grace laughed.

'It might blow some of that make-up off.'

'Is it that bad?'

Grace nodded. 'Amy has tidied your eyebrows up in the middle but, apart from that, they've grown rather significantly.'

'How so?'

'Well, you know if you went outside and found two big black slugs then perched them above your eyes…?'

'Oh, dear.'

Grace shrugged. 'It's fashionable these days among teenagers, so I hear.'

'What is?'

'To have barcodes above your eyes.'

'What?'

Grace snorted and Zoe joined her until her sides ached and she could barely catch her breath.

'Now, come on – let's head on out to that family of yours so I can thank them for letting me join you.'

'It was a pleasure, Zoe. We all had a lovely time.'

Grace linked her arm with Zoe's and they walked out into the sunshine. Zoe's heart was filled with happiness, because not only did she now know what she needed to do, but for the first time in a long time, she had a female friend she could trust. And that was something she had once thought she'd never have again.

Chapter 12

Nate handed his mother the last plate from the dishwasher and she put it in the cupboard.

'Shall we have a coffee now?'

'Yes, please.'

Lunch had been an interesting affair as his usually confident and somewhat superior stepfather had revealed a side to himself that Nate had never before seen. In fact, Richard had got through two bottles of wine with lunch – while his wife had only managed a glass and Nate had stuck to water – then he'd finished off with a large brandy, apparently *to burn a hole in it*.

Richard was the physical opposite of Nate's father and he suspected that might be one of the things that his mum had been glad about. Nate's father had been tall and broad-shouldered with fair hair, and Nate resembled him – his mother told him so every time she saw him. Richard was a few inches shorter, his hair had been brown but was now thin and receding and he wore designer glasses, seeming to have a different pair to match his outfits. Whereas Nate's father had worn jeans and T-shirts, hating being confined in suits and shirts, Richard often wore a tie – even when he was at home – and Nate couldn't imagine him wearing jeans. He was usually quite portly but seemed more so at the moment, as if recent stresses had led him to seek comfort in food and drink.

While Nate and his mother had cleared the plates away and stacked the dishwasher, Richard had retired to his study. Nate had popped in there to ask if Richard wanted coffee and found the older man snoring his head off in his leather recliner. So Nate had sneaked back out and helped his mother to put everything away once the dishwasher had finished its economy cycle.

'Let's go and sit in the conservatory again, shall we, darling?'

Nate nodded and followed his mother into the glass room that overlooked their beautiful garden. The sky had become cloudy as the afternoon wore on and the room wasn't as warm as it had been that morning when Nate had arrived.

Paula perched in the edge of her seat and placed her coffee cup and saucer on her knees. She'd barely eaten at dinner and had pushed a sprout around her plate for so long that Nate had been tempted to reach over and flick it across the room into Richard's glass, just to get a reaction out of him.

'I'd like to help if I can, Mum.'

She sighed and when she met his gaze, her eyes were tired, the lines around them deep and dark with stress as much as the mascara that had bled into them.

'I know, love. It's simply one of those things, though. You know, after I lost your father, I thought that was the worst thing I could ever go through... apart from losing you, of course. That would have been unbearable. But seeing Richard like this makes me realize that there are varying degrees of awful. Your dad passed suddenly but it's like I'm watching Richard slowly crumble before my eyes and it's hard. I love him so much.'

'I'm sorry, Mum.'

'It's not your fault, darling.'

'So what will you do?'

She sipped her coffee then used her thumb to wipe away the smudge of lipstick that she'd left on the rim of her cup.

'I guess we'll sell the house to pay off what we owe. Or some of what we owe. With it being remortgaged, we might only break even.' She shook her head. 'I don't know the full extent of it because every time I ask Richard to discuss it with me, he clams up and finds some reason to go out or to leave the room. I haven't wanted to push him because it's broken my heart to see him like this but now… I'll have to push.'

'Do you want me to speak to him?'

'That's a very kind offer, love, but I'm his wife and he's a proud man. I'll have to do it myself. We are meant to be partners in this life, after all.'

Nate took a sip of his coffee. It was rich and nutty and obviously very good quality.

'I could well be drinking instant coffee soon.' His mother smiled at him.

'Instant coffee's pretty good these days, you know.'

'I always used to drink it and your father loved it. Mind you, he'd drink anything I put in front of him, that man would. And it would always be the best he'd ever tasted.'

'He was a good dad.'

'He was. And a wonderful husband.'

'Richard is a good man, too.'

'He is, darling. Such a good man and that's why I have to be at his side as he deals with this. He's made some silly mistakes but he only did what he thought was for the best. It's just the current economy is so up and down, and while some businesses are thriving, some are floundering. Add to that a few chances he took and, well…'

They sat there in silence for a while, gazing out at the garden where birds swooped in and landed on the feeders, then pecked at the nuts and seeds on offer. Some of the smaller ones fluttered to the grass where their heads bobbed as they collected the seeds that had dropped to the ground.

'I'll miss the birds when we move,' Paula said. 'I love my birds. They come back every day because they know I always have food for them.'

'Give them a forwarding address.'

'Ha! Yes, such a good idea.' She put her cup and saucer on the glass-topped coffee table. 'Do you have any good news to cheer me up, Nate?'

'Good news?'

'Yes, you know, like you've won a surfing competition or… perhaps there's finally someone special?'

He cleared his throat.

'Oh, there is, isn't there? How wonderful! My goodness, Nate, at last! What's her name?'

'No, there's no one.'

'Nathaniel Theodore Bryson!' Nate winced as his mother used his full name, the name he'd been keen to escape from as a child because it always made his school-friends giggle. 'You are fibbing to your poor old mother. Tell me the truth this instant. There's a woman, isn't there?'

'Okay… kind of.'

'Name?'

He met his mother's eyes and saw a sparkle there, the one he knew well, so he knew that if this was providing her with a well-needed distraction then he wasn't going to ruin that for her.

'Zoe.'

'Aw… I like that name. And who is she?'

'Well, she owns the diner at the cove. But it's complicated. I like her but I've made my decision now to go travelling.' He held his breath. He hadn't wanted to tell his mother that today, after seeing her so upset, but now she'd asked about Zoe, he had to give her the full explanation about his plans.

'You've decided that now's the time to jet off around the world?'

'Yes. But now I know you're having problems, I won't go. In fact, I have savings, Mum, that you can have. And you can sell the van – it's as good a time as any.'

'Don't be ridiculous!' His mother bridled. 'You can't put your life on hold because of Richard and me. Nate, I'm a grown woman, old enough to take care of myself, and I have plenty of skills and a good brain I can utilize. I won't be down for long. We are certainly not going to take your hard-earned money or sell your campervan. Your dad would never forgive me.'

'I think Dad would be quite understanding, actually.'

'Well, I would never, ever forgive myself, but thank you for offering, my darling. However, Richard and I will emerge from this. I'm like a phoenix, me.'

Nate smiled. 'I know that. You're a tough old bird.'

'Less of the old.'

'You said it first.'

'So I did, but in jest.'

'I'm joking too.'

'I know that.'

'Anyway, I can hardly allow myself to get involved with Zoe then leave her so I can travel. What kind of idiot would that make me?'

'Well, take her with you. Best way to find out if you're compatible is to travel together.'

'I would but she has a business and… there's also something that she's not telling me.'

'Oh god, is it a secret husband or a baby, or she's come out of a cult and they're chasing her?'

'I don't think so, Mum, but thanks for bringing your gossip mags and daytime TV into this.'

'Well, you never know. One of the girls I go to bingo with had a lucky escape after using Tinder, you know. Some man who'd been courting her on there turned out to be married twice already and wanted to make her his third wife so he could steal all her money.'

Nate swallowed his comment about courting on Tinder. 'Sounds like a lucky escape indeed.'

'You be careful, Nate, and find out all you can about this Zoe before you get involved. Then… and only then… you have my permission to fall completely and utterly in love.'

'Well, thanks, Mum. I couldn't have done it without your permission.'

'You know I'm pulling your leg.'

'As always.'

'You should have an open conversation with her and tell her how you feel and ask her to go with you. If she says no, then you know where you stand.'

'It's hard to be that open, Mum. Besides, I think she would say no. She has her business to run.'

Paula shrugged. 'And someone could step in and hold the fort, I'm sure, although it would need to be someone with the right experience and someone she could trust.'

'It also seems a bit… sudden and impulsive. I mean… I've only just started to get to know her and she might think I was mad if I asked her to come with me. It probably would be mad of me to ask her.'

'Oh, my darling, I understand why you feel that way, but I've never heard you mention a woman you really liked before and… well, life is so short. Sometimes, when I look back, I wish I'd been a bit more impulsive. We should all have got into the campervan and driven around the country. I wish…'

'I didn't know you felt like that, Mum.'

'I would've loved to have the chance to spend quality time like that with you and your dad. Hindsight can be painful, can't it?'

Nate nodded. 'Missed opportunities.'

'Exactly. Better to take a few chances, love, than to look back and regret the things you didn't do. Now, shall we have another coffee? Might as well enjoy the good stuff while I can.'

'Sure, why not?'

Nate picked up their cups and followed his mother into the kitchen. He knew she was right about being open but he also knew that it wasn't quite that straightforward. There was still a possibility that he liked Zoe far more than she liked him, and if he asked her outright to go away with him, she'd probably think he was completely mad.

He'd have to think about how to approach this *honest* discussion and to find the right time if it ever arose. But for this afternoon, at least, he was going to try to help his mother to think through her problems and hopefully find a way forward for her and Richard. Nate knew that he'd never be able to go away if his mum was stuck in Penzance, penniless and homeless; there was no way he'd let that happen. He'd give her all his savings if he needed to – even though she'd said she wouldn't take them – and find a way to support her if she couldn't get another job.

Nate loved his mum and she had been wonderful to him over the years, always putting him first and never worrying him with her troubles or concerns. Nate would be there for her, the same as she had been there for him. It was what his father would have wanted and it was what Nate wanted. He just hoped Richard would be able to put his pride behind him and accept whatever help Nate could offer, because otherwise it would be more awkward than it needed to be.

'Is there coffee, Paula?' Richard appeared in the doorway, rubbing his eyes.

'Yes, love, go and sit down and I'll bring you a cup.'

Richard nodded then shuffled away in his checked slippers. His shirt was hanging out of the back of his trousers, his tie was askew and his hair was sticking up where he'd been sleeping on it. He didn't look like the strong, resilient man Nate had known and it worried him.

'Let me talk to Richard with you, Mum. Let me at least help you speak to him. I think he might need someone else around and it's possible that I'll be able to offer some suggestions or think of someone who could help.'

His mother released a long sigh. 'Okay, Nate. Thank you. To be honest, I'm not sure if he would listen to me alone. Believe me, I've tried, but it's like he doesn't want to tell me the full extent of things.'

'Give me the tray and we'll have a chat with him now.'

Paula nodded. 'I love you, Nate.'

'I love you too, Mum, and I'll always be here for you.' His mum's eyes glistened and she pressed a hand to her lips. 'But, Mum?'

'Yes, Nate.'

'Please don't ever call me Nathaniel Theodore in public, will you? I'm not sure my reputation could stand it.'

He smiled to show he was joking and his mum smiled too, and it was the best thing he'd seen all day, because he knew that her smile held a glimmer of hope that her son would be able to help her out of the mess she had found herself in.

And for Nate, that was what family was all about.

Chapter 13

Nate opened the door to Riding the Wave and went in. The owner, Lucinda Norris, smiled at him then gestured at the phone she was holding between her chin and shoulder.

Nate nodded and had a browse around the shop while he waited. Riding the Wave was like an Aladdin's cave, full of treasures that he could spend hours looking through. From surfboards, paddleboards and foam boards, to wetsuits, rash vests, board shorts and more, the shop had everything he could want for a day in the sea. He read the labels of the range of surf wax: Mrs Palmer's Ultra Sticky Surf Wax, SexWax Dream Cream Surf Wax Gold and Matuna's Organic Surf Wax. There was a whole industry dedicated to surfing, and more and more brands kept popping up all the time. The clothes in the shop were fantastic; there was so much choice. As he moved around, he came across some women's kaftans, and a white and indigo one caught his eye. It was tie-dyed with loose, cropped sleeves and would fall to mid-thigh. He ran a finger over the soft and silky material. It would look amazing on Zoe and he could imagine her wearing it at the beach.

'Nate?' Lucinda to called him as she walked over and kissed his cheeks. 'What can I do for you?'

'Hi, Lucinda.'

Nate took in her wavy blonde bob, tanned skin and weathered face. Hours spent in the sun had etched deep lines around her eyes and mouth and she had a jagged scar on her jaw where she'd sliced her face open on a surfboard fin. Nate knew from previous conversations that she also had several scars on her back where she'd had a collision with a reef in Australia when she surfed professionally. Her green eyes twinkled as she smiled at him and he relaxed instantly; she was warm and friendly and their shared love of surfing meant that he felt a certain affinity with her. There was no pressure to conform to anything around Lucinda; he could be himself.

'I wanted to update you on progress for Surf for Sighthounds. I've secured the dates with Luna Bay council, so we're good to go there, and Conwenna's on board too. Have you managed to rope anyone in?'

Lucinda's smile widened. 'I have, you'll be pleased to know. I have three professional surfers keen to be involved and one of them is quite a celebrity, so he should draw the crowds. Let me show you.' She led him around the counter and opened her laptop, then fired it up. 'Here's the list.'

Nate's jaw dropped as he read it. 'Wow! How'd you manage that?'

'Oh, you know… I called in a few favours and, lucky for us, these guys happen to be in the UK that weekend in August.'

'You're fabulous, Lucinda, you know that?'

She shrugged then laughed. 'Happy to help, sweetie. And it's good for the dogs and for tourism, which we all need to survive, right?'

'Indeed we do.'

'How are things with you, anyway? Have you thought any more about that trip you mentioned?'

'Well, I haven't firmed up my plans yet as I've been busy working and organizing Surf for Sighthounds, but I am hoping to head off in August.'

'Good for you. You only live once and life's not a rehearsal.'

Nate nodded. 'So true.'

'Do you want a coffee? We can go through what I've got lined up as a prize from Riding the Wave.'

Nate checked his watch. 'Sure. I have half an hour of my lunch break left, so as long as I get back to the cafe by three, it'll be fine.'

Lucinda went through to the back to switch the kettle on, and Nate gazed at the screen of her laptop in awe. She'd really excelled this time by getting not just one but three of the surfing industry's big names involved, and he knew for certain now that Surf for Sighthounds was going to be even better than before.

—

Zoe checked her reflection in the mirror on the diner wall for the hundredth time that hour. She couldn't believe she was doing what she was, but she needed to see him again, and soon. Preferably alone.

That morning, she had sent Nate a text to ask him to come to the diner after closing. She'd told him she had a surprise for him, and his reply had been one that could have been interpreted as bordering on flirty, especially because of the winking emoji at the end, along with a kiss. Speaking to Grace on Sunday had helped Zoe to work through some of her thoughts and feelings, and she felt better for it. Whatever happened now, she knew she had to put her big girl pants on and face her past, in whatever form that was, and she also knew where she had to start. But first, she wanted to see Nate and to do something nice for him because he'd been nothing but nice to her. Zoe knew she'd been a bit up and down with him, probably confusing him with her softening towards him, followed by pulling away then softening again, but she was so confused herself that it had been hard to be direct with him. If only he wasn't going away... but then if he'd been staying around, she might be in trouble.

She heard a knock at the front door so she went to open it. The diner was dark except for the lights behind the counter, as she'd closed two hours ago and it was now eight-thirty. The shadows outside were lengthening as dusk was beginning to fall outside.

Zoe smiled as she met Nate's gaze.

'Evening.'

'Good evening to you. What's all this about, then?'

She breathed in his scent, savouring his sandalwood aftershave that made her stomach flip. Wearing washed-out jeans and a black T-shirt that clung to his sculpted frame, he looked good enough to eat.

'I have something to show you.'

'Well, I have something to show you too. Come out here for a moment.'

Nate took her hand and led her outside the diner and down to the harbour rail.

'Look.'

'It's breathtaking.'

They gazed out at the horizon where pinky-purple streaks were set on a canvas of orange. It was utterly beautiful. The air was filled with the heady fragrance of flowers from the baskets attached to the rail and the heavy stone planters that were set at intervals along the front.

'It is, right?'

Nate was still holding her hand and his fingers were warm, his body so close she could have leant against him had she wanted to. And she did want to. But she was trying to control her impulses.

'When it's this lovely, I don't think I want to be anywhere else.'

'Me, neither.'

'Will you stay here now, Zoe? For ever?'

'I guess so. As long as I can, anyway. I feel a sense of peace here. Not all the time, you know, but most of it, and I've never had that anywhere else. Of course, lately it's been a bit different but it'll settle down again.'

'Why has it been different?'

'Well… because of you.'

'I'm sorry.'

'Don't be.'

'But I didn't want to steal away your peace of mind.'

'It's not just you, Nate. It's losing Raven, my past repeatedly creeping into my dreams, and the range of emotions I've experienced as I've got to know you. So… you are partly responsible but not totally to blame.'

He smiled, then raised her hand and pressed it to his lips.

'If only life was simpler, right?'

'But then it probably wouldn't be so much fun.'

'There is fun to be had, I have to agree with that. So what did you want to show me?'

'Come inside.'

Zoe led him into the diner then locked the door behind them and gestured at the counter.

'Wow! Did you make these?'

'With some help.'

'What, from one of your chefs?'

'No, from Simon. He was here all afternoon, baking.'

'They're amazing. Great way to spend a Wednesday!'

Zoe watched as Nate took in all the details of the cakes she and Simon had made. There were cupcakes in different flavours with chocolate, vanilla and strawberry. Each one was decorated with a swirl of buttercream, then on top were marzipan decorations that Zoe and Simon had created. Some were greyhounds in different colours and sizes, while others were tiny surfboarders riding on the top of waves. They were intricately detailed and had taken hours, but Zoe had wanted to practise them and ensure that they were perfect, and with Simon's help she'd been able to do that.

'It was a trial run ready for Surf for Sighthounds. We'll make a load of them for the event and sell them to raise money.'

Nate was shaking his head as he stared at the cakes, a muscle in his jaw twitching.

'Nate, are you okay? I didn't do the wrong thing, did I?'

'No, Zoe… I'm really grateful. These are fantastic. You are incredibly talented.'

'I didn't just invite you here to see the cakes, though.'

'You didn't?'

As he turned to her, her breath caught in her throat at the intensity of his gaze.

'No. I… Nate, I like you so much and I…' Her heart thundered and heat flooded her face. 'This is a bit harder to say than I'd imagined.'

'Say it. There's no judging here.'

'I… I've reached a point in my life where I know that I have some things to sort out. I'm carrying a lot of baggage from my past and I need to try to put it behind me. Until I do, I won't be able to move on.'

'Do you want to talk about it?'

She worried her bottom lip. 'Not yet. I'm still working through it – but soon. Once I've addressed some issues…'

'Do those issues include other people?'

She nodded.

His eyes roamed her face and he raised his hand as if he was going to touch her, but just before his fingers met her cheek, he lowered his hand and tucked it into his jeans pocket. Her heart squeezed because she ached to touch him, to hold him and to surrender to her feelings for him, but she knew why he was holding back. He was being sensible and strong and that was good. They needed to be strong, because whatever it was that was growing between them couldn't go anywhere right now. Not until everything was sorted and maybe not at all. Perhaps he would return to Conwenna Cove after he'd been travelling and they would have the possibility of a future, but she thought that unlikely and didn't like to hope. Instead, she would take each day as it came and try to find peace of mind. It was a good starting point.

'Try one.'

'Sorry?'

'Try a cupcake and I'll get us a drink.'

'Oh… okay.'

Zoe broke away from the tension that had pinned her mere inches away from Nate and went behind the counter to make some milkshakes. A brandy would have been better but she knew that alcohol would weaken her and probably make it far more likely that she'd throw herself at Nate. Better to have a sweet, creamy milkshake and to keep the counter between them; better to avoid letting her longing overpower her as it was threatening to do.

She made the milkshakes then sprayed whipped cream onto them, knowing that this would be the only sensual delight she'd be enjoying this evening. But at least she'd done something nice for Nate, and that could only help to assuage her guilt at creating so much turmoil for them both, and for pushing him away when all she really wanted was to hold him close.

–

The next day, Zoe had arranged for her chefs and her waiting staff to run the diner, as she prepared to try to deal with some of the issues that were haunting her. The only way to deal with them was to face them head on, so she needed to see the woman who had caused some of the issues in the first place, and that meant returning to her home town of Brixham in Devon.

She spent the car journey thinking about the diner and what she would like to add to the autumn menu. She'd discuss it with her chefs, obviously, but also liked to think about what local seasonal produce could be brought into the food they offered the customers. It was easier to think about the diner and food than to think about her past or about her present. She did this whenever she needed to let her subconscious mull something over, and it had proved to be quite effective when emotion threatened to overwhelm her.

With it being a Thursday, the traffic wasn't too bad. When she reached her destination, following three hours of travelling – which included two comfort breaks along the way – her stomach clenched. Perhaps this wasn't such a good idea, but then what else could she do? She didn't even know if either of the people she wanted to see would be there – highly doubted that *he* would be – and wondered again at her wisdom in coming back.

But she was here now, so she'd just as well stretch her legs and see what happened. She found a space in the car park then strolled down to the harbour. It was strange coming back after so long. She'd moved around a lot in her previous life, the one she'd led before settling in Conwenna, and the only place she'd had roots before Conwenna Cove was in Brixham. But now that was like a dream she'd once had.

Zoe wandered along the harbour, taking in the familiar views that also seemed so different. The day was warm and the sun now high in the sky, shining down on the numerous fishing boats at the quayside where she knew locals would be selling their daily catch caught on their trawlers and day boats. She glanced behind her at the town, admiring the colourful houses that cascaded down either side of the harbour, the mixture of old and new architecture. This had once been her home, she had grown up here; now she was like a stranger in a place full of ghosts.

She hugged herself, suddenly cold in her white T-shirt, jeans and sandals. She'd left her cardigan in the car and could go back to get it but she worried that if she did, she might drive straight back to Cornwall. No, she was here, and she would do this. If she left now, she'd regret it and she was getting tired of regrets.

All along the front sat shops and cafes. Zoe wandered past pink and blue buildings, moving aside to let tourists by, until she reached the small gift shop that she'd once known so well. She paused and gazed through the window. The interior of the shop was dark and she knew that inside it would be cool and smell of old paper, varnish and peppermint. That familiar smell had been one that she'd loved in her childhood and adolescence. Then everything had changed, and she hadn't been able to return there.

She pushed open the door. The familiar tinkle of the bell that she was expecting had been replaced with an electronic noise that made her start. But things change and she should expect that. She didn't know if the shop had changed owners, after all.

The shelves groaned with knick-knacks, from ornaments featuring the harbour to snowglobes filled with mermaids and glitter. She picked one up and shook it, filled with a strange melancholy as the mermaid was surrounded by a whirlwind of multicoloured glitter, her blue eyes staring out unseeing, her tail fixed to the rock she sat on. Zoe put the globe back then picked up a model of the iconic *Golden Hind*, Sir Francis Drake's ship from the 1500s, a replica of which sat in the harbour and was a big tourist attraction. Zoe had always liked the stories of Drake her teachers had told her as a child, enjoying how adventurous he had seemed, setting off on his ship with his crew, not knowing if they'd ever return. Some of them didn't. Sometimes, you just had to squash your fears and doubts and sail off into the sunset. But Zoe had done that once and look where it had got her. Subconsciously, she touched her fringe, feeling the scar that lay beneath her soft hair. Sometimes, taking a risk backfired and led to heartbreak.

'Hello? Are you looking for anything in particular?'

Zoe turned to meet the friendly grey eyes of a man who was about her height, with short ginger hair and lots of freckles. His T-shirt was baggy but it didn't hide the fact that he had a slight paunch, and his jeans were baggy and stained.

'Excuse the state of me.' He smiled, then pulled at his T-shirt. 'We're in the middle of painting the flat upstairs.'

'Oh! You live there?'

He nodded.

'I uh… I came here looking for someone I used to know but I guess they've gone now. Do you own the shop?'

'No. Well, yes, actually. I keep forgetting.' He offered her that friendly smile again and she realized he looked familiar. Her mind tried to place him but it was a hazy memory. She suspected he could have been at her high school but was someone she hadn't known well.

'Do you know the previous owners?'

'Yes, very well, actually. Pat and Geoffrey don't live above the shop any more as they moved into Pat's mother's bungalow along the way.' He pointed behind him as if the streets were visible. 'But Amelia is still here. In fact, she's my—'

'Wife.'

Zoe gasped as her old friend stepped into view behind the counter; she must have been in the shadows of the corridor that led off the shop and to the stairway up to the flat.

'Amelia?'

'You two know each other?' the man asked.

'We do.' Amelia's tone was flat, cold, unwelcoming. 'Pete, this is Zoe. Zoe, meet my husband, Pete. You probably don't remember him, but he was two years above us at school.'

'I thought you looked familiar.'

Zoe stepped forward and held out her hand and Pete took it, but not before glancing at his wife as if seeking her approval.

'It's okay, Pete. I've got this. You carry on painting.'

'Are you sure?' He touched Amelia's arm and Zoe caught the look that passed between them, a look of two people who trusted each other and were intimate friends.

'Yes, love. I'll call if I need you.'

Pete shambled off, back up the stairs, whistling under his breath.

'So, Zoe, are you in town for anything special or is this a social call?' Amelia scanned her with her piercing eyes: one blue, the other brown. Her black hair was tied into a bun perched high on her head and her face was bare of any make-up.

'I came back to see if you were here. I need to talk to you.'

Zoe's stomach churned as if it would explode and release the butterflies battling for room into the shop. Her neck ached with tension and her mouth was dry, but she had to speak to Amelia, to try to figure out what had happened, how things had all gone so wrong.

'I thought you said you never wanted to speak to me ever again.' Amelia sniffed. 'And I don't blame you.'

'I know. I did feel that way but I've had time to think, too. In fact, time is all I have had. You weren't solely responsible for how things panned out and I want to speak to you about it.'

Amelia nodded but her eyes were still wary.

'Would you like to grab a coffee? I promise I'm not here to upset you.'

'It would be nice to escape the paint fumes for a bit. We bought that paint that's supposed to be fume-free but I think my nose is just extra sensitive at the moment. Hold on. I'll be back in a tick.' Amelia turned and Zoe heard her climbing the stairs then the murmur of voices from above, before hearing the footsteps descend again.

'Right, Pete said he'll hold the fort. It hasn't been busy today but you can guarantee that if I shut up shop for an hour, someone will suddenly want a snowglobe or a kite, and we need every sale we can get at the moment.'

Amelia came around the counter and Zoe had to swallow a gasp.

'You're…'

'Pregnant? Yes, and I feel gigantic.'

'Wow!'

'Zoe, it's not that surprising. I'm a thirty-three-year-old married woman. I always wanted a family and my parents are delighted to be grandparents again.'

'Again?'

'Oh… not me, no. My two brothers have both had kids, so Mum and Dad are living their dream with babies popping out all over the place.'

Zoe nodded, not trusting herself to speak. She realized she'd missed so much over the years; people she'd once known and been close to had lived their lives while she'd been gone. And so they should. But it still seemed strange to think of Amelia's parents as grandparents, and of Amelia's older brothers – with their constant teasing of Amelia and Zoe growing up – as old enough and mature enough to have families of their own. How did that happen?

Pete appeared in the shop again, wiping his hands on a cloth. 'Darned paint.' He shook his head. 'Amelia's managed to get it everywhere in the nursery except for on the walls.'

'You!' Amelia giggled, then she squeezed his hand. 'I'll be about an hour. Is that okay?'

'Of course. Take your time, angel. I'll be here.'

Zoe went through the door and into the brightness of the afternoon on legs that shook like jelly, but she was glad she'd come, if only to know that Amelia had moved on with her life and hadn't remained trapped in some awful stasis of guilt and remorse.

Chapter 14

Zoe found them a table outside one of the harbour cafes and they sat down. She couldn't stop looking at her old friend's bump. Amelia had always talked about having children but Zoe had imagined that being years off in the future. But then, this was the future.

'How far along are you?' Zoe nodded at Amelia's bump.

'Just over six months. I can't believe that in less than three months, I'll be a mum.'

'It's wonderful. I'm really happy for you.'

'Truly?' Amelia met Zoe's gaze and they sat that way for a few moments. 'I didn't know if you would be. I mean… why would you be?'

'I didn't know if you'd still be with… *him.*' Zoe forced the last word out.

'With Finn?'

Zoe nodded. 'I thought you might have still been together.'

'And how would that have made you feel?'

'I honestly don't know. A few years ago, I'd have… well, I did feel dreadful. Broken. Destroyed. I never thought I'd get over it, but I guess time moves on and feelings change.'

'He did the same to me, you know?' Amelia said it matter-of-factly, as if cheating was an everyday pastime for the man they'd both fallen for.

'I didn't know and I'm sorry.'

'It only took him eight months. I did stay with him for a while, in hotels and rented apartments – when he was around, that is, and not travelling abroad or to London for TV appearances. But he was never around for long so, in between, I'd come back here. I suppose it was like I was on tap for him. Sorry not to have a more eloquent expression but that was how I ended up feeling. Then, after a particularly heavy night out, I woke in a hotel bathtub with a cracking headache and virtually no memory of the night before. I mean, this was only about four years ago. I was twenty-nine and suddenly everything hit me at once. There I was, living day to day, desperate for scraps of affection from a man who would probably only ever love himself. I'd sacrificed our friendship for him and for what? I knew he didn't love me and never had done. To be honest, I think Finn is only capable of loving himself. You were his wife of eleven years and look at what he did to you. Why would he treat me any differently? So… I washed my face and brushed my teeth then headed into the bedroom to confront him.'

'And…'

Amelia grimaced. 'He was in bed with not one, but two women. I went crazy.'

'What did you do?'

'I wish I could say I chopped off his bits but I wasn't quite that gutsy. Mind you, I wouldn't be in the situation I'm in now if I'd done that, and I don't think I could have

155

coped with prison. No… I simply decorated his favourite surfboard. It was out on the hotel balcony.'

'You didn't!'

'It was the latest one he'd received from that brand that sponsors him. He loved it and kept telling me how much it would cost to buy and how he could have ten thousand of them free if he wanted them. So I decorated it with three bottles of nail varnish and a letter opener. No way he was getting those marks off.'

Zoe smiled, imagining how furious that would have made Finn. 'If there was one thing that would be guaranteed to get to him, it would be the destruction of his *board, man*.'

'Yep. Sadly, I didn't hang around to see how gutted he was, because I just had to get out of there. I kind of wanted to maintain some dignity too. Speaking to him in front of his latest conquests wasn't high on my list of priorities.'

A waitress arrived and took their orders. When they were alone again, Amelia leant forwards. 'Zoe, I am so sorry. I'm sorry for hurting you and for doing what I did. It was unforgiveable to sleep with Finn. I regret it with all of my heart.'

'It wasn't only sleeping with him, though, was it?'

Zoe kept her hands clasped on her lap, pressing her nails into her palms. This was every bit as difficult as she'd imagined it would be and yet, she was still glad she'd come.

'No. I was seeing him for a while. The deceit…' Amelia looked up and her eyes were glistening. 'We deceived you for months. But I thought… I believed him.'

'He told you he loved you.'

'He said it had always been me and I so wanted for that to be true.'

Zoe touched her head and caught Amelia watching her.

'Does it still hurt?'

'What?'

'The scar.'

'Not really. Sometimes it aches a bit and sometimes it itches, but it's not painful.' Zoe swallowed, not wanting to talk about the nightmares in case they got worse. Besides, she'd come here to start letting go of those fears.

'It was the catalyst, I suppose, wasn't it?' she asked.

'The accident?'

'Yes. After it, I changed. I know that.'

'Well, that's not surprising; you could have been killed.'

'But up to that point, I was doing what Finn wanted. I was living his life with him, even if it wasn't really the life I wanted.'

'You were a good wife to him. You made so much effort to—'

'—be what he wanted me to be. And then… after this.' Zoe touched her head again. 'I just couldn't do it any more.'

'Well, you can't blame yourself for that and it makes me seem even worse. I took advantage of the situation.'

Zoe shrugged. 'It would have been someone else if it wasn't you. In fact, I suspect there were others, anyway.'

'You're not wrong there.' Amelia winced. 'Although I didn't know anything about any other women at the time. I never would have allowed that to happen right under your nose. Oh god, Zoe, I'm making this worse, aren't I? I'm, like, I wouldn't let anyone else hurt you but I was happy to do it myself.'

Their drinks arrived and Zoe thanked the waitress.

'I'm not allowing myself much caffeine at the moment, but I need this.' Amelia sipped her latte.

'I'm sure you're allowed the odd coffee.'

'Zoe… I never thought I'd see you again but I've had this conversation with you so many times in my head. I've even spoken to Pete about it.'

'You told your husband what happened?'

'I did. Pete's a good man and he deserved honesty. When we got together, I didn't want a relationship, but he's so kind and caring and so understanding. He knew I was hurting and damaged but he waited for me to heal. He helped me to heal, I guess. He said he always liked me at school but thought I was way out of his league.' She laughed. 'As if there's a league of people and you can only date someone on your *level*.' She air-quoted 'level'.

'That's high school for you.'

'Yes, but who did we have eyes for?'

'Finn and his buddies.'

'Yep. How sad were we?' Amelia sighed. 'That's why me being with him after all those years, and knowing he was your husband and that you adored him, was just horrid. I hate that I did it, Zoe, and if I could go back in time…'

'I know. Me, too.'

'How so?'

'Well, recently, the more I've let myself think of the past, of the anger and the pain and the initial reaction I had to it all, the more I've seen it all clearly. Yes, you hurt me. You and Finn broke my heart, but I was never really happy with him. If it hadn't been you, it would have been someone else. But… you were my best friend.'

'I betrayed you. It's unforgiveable.'

'Look, Amelia, I tried to be what Finn wanted and it was so hard. After the accident, I couldn't maintain the façade any more and, to be honest, I didn't want to. It's tiring being the version of yourself that someone else wants you to be. Finn didn't love me like I wanted, and deserved, to be loved. I can see that now and recently I've actually started to believe that I had a lucky escape. So, while I'll never be grateful to you for stealing my husband, I can finally forgive you. I need to forgive you now and to move on.'

Amelia gazed out at the boats bobbing on the water and Zoe followed her gaze. There were so many of them, bright white in the sunlight, their windows dark as eyes full of secrets.

'I've dreamt of you saying that for such a long time but I never thought I'd hear the words,' Amelia said, breaking the silence that had fallen between them.

'I'm not saying I won't remember, because I can't zap my memory, even though sometimes I wish I could wipe some areas of it clean and start again.'

'That would be nice, right? Just keep the bits you want.'

'So nice. But I don't want to carry the anger or the pain any longer. There's no point. Finn has, it seems, surfed off into the sunset and we're the ones left behind.'

'Well, I am. You're living elsewhere now and good for you. By the way, where is that? I didn't even ask, I was so shocked at seeing you.'

'I live in a beautiful village called Conwenna Cove in Cornwall. It's about two and a half hours away.'

'Did you drive all that way today?'

Zoe nodded. 'I got it into my head and I had to do it. I've been thinking about it for a while, that the anger and bitterness in my heart have been holding me back, and a few things in my life have shifted and it felt like the right time.'

'I'm glad you did come. With my marriage to Pete and the baby on the way, I'd like to feel like this is a proper fresh start. Having the guilt hanging over me has been tough. Not that I'm asking you to feel sorry for me, of course.' Amelia wrinkled her nose and Zoe saw the little girl she'd once been, at one time her closest friend in the whole world, the friend she'd sworn to love forever.

Zoe reached over the table and took Amelia's hand. 'It is a fresh start, sweetheart.'

They smiled at each other and it was as if they'd gone back in time to when they used to sit at the harbour as teenagers, drinking cokes and chatting about school, music, fashion and boys. Back then, Zoe had thought they'd be friends for the rest of their lives. Back then, she had thought their friendship was invincible. Then Finn had showed an interest in them in turn and that had been that; their relationship had changed irrevocably, even though they hadn't known it at the time.

They stayed at the cafe for much longer than an hour, talking and catching up on the years that had passed since they'd last seen each other. It was gone four when Zoe finally walked Amelia back to her shop and her home above it. Amelia asked her in but Zoe declined on account of her needing to get back on the road. They exchanged numbers and even though Zoe suspected that they probably wouldn't do much more than text now – because life had moved on and so much water had passed under the bridge – she still felt lighter as she drove away from Brixton. She'd put one of her past sorrows to bed and made peace with the woman she'd once loved as her best friend.

Now she could take another step into the future, with one less concern holding her back.

—

When Zoe got back to Conwenna Cove, she drove over the brow of the hill and had to blink hard as tears filled her eyes. She'd held it together as she'd driven all that way, even when she'd stopped at the services for coffee and cake to keep her going, but arriving home and seeing the pretty little village lit up before her, glowing invitingly, tipped her over the edge. The sky was pitch black but the windows of the village houses that spread out to her left and right glowed gold and orange and, beyond them, lay the cove and the sea. There was such a sense of openness yet security about the cove, and Zoe knew that she was home.

She drove slowly, taking the road that veered left, then parked in front of her cottage. Inside, it would be quiet; no one would be waiting for her, but at least she'd be free of some of the ghosts from her past. When she'd gone to Brixham, she'd been hoping that forgiving her old friend would let her move on. It was obvious that even though Amelia had moved on with her life, Finn had hurt her too. Handsome, daring, arrogant Finn, the man she'd married at eighteen and who had once loved her in his own way. They'd been close for a while but fame and fortune had changed him, taking him away from what he'd once held dear and making him think he was destined for better things. Better things than his teenage sweetheart, better things even than her best friend. When she really thought about it now, Finn had come to think of himself as being above fidelity, as if it were a concept for lesser mortals.

And that was something Zoe feared now; that if Finn, someone she'd know for so long and had been married to could change, then couldn't anyone? Someone could seem like the nicest person in the world, as if they had the kindest heart, but life could change them. It was possible, wasn't it? Or did some people deserve a chance to show that they were different?

She sighed as she got out of the car and trudged towards her front door. Just as she got inside, her mobile buzzed in her bag, so she pulled it out and swiped the screen. It was a message from Nate, as if he'd sensed that she was thinking about him.

> **Zoe,**
> **Hope you're okay? Went into diner but they said you'd gone out for the day. Have a surprise for you. Meet me at the cove tomorrow evening around eight.**
> **Sweet dreams,**
> **Nate X**

Zoe read the text through three times then held her mobile to her heart. She so wanted for this to be real, for Nate to be as good as he seemed to be. Even if nothing came of this and she only had the next few weeks with him, then at least she could learn to let herself care again. She wanted to, because she wanted to feel love again, fully, deeply and truly.

Perhaps Nate could show her the way...

Chapter 15

At seven forty-five that Friday evening, Zoe left her cottage and walked down to the cove. She'd dressed in navy linen trousers and matching T-shirt, white Converse daps and carried a white and navy striped cardigan in case it was cooler on the beach.

The evening air was warm and sweet. Above the cliffs, the sky was painted with shades of cobalt and sapphire that stretched out across the sea, where they entwined with tangerine and amethyst. The sparse clouds were like puffs of pink cotton-candy dusted with icing sugar as they floated languidly across the open expanse of the horizon.

When Zoe reached the top of the path that led to the beach, she paused and gazed around her. She took a few moments to breathe deeply, to appreciate the sensation of the breeze on her skin and the clean, briny scent of the air as it blew in from over the water. There was such a deep sense of peace to be had from living near the sea, and she felt she could lie down on the grass right there and sleep peacefully.

A flock of birds passed overhead, silky black silhouettes against the beautiful sky, and she tilted her chin to watch them as they swooped and turned, working in harmony, then headed back inland, presumably to the open farm-land and quiet outbuildings of the farms where they'd roost for the summer months, raising their chicks in the rich Cornish environment.

When Zoe lowered her gaze again, she could see a lone figure down on the sand, walking towards the cliffs off to her left. It could be Nate, but from this distance and in the twilight, she couldn't be certain. Her stomach gave a flutter and she realised that she was looking forward to seeing him more than she'd admitted to herself earlier. She'd taken time to think through what had happened when she'd returned to Devon, and she had no regrets about going to see Amelia. It had been an entirely positive experience and although part of her hoped she would see her old friend again, she knew that even if she didn't, she had at least been able to let her anger go and to forgive Amelia.

Zoe took one more deep breath then made her way down the path to the beach. The long grass swished against her ankles and the sandy path was loose beneath her soles, so she took her time, although she'd walked the path so many times over the past few years that she knew she could probably get to the bottom blindfolded.

Once on the sand, she looked around for Nate. There were a few stragglers still in the sea, making the most of the warm water after a day of sunshine. Off to her right, some of the local teenagers were having a barbecue. The strains of an acoustic guitar reached her ears and she smiled. Who'd have thought kids their age would even know 'Hotel California'?

Deciding it was more likely Nate would be off to the left, she went in that direction. She soon spotted him and a sigh escaped her lips when she saw what he'd done.

In the shelter of the towering grey cliffs, Nate had spread out a large blanket that he'd weighted down with rocks. Around the edges were four solar-powered lanterns, casting their ethereal pale blue light over the sand, and in the centre of the blanket were four glass votive holders that created a warm circle of light. To the side of the blanket sat a cooler box; next to it, Nate was on his knees with his back to her, rooting around in a rucksack.

She approached slowly, hoping he'd turn around as she didn't want to startle him. When he did turn, she raised a hand in greeting then picked up her pace.

'Evening, Nate.'

'Zoe.' He stood up and walked towards her. 'So good to see you. It feels like weeks since you showed me the cakes.'

'It has been a busy week.'

As he took her hands and kissed her cheek, his sandal-wood scent washed over her and she closed her eyes briefly to savour it.

'What's all this about, then?' she asked.

'I wanted to thank you for all your effort with the cakes.'

'You didn't need to. I'm glad to help out.'

'I wanted to. And not just for the cakes but for everything.'

'Everything?'

He nodded. 'I'll explain, but come and sit down first.'

He led her towards the blanket and she sat down, then he produced two plastic cups from behind the rucksack and a bottle of cider from the cooler.

'Cider?'

'This one's delicious. It's from the cider mill at Luna Bay.'

'I haven't drunk cider in years. Not since I was a teenager, in fact.'

'What, since you used to drink White Lightning or something similar?'

'That's the stuff.' She giggled. 'Those were the days, eh?'

He nodded. 'To be honest, I didn't do a lot of teenage drinking. It was all about swimming and surfing.'

'If only some of the kids today could be like that.'

'Hey, grandma!' He nudged her. 'The youth of today, right?' He stroked his chin with his thumb and forefinger as if lost in thought and Zoe nudged him back.

'So you wanted to thank me for the cakes – and something else?'

'First a toast.' He popped the cork from the bottle then poured the bubbly liquid into the two plastic cups. He handed one to Zoe and she caught a whiff of a fruity floral scent that made her mouth water.

'Zoe,' Nate raised his cup, 'this is to friendship and everything else that comes with it. Also, to you for being so sweet and thoughtful and to the greyhounds and finding them their forever homes.'

Zoe tapped her cup against his then sipped the drink. The bubbles tickled her nose and she pursed her lips at the sweet, sharp contrast of flavours.

'Mmmm. That's good.'

'I know. I picked some up from the farm shop when I went to check that everything was organized for Surf for Sighthounds.'

Zoe took another sip, enjoying the simple pleasure of drinking organic cider on a beach with a man she liked very much.

'The candles are pretty… it's a nice touch.'

'I'm glad you think so. I wanted to do something special. I also have supper in the cooler, so I hope you haven't eaten. I forgot to add that in my text.'

'I haven't and I am peckish, now you mention it.'

'Hold this and I'll get the food out.'

Zoe held Nate's cider and watched as he spread the contents of the cooler out on the blanket. There were three wedges of different coloured cheese, a salmon and asparagus quiche, a Tupperware container of potato salad, a large bag of sea salt crisps and four large, fresh peaches.

'That looks incredible, Nate.'

'We should eat well, right? The quiche and the potato salad are courtesy of Uncle Kevin, but I picked the rest up in Truro earlier.'

'You went into Truro especially to get this?'

Nate dropped his gaze to the blanket and his cheeks coloured slightly. When he met Zoe's gaze again, his smile lit up his whole face.

'Yeah.'

'Thank you.'

Zoe leant forwards and went to kiss his cheek but he moved and instead their lips met. She jolted as if shocked by the spark she'd felt.

'Must be nylon in this picnic blanket.' Nate patted the blanket. 'If not, there's definitely some serious electricity between us.' His grin warmed her heart.

Zoe handed him his drink, then he gave her a paper plate and they ate, pausing only to comment on the creamy richness of the cheese, the flaky perfection of the quiche pastry and how well it all went with the cider.

When they'd eaten their fill of the savoury food, Nate handed her a peach. It was perfectly ripe, the silky skin a pinky-orange. When she bit into it, the flesh was sweet and aromatic, the wonderful taste of summer.

'You have juice running down your chin,' Nate said and Zoe nodded. She didn't have a free hand to wipe it away so Nate came to her rescue, gently dabbing her chin with his napkin. It was such an intimate gesture that Zoe's heart sped up and she had to tear her gaze from his perfect features. He was so handsome it almost hurt her to look at him, because she knew she couldn't have him. He wasn't available, he wasn't free, he was leaving and it wasn't fair. Then her thoughts about enjoying her time with him until he went away came back and she nursed them inside like a precious infant, wanting them to be possible, yet not sure if she could give them life.

'Tell me about you, Zoe. I want to know more.'

'Like what?'

'Who are your parents?'

'My parents?'

'Yes. Who are they? Where do they live?'

Zoe drained her cup then placed it next to her on the blanket.

'They're long gone.'

'I'm sorry.'

'It's okay. They were older having me and quite set in their ways. We weren't really close because we didn't agree on a lot of things. I grew up in Devon, in a pretty harbour town, and my parents were good to me, in their own way, but I was never close to them. I saw school friends with their parents and sometimes envied them the relationships they had with their mums and dads. My parents never left me wanting for anything financially; I had a good education, music lessons, private tutors, and they wanted me to be a professional of some sort, like a doctor or a lawyer or something similar. But they never asked me what I wanted and, as I grew older, the pressure mounted. I was stuck in studying while my friends went out enjoying themselves and I grew resentful.' She glanced at Nate to gauge his reaction but he was nodding in understanding.

'When I turned seventeen, I rebelled, and instead of a daughter they could be proud of, I became their biggest disappointment. When you've become someone's disappointment, it puts a wedge between you that's pretty tough to budge. They never got over me refusing to conform and I never got over them not loving me for who I was.'

'Again, I'm sorry.'

'Again… don't be. It's not your fault. Besides, I think it all made me stronger. If they'd been loving and indulgent, then what came afterwards would probably have reduced me to dust. It almost did, but I'm kind of like the phoenix, I guess.' She gave a laugh to show she wasn't being arrogant. 'I rise from the ashes.'

'You are strong. I can see it in you, that inner strength. It radiates from you, even though you've been hurt in the past.'

'Experiences shape us, don't they?'

Nate nodded.

'Anyway, they're gone now. Both cremated because that was what they wanted and both scattered at the beach where they met all those years ago. Quite romantic, really, although the fruit of their union kind of ruined it a bit.'

'I'm sure they loved you.'

'They did, I think, but they loved each other and their lifestyle more. Which is fine.'

Zoe stared out at the sea in the fading light. The colours of the sunset had blended to mauve and the clouds were darker now, dove-grey shapes that floated across an indigo background.

'Not everyone should be a parent.'

'That's true.'

'How do you feel about them now?'

'Sometimes, there's a flicker of the old resentment, but then I remember that they did their best. The best that they thought they could, and I can't fault them for that. Perhaps their parents weren't particularly loving, and we learn from our families, don't we?'

'We also learn how to make things better from our mistakes and from those around us.'

'True. I'd be a different kind of mum.'

'You'll be a lovely mum.'

Zoe peered at him from under her lashes. His face was warm in the candlelight and it was a face to melt hearts.

'If I ever have kids.'

'Same here.'

'What? You'll be a lovely mum, too?'

'Ha ha! I like to think I'd be a good dad.'

'If only we knew what lay ahead for us.'

'Sometimes I think it's better not to. I mean, if my father had known that he was going to die young, he might not have enjoyed his life as much as he did.'

'He died before you came here, right?'

Nate nodded. 'Suddenly. But that's the way I'd prefer to go. I'd hate to be incapacitated by an illness or to know how long I had left and end up counting the days.'

'Was he a good dad?'

'The best. He taught me so much and was funny, kind and understanding.'

'It's nice when you have that. I mean… I imagine it must be nice. I think I got married so young because I was looking for that kind of love and security. I just wanted to be accepted by someone for who I was.'

'And were you?'

'In all honesty… no. But I picked the wrong guy.'

'How old were you?'

'Eighteen when we married, but I met him at seventeen and he turned my world upside down.'

'Young love, eh?'

'Kind of a Romeo and Juliet in that my parents disapproved of him and his lifestyle and our parents would never have got on.'

'Yikes.'

'Exactly. But I learned from being married to him, and I know I'd never put myself through all that again.'

'I wish there was a way to make it all better for you.'

'To turn back the clock?'

'If I could.'

'I'd rather stay right here.'

'Right now?'

She nodded. 'We can't change the past, Nate. As much as we sometimes wish we could. We have to let go and embrace today.'

'Would you travel if you had the chance?'

Zoe lay back on the blanket and gazed up at the sky, where the stars had appeared.

'I think so. I've settled here and I love the cove but there are places I want to go.'

'Where?'

'Oh, all the usuals… like New York, perhaps. I'd like to walk through Central Park, see the view from the top of the Rock, take a carriage ride…'

Nate had fallen silent and when she turned her head to peer at him, she found him reclining on his side, his arm supporting his head.

'Are you smiling?'

'I am. I think you should take the time to travel. It would be good for you.'

'You do?'

'Zoe… this might seem crazy but… I've been thinking… you could come with me.'

'What?' She sat upright. 'Come travelling?'

'You could…'

She allowed herself to entertain the idea for a moment, allowed images of her and Nate taking selfies in front of the Empire State Building, at Strawberry Fields and possibly even on a beautiful beach somewhere warm, to flicker through her mind. They would eat cheesecake in Times Square, drink beer at a genuine sports bar, soak up the sun on luxury loungers beside a sparkling pool, and then rush back to their hotel where they would…

'I can't.'

'Why not?'

'Nate, I have the diner. See, my parents left me money in trust that I couldn't access until I was thirty. That was a good thing as it turned out, because my ex might well have wasted it, if I'd had it sooner. Or I could have blown it on him, more like. But I wanted to invest it, to have some security and something that belonged to me after so long just drifting and rebelling against what they'd wanted for me. The diner is all I have and I can't give it up.'

Nate sat up then and moved closer to her, taking her hands in his.

'I understand that, Zoe. I honestly do. I've been the opposite I suppose, not wanting to be tied to anything and I have had a good time since I moved here. I haven't taken life too seriously but I've saved for my trip. The thought of going away and seeing some of the world kept me going when the pain over my dad was at its worst. He always wanted to travel and he inspired me. What if…' He bit his bottom lip as he scanned her face. 'What if I didn't go away for so long in one go? You could come with me then and get someone to watch the diner for you. You could come with me for all or part of it; that would be up to you. We could go through my plans together, alter them if need be, but then we could sort something out for the diner, too. We could find someone to take care of it for you.'

Zoe smiled as he squeezed her hands. He was being so sincere and so convincing, it actually sounded as if it could be possible.

'Oh, Nate, I don't know. I mean… it sounds so good but I don't know if I could trust anyone else to take care of the diner, long term. What if they didn't run it properly? My whole reputation would be at stake and I could lose business, lose it all.'

The fear gripped her again, the one she tried to keep at bay. She couldn't drift along again as she once had. Look at how badly she'd been betrayed and how, if her parents hadn't left her that money, she'd have been jobless, destitute, and hopeless. The diner was solid, bricks and mortar, but what she had here with Nate was emotional, intangible. Nate might like her now but that could change, someone better could come along and steal him away. He could lose interest in her or she could in him; after all, he was the first man she'd looked at properly in ages and what if they went away together and she found that she didn't like him as much as she'd believed she did. What if he discovered something about her that he didn't like? It could turn out to be disastrous...

'That wouldn't happen, Zoe. We'd make sure of it.'

She sighed then, long and deep, and he released her hands and wrapped his arm around her shoulders.

'I know you've been hurt, Zoe. I understand that and this is a big ask. Hell, it's a big risk because we don't know each other that well. But please consider this because I truly believe it's a risk worth taking and because... the more time I spend with you, the harder it's going to be to leave.'

'You could avoid me until you go,' she murmured against his chest as she slid her arms around his waist.

'That's not going to happen.'

'I hope not.'

They stayed that way, holding each other tight until the moon was out and the temperature dropped enough to make them shiver, then they packed up the picnic and Nate walked Zoe back to her cottage and kissed her softly on the lips before saying goodnight.

Zoe watched him walk away, his rucksack on his back and the cooler under his arm like a bulky suitcase, and she knew that saying goodbye to him when he left to go travelling was going to be extremely hard indeed. But she couldn't imagine how it could be any other way, unless she could find someone to run the diner as well as finding a way to put her fears and doubts aside and take the risk that Nate had asked her to take.

Chapter 16

The days passed quickly as Nate and the villagers prepared for Surf for Sighthounds and it was Wednesday before he knew it. Nate was busy making phone calls and sending emails, visiting sponsors as well as working at the cafe. He needed to help train his replacement – a young local woman who'd studied catering at college and who was taking a gap year before going off to university – so that he didn't feel as if he'd be leaving his aunt and uncle in the lurch.

He'd just sent a brief text to Zoe, asking how she was and telling her he'd try to get down to the diner later to see her, when he heard a familiar voice. He looked up from his mobile to see his mother embracing his aunt and uncle.

'Mum!' He went from behind the cafe counter and hugged her. 'What're you doing here?'

She smiled but her eyes were watery and the smile wobbled. 'Oh, love…' She covered her mouth as if it was too awful to tell him.

'Nate, take your mum up to the flat and make her a cup of tea. We'll be fine here.' June patted his arm.

'Thank you.'

He led his mother behind the counter then gestured for her to go in front of him, but she froze and he bumped into her.

'My things!'

'What things?'

'My suitcase, clothes and photographs. It's all in the campervan.'

'You came in the VW?'

She nodded and a tear escaped her eye and slid down her cheek.

'Where have you parked?'

'Just outside.'

'Let's go and park her around the back of the cafe.'

They went back through the cafe and out into the brightness of the afternoon. Paula opened her handbag with trembling hands and took out a pair of sunglasses. When she put them on, they covered most of her face.

'Very Jackie Kennedy, Mum.'

She nodded.

'They suit you.'

'I grabbed the sunglasses before they could take them, too.'

He stopped walking and shook his head. '*They*?'

'It was the bailiffs, Nate. They came this morning with a large white van and they started taking everything from the house.'

'What?' Fury bubbled in his gut. It wasn't often that Nate experienced anger but if anything was likely to stir it, then injustice would do it. 'The bailiffs took your belongings?'

'Yes, love. It's all gone other than what I could pack into the campervan before they saw it, and the things that were of no use to them.'

Nate reached out and squeezed her shoulder, then tried not to wince at how bony she was. 'Okay… okay. It'll all be okay, Mum.'

She stepped forwards and as he hugged her tight she folded against his chest. People passed them as they stood in the middle of the street and a few cast concerned looks at Nate, so he gave a small wave to let them know he had the situation in hand.

'Where was Richard while all this was going on?'

'Desperately ringing around… trying to raise some money to stop the bailiffs… taking things. They took his drinks globe, the one that he bought direct from Italy, and his golf clubs… the ones I had his initials engraved on last Christmas. They took… they took your dad's watch, too. I'm so sorry, Nate, I was keeping it for you for your fortieth birthday… I gave him the watch on his fortieth and I thought it would be nice for you to have it, but they said it was worth something.'

As she looked up at him, mascara ran down her cheeks, carried on her tears, and pain surged through him. His poor mother, and after all she'd been through already. Now they'd done this to her.

'Mum… don't worry. It was a watch. I have you and you said you have the photos, so we have what matters. And they can't take our memories of Dad away. No one can.'

She nodded, her front teeth buried in her bottom lip as she tried not to cry.

'Come on, let's get you up to the flat.'

He wrapped his arm around her shoulders and walked her to the campervan, then opened the passenger door for her before climbing in and starting the engine. The fuel gauge was on red and he realized she must have coasted into Conwenna Cove on fumes.

Once he'd parked the van around the rear of the cafe, he helped his mum out and took her up the steps to the flat.

'You put the kettle on and I'll start bringing your things up. We can put them in the bedroom for now.'

'Thanks, darling. I don't know what I'd do without you.'

'Mum, is Richard coming too?'

She shook her head. 'He's staying there to see what he can salvage. He told me to come to you and said he'd follow in a few days.'

'Right.'

A few trips up and down the steps and Nate had brought in the small amount of belongings his mother had saved. She had two suitcases full of goodness knows what, a box of what appeared to be make-up and hair products, a wicker washing basket full of photo albums and two Waitrose tote bags bulging with recipe books.

The final thing he found in the van was a small wooden rocking chair that looked as if it would fit a toddler. He carried it into the flat and set it down in the lounge area.

'What's this?'

'Don't you remember?'

He shook his head.

'That was yours, Nate. Your dad bought it for you when you were still in my belly and when you were big enough to sit in it, you'd watch TV, eat your dinner and sometimes even fall asleep in it.'

'Really?'

'Yes, darling. I had to save it… I went into the attic to get it. There were other things there too, but that was the closest one and I had to get away before they saw what I'd taken.'

She handed him a mug of tea then went and sat on the sofa, crossing her legs beneath her. Nate followed her and sat down. He wrapped his hands around the mug and let the heat warm his palms as he tried to make sense of the situation.

'So are you…'

'Homeless?'

'Yes.'

'We are. I'm so ashamed.'

'Well, don't be. None of this was your fault.'

'I could have asked what Richard was doing with our money… I could have shown more of an interest in the business.'

Nate shook his head. 'You trusted him and there's no shame in that. Look… I know this is an awful situation and I wish with all my heart that you weren't going through this but it's what you do from here on in that matters.'

'Yes, love.'

Her dark green eyes roamed his face, her hands clutching her own mug so tightly the blue veins showed through her papery skin. When had she got so thin?

'You'll be safe here.'

And I'm going to make sure you eat.

'I can stay?'

'Of course you can.'

'Oh, Nate… thank you. I didn't want to come and be a burden to you.'

'How could you ever be a burden?'

Paula yawned, covering her mouth with her hand. 'Darling, please excuse me. I'm so tired.'

'Right, you need to take a nap. I'll go and change the bed, then you can go in there and get some rest.'

'Oh, there's no need—'

Nate held up a hand. 'Don't protest, Mum. I need to change the sheets anyway, and I'll put the nice ones on that you bought me last Christmas.'

Paula smiled, the shadows under her eyes seeming to darken by the minute. 'All right, love.'

When Nate had ensured that his mum was going to take a nap, he went into the kitchen and washed their mugs then set them on the draining board. He was really worried about the effect that the situation was having on his mum and it broke his heart to see her struggling after everything she'd been through in her life. After all, Richard was meant to be her fresh start, her second chance at happiness, and look what had happened. It just went to show that there probably was no happy ever after – or not for everyone, at least.

Well, if there was one thing he did know for certain, it was that being in Conwenna Cove would be good for his mum. The village was so pretty and the atmosphere so positive, that he was sure it would have a positive effect upon Paula. She would be able to take a breather from her life and decide where to go from here. She loved Richard, Nate knew that, and perhaps it would be good for his stepfather to come and stay too. Then his mum and her husband could take some time to think and plan. Some time out never did anyone any harm.

—

'That was another delicious meal, thank you.'

'You're welcome, Nigel.'

Nate smiled at the friendly Welsh man and his wife, Gaynor. They weren't staying in Conwenna but had been back several times since he'd bumped into them on the beach.

'So, can you extend your holiday and hang around a bit longer? It's the greyhound event on Saturday.'

'I wish we could.' Gaynor shook her head. 'But we're heading home on Friday, sadly. We'd love to stay in Cornwall for longer but we've had nearly three weeks and have to get back to reality.' She rolled her eyes.

'That's a shame.' Nate handed Nigel his change. 'You think you'll be back?'

'Definitely.' Nigel nodded. 'We love this part of the world and Ash has had an amazing holiday, haven't you, boy?'

The dog panted next to his owner, seeming to grin in agreement.

'See you again!' Nate waved as they left the cafe.

'Who was that, darling?' Paula appeared in the doorway that led to the stairs up to the flat.

'Nigel and Gaynor Maggs. They were here on holiday with their greyhound, Ash.'

'You make friends with everyone, don't you?'

He smiled. 'You think?'

'You've always been the same, love. Such a friendly lad.'

'I don't know, Mum. I was quite shy as a teenager.'

182

'Yes, you're right. You were always lovely but you did come out of your shell once you started swimming and surfing.'

Nate groaned as a familiar face peering through the cafe window.

'What's wrong?' His mum rushed to his side.

'It's nothing.'

'It surely is to make you groan like that.'

He sighed. 'There's this woman... she's on holiday here, must have a holiday cottage or be staying with relatives as she's been around for a few weeks, and she seems to... like me.'

Paula peered around him. 'That blonde girl who's standing in the doorway?'

'Yep.'

'You mean she's got a crush on you?'

'Her name's Calista and she caused some problems for me when I was at the wine bar with Zoe recently.'

'Problems?'

He shrugged. 'Oh, I don't know. She was jealous, I guess, and she called Zoe some names and upset her. But I'm not interested.'

'In Zoe?'

'In Calista.'

'Oh, love.'

'I'd hoped she'd have gone by now.'

'Do you want me to deal with her?' His mum touched his arm. 'I can have a word?'

Nate laughed. 'It's okay, I can deal with it. I'm not thirteen any more.'

'No, you're not, darling. You're a tall, handsome man but you're such a nice person that it's easy to see why some of these girls do get the wrong idea. You might need to be a bit firmer with them.'

'Perhaps. Probably. But I find it difficult to be mean.'

'Not mean, darling, just firm.'

'I'll try.'

Calista sashayed over to the counter and Nate tried to keep his eyes on his notepad and the Surf for Sighthounds plans.

'Nate?'

He ground his teeth together.

'Nate? Hello?'

Having no choice, he looked up, and winced. Calista was wearing an outfit that looked about four sizes too small for her. How she could walk in the tight denim shorts, he had no idea. She'd paired them with a pink halter top that was barely there.

'Hello, Calista.'

'How are you?' She flicked her long hair over her shoulders and stuck her chest out.

'I'm fine, thanks.'

'Oh… good. Uh… I wanted to, uh… ask if you—'

'Look, lovely, my son isn't interested.'

'What?' Calista's gaze flicked from him to Paula, who was standing next to Nate with her hands on her hips.

'I said my son isn't interested in you. So why don't you either order or take your… camel toe elsewhere.'

Calista's jaw dropped. 'How… dare you!'

'How dare I?' Paula placed her hands on the counter and leant forwards. 'You might not realize it, but you're making Nate very uncomfortable.'

'I am?'

Calista's mouth opened and closed and her eyes flickered between Nate and his mother repeatedly, as if she was unsure which one of them was to blame for this confrontation.

'Okay,' she finally squeaked, then she flounced out of the cafe.

Nate turned to his mother.

'Mum! That was… embarrassing.'

'Sorry, darling, but it needed to be said.'

'But… camel toe?'

'I'll blame the menopause for that one. Sometimes I speak before I can filter.' She winked at him.

'She's probably really upset now.'

'Nate, you are such a softy. She'll be fine and she needs to get some bigger shorts or she'll end up with a nasty case of thrush. They were far too tight and must have been uncomfortable. Although I know that these days you can get a designer vagina so she could go and get one of those…' Paula looked up and bit her lip. 'Am I prattling on? Sorry, Nate, I had such a good sleep that I'm feeling much better and I couldn't help jumping in then.'

'Don't be sorry. And thank you. I hate having to be… *firm*.'

'My pleasure. Now, can I have something to eat? I don't know if it's the fact that I slept or the sea air, but I'm suddenly ravenous.'

'Of course. I'll make you a cheese and roasted tomato panini, shall I?'

'That sounds amazing.'

'Go and sit down and I'll bring it over.'

'You're an angel.'

As Nate made his mother's snack, he thought about what had just happened. Paula might well be right; perhaps he did need to be a bit firmer. He'd hate to be out with Zoe and have another woman make her uneasy again; that simply couldn't happen. It was also nice to have his mum here in Conwenna. He didn't see much of her these days as they were both busy with their lives but he knew that she loved him and vice versa. In fact, he hoped that she'd stay around for a while now, as it would be nice to spend time with her before he left. A chuckle escaped as he thought about what she'd said to Calista. He'd never say something like that but, coming from Paula, it seemed acceptable. She was his mum, after all.

It also reminded him of the mum he'd known growing up, before his dad had died. She'd had a great sense of humour and was always smiling and joking, and at times, she had been a bit wicked too. Had losing his dad changed her that much then, stolen her easy smiles and relaxed demeanour and replaced them with a wariness that seldom gave way to humour? Grief was a terrible thing and it affected people in different ways. Nate supposed that he had run away but his mother had stayed to face it, worked her way through it, then found love again with Richard. And now… Richard had screwed that up. Or at least, life had. He just hoped they'd be able to salvage something from the mess so they weren't facing complete financial ruin.

He took her panini over with a large mug of Earl Grey tea, made exactly how she liked it, then he sat opposite her. The cafe had gone quiet, so he could take a short break and spend the time chatting with his mum, making sure that she was able to think about things other than how frightening her life had become. Hopefully offering her some ideas about where she could go from there.

Chapter 17

Zoe was clearing a table when the door of the diner opened and Nate walked in, accompanied by an older woman. She carried the plates over to the counter, then smiled as she approached them.

'Hi, Nate. Do you want a table?'

'Yes, please, Zoe. For two.'

'Of course. How about the corner booth, there? Or do you want something closer to the window?'

'The booth will be great, thanks.'

'So you're Zoe?'

Zoe looked at the woman and realized there was something familiar about her. In fact, she reminded Zoe of Nate. She had the same blonde hair and a similar nose, although hers was smaller, and when she smiled, it lit up her whole face exactly as Nate's smile did.

'Yes, I'm Zoe.'

'Aren't you beautiful?'

'Uh… thank you.'

Nate was grinning as he looked from the woman to Zoe and back again.

'Zoe, before she says anything else, this is my mum, Paula.'

'Nice to meet you.'

They shook hands.

'Do you want to go over to your table and I'll get the menus for you? Would you like to order drinks now or take a few minutes?'

'I'd love a glass of prosecco, please.' Paula nodded. 'Nate?'

'I'll have a glass of beer, thanks, Zoe.'

'Coming right up.'

Zoe went behind the counter and poured the drinks, then got two menus.

When she delivered the drinks and menus to the booth, Paula asked, 'This is your diner then, Zoe?'

'It is.'

'Very nice.'

'Thank you.'

'Will you join us?'

'Oh… uh…'

'Mum, Zoe's working. She hasn't got time to have dinner with her customers.'

'We're not *just* customers, Nate. Well, you're not, at least.'

'Mum!'

Nate's cheeks flushed and Zoe bit her lip to hold back her smile. It seemed that Nate's mother had a habit of saying whatever was on her mind.

'Thanks, Paula, but I can't right now as we're a bit busy. Perhaps after you've eaten, I'll be able to grab a drink with you.'

'I shall look forward to it, Zoe.'

An hour and a half later, the diner only had a few customers remaining. Zoe went to the booth table to clear Nate and Paula's dessert plates.

'Can I get you anything else?'

'Yes, we'll have three coffees and you can come and have a chat with us.'

'She's not going to give up, Zoe, so you'd just as well surrender now.' Nate winked at her and she smiled in return.

'Okay then, you've twisted my arm.'

Coffees made, Zoe sat with Nate and Paula. She wondered how the diner looked from their perspective with its checked floor, red seat cushions, mirrors and pictures on the walls, and the clean shiny white counter. Right then, Buddy Holly was singing about Peggy Sue and she noticed that Paula was moving in time with the beat.

'This is a lovely diner, Zoe.'

'Thanks, Paula. I've tried to make it a relaxing place to be.'

'The atmosphere, the decor… oh, I could spend hours in here. In fact, while I'm in Conwenna Cove, I actually might.'

'You're very welcome.'

'Thank you. I don't suppose you have any jobs going, do you?'

Zoe watched as Nate turned to his mother, surprise registering on his handsome face.

'You want a job, Mum?'

'Well, love, it's not like we didn't discuss the possibility that I'll need to find work again.'

'Yes, I know, but… you've only just got here.'

'No time like the present. You know me, Nate, I can't let a situation unfold around me. I was made redundant and that was hard but with things as they are…' She glanced at Zoe. 'I need to work. And the sooner the better.'

Nate nodded.

'Sorry, Zoe, I know you don't want to hear all my woes, but, in short, I was recently made redundant and my husband and I… well, we're in a bit of a sticky situation. Nothing I can't deal with.' She plastered on a smile. 'But I am going to try to find employment and I'd love to work in a place like this.'

'Um, there's nothing solid at the moment but one of my waitresses is going on holiday soon, so you'd be welcome to try out then, if you want. I say "try out" because you might not like it…'

'Don't worry about that, Zoe! I worked in the catering industry all my life. I took a few years off when Nate was born but apart from that, I've always worked. Gosh, my feet are so tough from all the time spent standing on them that I don't really need to wear shoes! Don't tell my husband that, though… don't want him knowing I've got hard skin an inch thick on the soles of my feet. He bought me one of those buzzing vibrator things.'

Nate's eyebrows shot up his forehead. 'A what?'

'You know, love, you put batteries in it and rub it over your skin.'

Zoe had almost choked on her coffee at the turn the conversation had taken.

'It's for your feet,' Paula explained, as she registered their expressions.

'Thank god for that!' Nate shook his head.

'It's a pedi vibrator. No… a pedi scraper. Nope. Oh, I can't remember what it's called exactly, but it basically vibrates and takes all the hard skin away, but I haven't actually had time to use it.'

'So, Paula…' Zoe was keen to change the conversation, aware that the customers at the next table had overheard the word 'vibrator' and were probably wondering if Zoe's Diner was the kind of establishment they wanted to visit with their children. 'You worked in catering?'

'Yes, love. I can cook, waitress, host… you name it. With my eyes closed.'

'Where did you work?'

'Oooh, all over the place before Nate came along. At some big London hotels and restaurants, at various establishments in Cornwall, and I did some freelancing too, when I needed flexibility. My last job, though, the one I've had for over fifteen years, was for a corporate catering firm. Sadly, they were undercut and lost several of their biggest clients, so they had to cut costs and I was one of those let go. It's my age, see – they usually get rid of those with one foot in the grave.'

'Bloody hell, Mum, you're hardly the walking dead.'

'No, love, not yet, but you know what I mean. I'm not exactly getting any younger. I've plenty of energy and experience, though, Zoe, so please, if you do need someone then let me help out here.'

'Of course. Thank you, Paula, I'll keep you in mind.'

'Have you decided yet if you're going to travel with this one?' Paula laid her hand on Nate's arm.

'Sorry?' Zoe's stomach flipped.

'Nate told me that he'd like you to go with him.'

Zoe met Nate's eyes and watched as they widened.

'He would? I… uh… he did mention something but I didn't know he'd told anyone else. Not that you're just anyone, of course, but… uh…'

'Of course he would! But he's too shy to tell you the truth about how he feels.'

'Nate is shy?'

Paula nodded. 'Not in most situations, but when he finds someone he really likes then he changes. It happened when he was a teenager and he had a crush on our neighbour's daughter, although, of course, that was a teenage crush.'

'Mum!' Nate nudged his mother. 'I was about thirteen and nothing ever came of it.'

'I know, and now you're a man, so this must be even more serious.'

'Besides, Mum, I have mentioned it to Zoe. We just haven't had a chance to discuss it further.'

Zoe's heart thudded as Paula's words sank in. Nate had spoken to his mother about her and told her he'd like Zoe to travel with him. He'd suggested it, yes, but they hadn't confirmed anything and there were still reasons why she didn't think it could work. And now his mother, a complete stranger who had made Zoe smile more in the last half hour than she had done in ages, had mentioned the idea of travelling with Nate as if it were the most natural thing in the world.

'We'd probably better get going.' Nate drained his coffee. 'I still have lots to sort out for Saturday.'

'Let me know if you need any help.' Zoe smiled at Nate, wanting to say more about travelling, but not sure what it was that she wanted to say.

'Thanks again, Zoe. That was a lovely meal and it was lovely to meet you.'

'You, too.' Zoe realized she wanted to see Paula again, to find out more about Nate and his family and if this woman really did think there was something between Zoe and Nate. 'Uh… Paula. Do you have plans in the morning?'

Paula looked at Nate and he shook his head. 'I'm working.'

'Then, no, I'm free.'

'Well, first thing, before work, I'm heading up to the greyhound sanctuary to exercise some of the dogs. Would you like to come?'

'The greyhound sanctuary? Nate's talked about the farm and the sanctuary many times, and I've always wondered what it's like up there. I'd love to come.'

'Wonderful. I'll pick you up about seven… if that's okay?'

'Fabulous! I don't sleep well anyway, not with how things have been, and without Richard next to me tonight, I doubt I'll get much sleep at all.'

'He'll be fine, Mum.'

Paula nodded, but a sadness had settled over her features.

'Honestly, Mum, Richard will be fine. He's probably sorting things out as we speak and will soon come and join you here.'

'But will he have good news?'

Nate slid his arm around Paula's shoulders and hugged her to his side. The gesture made a lump rise in Zoe's throat. Nate was so kind and clearly a good son. Side by side, the family resemblance was even more evident.

'Whatever the news, we'll face it together then find a way forward.'

'Yes, love. We will.'

Nate and Paula stood up and followed Zoe to the counter where Nate paid for the meal.

'I'm going to grab a breath of air, Nate. Thanks again, Zoe. I'll see you in the morning.'

Paula waved then left the diner.

'Is she okay, Nate?'

He sighed. 'Not really. She's very up and down.'

'I don't know the full story obviously, but I gather from the things she said that they've some money troubles.'

'She's usually a very private person but it's like coming here and being away from my stepfather has loosened her tongue. Or perhaps it's just you, Zoe. Perhaps you relaxed her and she can tell you're a good person.'

'You think?'

'I do.'

'Well, I'm happy to give her some hours here, but at the moment it won't be much.'

'You don't have to do that, Zoe. You don't know her or know if she's any good.'

'Is she?'

He smiled. 'She is and I'm not saying that because I'm her son. She knows her way around the catering business.'

'Okay, well, I'll be extra busy tomorrow with the preparation for Saturday, so after we've been to the sanctuary, I'll ask her to help out for a few hours here. How does that sound?'

'Brilliant. It would boost her confidence if nothing else, and she's taken an extraordinarily quick shine to you. A bit like I did once I got to know you properly.'

Nate held her gaze then and slid his hand over the counter. Zoe took it and he squeezed her fingers.

'We have things to talk about but let's do it after Saturday, shall we?'

'Yes.'

He lifted her hand and pressed his lips to her fingers then turned and left the diner.

Zoe raised her hand and kissed where Nate's lips had just been. She could smell his aftershave on her skin and feel the warmth that he exuded filtering through and wrapping itself around her heart. It was one of the best feelings she'd ever had.

Nate Bryson was a very special man indeed.

Chapter 18

The next morning, Zoe drove down the main street of the village to the cafe. It was six-fifty and she knew she should be tired but she felt good. She'd slept well, thankfully without nightmares, and woke refreshed and ready to face the day. Tomorrow was Surf for Sighthounds, which she was looking forward to, and she planned to get the bulk of her baking done that afternoon after she closed early.

She parked outside the cafe and cut the engine. Not wanting to put any pressure on Paula by beeping or knocking, she sat and waited, taking the time to enjoy observing the village shops. The grocer's was already open, taking in a bread delivery, and the sounds of the crates being unloaded and the small talk between the shopkeeper and the delivery man made her smile. They sounded so cheerful, in spite of the hour, but then it was a beautiful August day in Conwenna Cove and that meant there was plenty to smile about.

A movement to her left caught her eye and she waved at Paula. Nate's mum walked towards the car and smiled broadly. Zoe noted that she was wearing jeans, trainers and a dark green fleece – good clothing for exercising the dogs in the cool morning air.

Paula opened the passenger door and got in, bringing with her a waft of floral perfume and the smell of toast.

'Good morning, Zoe, and how are you this morning?'

Zoe tightened her short ponytail then automatically ran her hand over her fringe.

'I'm good, thank you. I slept really well.'

'Do you know, so did I! I was shocked when I woke up at six. I thought I wouldn't sleep a wink but the combination of the sea air and a comfy bed meant that I went out for a good seven hours.'

'That's great.'

Zoe appraised Paula's blue eyes, brighter than yesterday, and her clear skin.

'Conwenna Cove is already working its magic on you.'

Paula laughed. 'You don't believe all that, do you, Zoe?'

Zoe pursed her lips. 'I'm not totally sure, but I've seen the cove have a positive effect on people. Almost… healing. I've certainly been quite happy since I moved here, and I know a few people who swear by the sea air and more relaxed pace of life.'

'Sounds idyllic.'

'Spend some time here and find out.'

Paula smiled. 'I don't think I have a choice. I spoke to Richard last night, and although he wasn't telling me everything, I know him and I don't think the news was good.'

Zoe touched Paula's arm. 'I'm sorry.'

'Me, too. But, hey, one door closes and another opens.'

'That certainly appears to be the case so often in life.'

'We just have to be careful not to get our fingers trapped as the door closes though, right?'

Zoe nodded. 'Absolutely.'

'So I'm going to try and make the best of a bad situation… excuse the clichés, Zoe' – Paula smiled – 'and simply get on with life.'

'Conwenna is a good place to start.'

Before Zoe pulled away from the kerb, her gaze was drawn to the windows of the flat above the cafe, and she saw Nate smiling down at her, his face tanned and his hair sticking up in all directions. She gave a small wave and he returned it, then she drove away, her heart fluttering at seeing him.

At the bottom of the main street, she took a right and went past the harbour then up the road that led out of Conwenna. As she drove, Paula made lots of appreciative noises about the beauty of the village and the surrounding scenery. And Zoe agreed wholeheartedly. It was a beautiful place to live and she was sure it could lift anyone's heart.

They reached Foxglove Farm and Zoe stopped the car, then climbed out to open the gate at the edge of the property. Once she'd driven through then closed the gate, she got back in and drove the car further along the track before stopping again.

'Why've we stopped here, love?' Paula asked.

'I want to show you something.'

They got out and Zoe led Paula away from the car then gestured at the view.

Paula gasped and placed a hand on her chest. 'It's magnificent.'

'It is.'

Conwenna spread out before them, a perfect Cornish fishing village. The different-coloured houses led down to the harbour, their pastel shades reminding her of sweets in the early morning light. The birds' morning chorus was enough to warm even the hardest heart, and the scent of earth, damp with dew, and the wild flowers in the hedgerows, filled the air with the promise of a lovely summer's day.

When Zoe turned to Paula, she found the older woman had tears in her eyes.

'Paula, the last thing I wanted to do was to upset you.'

Paula shook her head. 'I'm fine,' she squeaked.

Zoe wrapped her arm around Paula's thin shoulders. 'The ups and downs of life, eh?'

Paula nodded then pulled a tissue from her pocket and wiped her eyes. 'Never works out how we think it will. You know, at your age I had everything. I was happily married with a wonderful son and life was good. It was calm, happy, and I didn't want for anything at all. Nate grew up and he was always such a lovely boy. He's a good man now, too. I know that as his mother I'm biased, but that's okay in his case because he really is a decent sort. People have tried to take advantage of him for it, but somehow he always bounces back.'

'Advantage?'

'Oh… women, people in the modelling industry.'

'Modelling?'

'Yes. Didn't he tell you?'

Zoe shook her head.

'Typical Nate, never one to boast. He was spotted on a beach at eighteen and they loved his look, apparently. He was the blond-haired, blue-eyed surfer some big London agency wanted for their books. He had a few meetings with them and they filled his head with promises of travel and success, then the client they had in mind for him fell through and suddenly they didn't want him.'

'Poor Nate.'

Paula nodded. 'I was so sad for him but he didn't seem to mind at all. He said they wanted more than he was happy to commit to and he didn't mind that they dumped him, but I did wonder if he was just saying that so I wouldn't worry. You know, he had no confidence when he was younger and only grew into his own skin when he hit his teens and started surfing. It brought him out of himself and gave him a focus, which meant that his shyness seemed to evaporate almost overnight.'

'It is hard to imagine him being shy.'

Paula chuckled. 'My beautiful boy. His father was so proud of him. Still would be…' She sniffed and wiped her eyes again.

'Let it out if you need to, Paula. Holding it in does you no good.' Zoe squeezed Paula's shoulders.

'I'm fine, sweetheart, but missing my first husband. It catches me sometimes. Usually when I'm somewhere that I know he would have loved.'

Zoe sighed. 'Life is a rollercoaster.'

'Every single day. And now… Richard, who happens to be a very good husband – I have been extremely lucky to find two fabulous men – is struggling to sort out our affairs. It's quite a mess, Zoe.'

'If I can help in any way…' Zoe didn't know what she could do but it seemed the right thing to say.

'It's not your problem, Zoe. But thank you. My immediate worry is that I'm taking Nate's bed. He said he didn't mind at all, but he can't sleep on the sofa indefinitely.'

'Come and stay with me.'

The words shot out of Zoe's mouth almost as soon as she'd thought them. She'd spent years being sensible and cautious but over the past few weeks, something had started to change inside her. Nate was having a positive effect on her and she liked the way that she was opening up to people. In this case, Paula needed a place to stay, so to hell with caution! Zoe wanted to help her and to help Nate, and what was the worst that could happen?

Paula pulled away and met Zoe's eyes. 'I couldn't do that, Zoe. You have a busy life and you don't want a stranger under your feet.'

'You're not a stranger any more and you're the mother of a good friend. Look, I am busy but I have a spare bedroom in my cottage and no one ever stays in it. I was hoping to use it as a guest room but I never have guests. It's yours if you want it.'

Paula released a slow breath. 'That's a very kind offer, Zoe.'

'To be honest, Paula, you'd be doing me a favour. I've been quite lonely since I lost my dog—'

'You had a dog?'

Zoe nodded. 'A greyhound from the sanctuary... named Raven. I lost her earlier this year and I miss her dreadfully. The cottage is so quiet without her.'

'Sorry to hear that.'

'Well, look, no pressure regarding the spare room but have a think and if you fancy it, let me know.'

Paula nodded.

'Come on, let's get up to the sanctuary and you can meet the dogs. I bet you'll love Monica.'

'They have a dog called Monica?'

'Yes, she's adorable.'

'Do they have one called Chandler, too?'

'I'm sorry?'

'Monica and Chandler.'

'Oh! Sorry, I wasn't quite with you there, but it would be funny if they did name one of the boys Chandler.'

'I loved that series and Nate used to watch it with me when he was at home.'

'Did he?'

'He did a great impression of Chandler.'

'I'll have to ask him to do it for me.'

'It made me laugh many a time.'

They walked back to the car, then Zoe drove them up to the farm where she parked in the yard. She liked Paula already; she had the same amenable personality as Nate, and Zoe's heart went out to her because of the predicament she was in. Everyone had their troubles and everyone had mountains to climb, but surely it was easier to do if you had friends and loved ones at your side offering their support?

–

'Gosh, they're so fast!' Paula said.

'I know! And the best thing about it is that they're running for the sheer pleasure of it.'

Zoe smiled as they walked across one of the fields at Foxglove Farm, watching three of the rescue greyhounds racing around together. The dogs occasionally stopped to sniff at the grass or one another, then off they'd go again, tongues hanging out, legs moving impossibly quickly as they careened around the field.

A magpie cawed irritably from high in a tree, clearly displeased that his peace had been disturbed, and the calls of sheep in a nearby field drifted on the fresh sea breeze.

When they reached the far end of the field, Zoe noticed that Paula was short of breath.

'Paula? Are you all right?'

The older woman put a hand to her chest. Her cheeks were ruddy and her eyes glistened.

'Yes, sweetheart… I'm fine, just not as fit as I used to be. With everything going on I've been a bit under the weather, I suppose. I haven't been eating well and that affects my energy levels.'

'It's bound to.' Zoe rubbed Paula's shoulder. 'Do you want to take a break? We could sit for a while.'

'I think I'll be all right if we walk a bit slower. If that's okay?'

'Of course it is.'

They turned back and began walking, although Zoe kept glancing at Paula, keen to check that she wasn't struggling.

'Tell me about you, Zoe. Distract me with your life story.'

Zoe swallowed a sigh. She didn't want to lie to Nate's mother but neither did she want to tell her the gory truth.

'There's not much to tell really. I grew up in Devon, my parents were older having me and quite strict. I had a good childhood… at least in comparison with some others. I rebelled a bit as a teen and disappointed them, so we drifted apart.'

'I'm sorry to hear that. I thought you'd have parents who adored you. I can't understand why they wouldn't.'

'Thanks. But, hey, you know… families, right?'

Paula nodded.

'They weren't bad people but I think what they wanted in a child and what they got turned out to be very different things. Apparently, I was more like my paternal grandmother. I never knew her but she was rather rebellious for her time.' Zoe gave a small laugh as she thought of the times her parents had muttered that she was just like her grandmother. 'She left her husband and son and ran off with an American chef. Her name was synonymous with trouble and whimsy, so naturally my parents likened me to her. Not that I would do something like that.'

'Well, it's sad that she left her family but we never know what's going on behind closed doors.'

'No, we don't. My grandfather was very strict with my father and that rubbed off on him and how he parented. He did marry again but his new wife was quite a bit younger and not ready to be a stepmother, so my father left home at a young age and set up his own antiques business.'

'Another entrepreneur.'

'Sorry?'

'Well, you're a business woman.'

'Yes. Thanks to my parents. See... they left me money in trust and when I turned thirty I was able to use the money to buy the diner.'

'Thirty?'

Zoe met Paula's eyes and saw the surprise there.

'Yes. They were worried my husband... my ex-husband, would squander it away. I think they suspected that he'd cheat on me, and they guessed right.'

'He must be an idiot.'

Zoe shrugged. 'I guess so.'

'Hey, don't doubt how lovely you are.'

'Ha! Thanks.'

'Seriously, Zoe. You're like a little doll with your silky brown hair and those doe-brown eyes. You're beautiful.' Paula stopped walking. 'And you have an inner beauty that radiates from you.'

Zoe's cheeks burned. She wasn't used to being complimented on her appearance, although Nate had said nice things to her. Having Paula telling her that she was beautiful too made her feel strange.

'Don't be embarrassed. You know, Zoe, one of the things that makes you even more beautiful is that you don't know how lovely you are. Nate thinks a lot of you, I can tell.'

Zoe took a deep breath and willed her colour to fade.

'Look at Monica!' Paula chuckled as they watched the greyhound stalking something in the long grass. Her ears were pointed and she took slow steps as she kept her gaze fixed on whatever it was that she'd found. Suddenly, she gave chase and a fawn-coloured rabbit shot out of the grass and bolted towards the hedgerow. It got there just in time and disappeared into the undergrowth.

'Monica! Come here!' Zoe waved the bag of chopped sausage she had brought to help with the dogs' recall and Monica came bounding back.

'Could I give her some?' Paula asked.

'Of course. Try to get her to sit if you can.'

Paula held a piece of sausage out and told Monica to sit. The dog looked at the sausage, then at Zoe, then at Paula, before deciding to sit.

'Here you go, Monica, you darling.' Paula fed the dog then stroked her chin. 'Such a good girl.'

Zoe called the other two dogs over and they went through some basic commands to help with their training, then the dogs raced off for one more circuit of the field before they went back to the sanctuary.

'Zoe, I hope you don't mind me asking, but how did you get that scar?'

Zoe's hand instinctively went to her forehead and her fingers stroked the bumpy skin. She grimaced.

'Forgive me, darling, you don't need to tell me. It's none of my business.'

'No, it's okay. I uh… I usually keep it hidden behind my fringe but the wind doesn't consider my feelings.' She laughed. 'I used to surf.'

'You did? Nate is a keen surfer.'

'I know. But I don't surf any more.'

'You don't?'

'This…' Zoe patted her head. 'Put an end to my days in the water. I was hit by a board, it knocked me right under and I almost drowned. I had to be dragged from the water. To be honest, I wasn't ever that keen on it all anyway, but I did it to fit in with my ex-husband and his lifestyle. I guess I've always believed that it was nature's way of telling me that you shouldn't try to do what doesn't come naturally. I am not cut out for surfing, or for dating surfers.' She smiled but as she met Paula's gaze, the disappointment on Paula's face tore the smile from her lips. 'Oh… I wasn't saying that I'd never consider dating someone who surfs… uh… you know, I mean…' She sighed and shook her head.

'It's okay, Zoe, I think I know what you're trying to say. Sometimes we need to look past what has hurt us and to embrace what's right in front of us. If you find someone you share a connection with, then you'll find a way around any obstacles. You can't just shut someone out because of what an ex did to you.'

Zoe sighed. 'I know that. And when I think rationally about it all, I see the sense in your words. I've thought the exact same thing a hundred times and more. But when I wake from one of my nightmares, tangled in the sheets and with my heart thundering, I feel that primal fear again. The one that grips me and makes me want to hide under the bed and close my eyes.'

'I know, love. I get that too.'

'Oh!' Zoe pointed at Monica, who had come to Paula's side and was now leaning against her leg. 'She likes you. That's what they do when they trust someone; they lean against you.'

Paula looked down at Monica and stroked her gently. 'And I like you too, Monica. What say I come back and see you tomorrow?'

'It's the Surf for Sighthounds event tomorrow, so she'll be down at the cove, I expect.'

'Lovely! Well, Monica, I'll come and see you every day while I'm in Conwenna. How does that sound?'

The dog's tail wagged in big arcs and she licked Paula's hand.

'Such a sweetie.'

'Nate likes her a lot, too. He said he'd adopt her if he wasn't going away.'

'Did he now?'

Zoe nodded.

'You know, Zoe, I understand that you've been hurt and that you're scared, but my son is a very good man. I know he would never hurt you.'

'Paula… it hasn't gone that far between us. We're friends and we…' Zoe swallowed as she thought about how appropriate it would be to tell Nate's mother that she'd kissed him.

'You've kissed? Possibly more?'

'No! I mean… yes, we've kissed, but that's it.'

'Well, that proves it then.'

'Proves what?'

'If it wasn't serious, you'd have spent the night together without worrying. But, because feelings are involved and you're both scared, you're taking it slowly.'

Zoe smiled at Paula's openness. She really liked Nate's mum and hoped she'd be around for a while yet so she could spend more time with her. Paula's honesty was refreshing and she was enjoying getting to know her, as well as learning more about Nate.

'Now, it must be breakfast time, so shall we take the dogs back, then go and get something to eat?' Paula asked. 'I've suddenly got an appetite and I want to take advantage of it.'

'I could eat,' Zoe said.

They linked arms and walked the dogs back to the sanctuary, chatting like old friends and enjoying the sweet morning air.

Chapter 19

'Morning, darling, how did you sleep?'

Nate sat up on the sofa and rubbed his eyes. He peered at the clock on the wall.

'Ah… it's only six-thirty.' He lay back down then wriggled as he tried to get comfortable. 'I had quite a good night, although…' He moved his head from side to side.

'What is it?'

'Nothing. I'm fine.'

'You have a stiff neck, don't you?'

He smiled at his mum. 'It's nothing.'

'Well, I can't push you out of your bed long term, Nate.'

'You're very welcome, here, Mum.'

'I know, love and I'm grateful. Uh… this probably sounds a bit strange, possibly impulsive, but… Zoe invited me to stay at her cottage. She said that she has room and would appreciate some company and that she wants to help. We got on very well yesterday and it might be a good plan for us all – get me out from under your feet, even if it's only for a few days or so.'

'I see…'

'What do you think?'

'Well, as long as you're both happy with that as an arrangement then it's up to you. It's a strange one, but then this is a bit of an unusual situation that we all find ourselves in. Have a think before you do decide anything, though, because you can stay here for as long as you like.'

'Anyway, I thought I'd better call you as you have a busy day ahead and I thought you'd want to get up early.'

'A busy day...' He frowned then ran a hand over his stubble. 'Shit!' He sat upright again. 'Surf for Sighthounds!'

'Yes, love, it's Saturday. Time to see all your hard work come to fruition.'

Nate swung his legs over the side of sofa and stood up.

'You might want to put something on, though, darling.'

Paula was averting her eyes and Nate realized he must have stripped off his clothes in the night. He grabbed the blanket and wrapped it around himself.

'Sorry, Mum, I'm not used to having someone else in the flat. Well… at least not someone who doesn't appreciate my penchant for sleeping in my birthday suit.'

'Now that's more information that your old mother needs, Nate.'

'I'm joking! About the appreciation bit anyway. But I do like to sleep without anything restricting me.'

'You were always the same, love. I'll make some tea and toast while you dress.'

Nate nodded then made his way to the bathroom. It was strange having his mother around but it was also nice. He liked knowing that he'd see her each day and that she'd be there for a chat or a cuppa.

Yesterday, she'd returned from her time at the greyhound sanctuary full of stories about Zoe and Monica and what a lovely time they'd had. He'd waited, expecting her to try to push him to admit that Zoe was adorable, but she hadn't. It was as if she'd either decided that Zoe wasn't a good match for him or she'd made up her mind to let things take their natural course. Nate shook his head. He had a busy day ahead and thinking about Zoe and how much he liked her would be counterproductive, so he needed to put thoughts of her to one side for the day and to focus on ensuring that the event ran smoothly.

Fifteen minutes later, Nate had eaten the three pieces of toast and two boiled eggs that his mother had made for him.

'I feel like a little boy again.'

Paula smiled at him.

'I like spoiling you. You might be six foot and have many female admirers, but you'll always be my little boy.'

Nate laughed. 'Okay, but don't tell anyone.'

'My lips are sealed.'

'I'm glad you had a good time yesterday at the sanctuary.' He thought he'd try to get her to talk about Zoe, just to see if she'd found anything out.

'Yes! I had such a wonderful time exercising the dogs and I helped out with some of the chores around the sanctuary while Zoe headed down to the diner. After that, I had tea and cake with the farmer's wife, Elena, and Mary Millar… the lady who owns the cottages up on the hill?'

'I know Mary.' Nate nodded.

'They're characters those two, especially Mary. She told me all about her niece Eve and how she got together with her tenant Jack and how happy they've been. It was so romantic!'

'So you had a good old gossip, Mum.' He raised an eyebrow.

'Not at all, just a good old natter. There's a difference, darling. Not a negative word was uttered. Mary also told me about Oli and Grace and how happy she was for them. Poor Oli went through such a hard time after losing his wife but then Grace came to Conwenna Cove with her parents and BOOM!' She clapped her hands together.

'I know all about it, Mum. I was here, remember.'

'I know, darling, but it's all so romantic. All we need now is for you and Zoe to admit your feelings and—'

'Mum! You have to stop this.' He sighed and put his mug down.

'But why?'

'I don't know if Zoe has feelings for me and it's all so complicated. One day, I'm on a high thinking we have a chance and the next, I'm doubting that she wants me at all. And it's not just her blowing hot and cold… it's me and my own confused feelings. Plus, I don't want to hurt her when I leave.'

'But you'll be back.'

'Yes… but don't you think it would be incredibly hard leaving her behind? And what about her? I know she's been hurt in the past so wouldn't she be worried that I'd be around other women and that she could get hurt again. If I wasn't going away then it would be different, but this is the way it is.'

'You don't have to go.'

Nate ran his hands through his hair then entwined his fingers behind his head. 'That's true, but if I don't go, I could end up resenting Zoe because I didn't.'

'Do you think you would? That doesn't sound at all like the Nate I know.'

'No, I don't. But I don't want to take that chance. I've always wanted to travel, or believed I did up to this point, and the time is right. I may not get the opportunity again. I don't want to be one of those people who regret things when they get older. I don't want to be sitting in some nursing home thinking about what I wish I'd done. And I don't want to die like Dad, young and sad because I never did what I wanted.' He started as the words left his mouth and he looked at his mum.

Her eyes had widened and her mouth gaped. 'What?'

'Mum… I'm sorry. I didn't mean that.'

'No. No, you did. You wouldn't have said it otherwise. What is it? Your father had regrets?'

Nate's heart pounded as he took in his mother's shock and he wished he could take the words back, but they'd been on his mind for a long time and now they'd been vocalized.

'I don't know for sure, but I think there were some things he wanted to do.'

Paula got up and went to the sink and placed her mug in it then turned around and leant against the unit. 'What did he want to do, Nate? He never said anything to me.'

'Or me. But not long after I came here, I was talking to Uncle Kevin about Dad. We were at the pub and we'd had a few beers. He said that growing up, Dad was very adventurous and a total daredevil. Apparently, Dad always talked about swimming the Channel and even swimming competitively but he never did. Then there were the maps and pictures in his study… I just got the impression that he'd have liked to see more of the world.'

'I wouldn't have stopped him… with any of that.'

'I know that and I bet he knew it, too. But you know what he was like.'

'He had such a sense of responsibility.'

'For you and me, and for paying the bills and making sure that everyone else was all right.'

'He was a good man. I hate to think that he didn't do what he wanted to.'

Nate got up and went to his mum and hugged her.

'He did in that he married you and he loved you and he was happy, but I think that he'd have liked to do a few more things with his time.'

'I didn't know that he wanted to travel extensively... he never confided in me that he had any unrequited longings, but we were planning a big holiday, you know... once we both retired. We were going to drive across the United States in a Mustang... cruise along Route 66 and all that.'

'I never knew that, Mum.'

She nodded against his chest. 'We were so looking forward to it.'

'You'd have had a great time.'

She leant backwards and met his gaze.

'But you are right. Your dad died suddenly and he didn't get to follow his dreams. I don't believe that everyone does, to be honest, but all we can do is try.' She placed a hand on his chest. 'You must do everything you want to do, Nate. Grab this life with both hands and don't regret a thing.'

'Yes, Mum. That's what I'm planning to do.'

And he knew that he had to travel and that he had to do it soon; he'd told himself for years that he should do it, possibly for his dad as much as for any other reason. But he also didn't want to regret not trying to make a go of things with Zoe, because he had a feeling that walking away from her would be a huge mistake.

–

Zoe was in the process of setting up her stall at the cove when a familiar voice made her pause.

'Hello, Zoe, can I give you a hand?'

'Hi, Paula, that would be wonderful, thank you. I need to get the boxed cakes set out and to display the banner advertising the diner. It took me a while to carry everything down here, so I'm feeling a bit frazzled.'

'I wish you'd called me, I could have helped.' Paula came around to Zoe's side of the stall. 'It looks amazing down here already, doesn't it?'

It was ten o'clock and people were already milling around the beach, waiting for stallholders to finish setting up so they could sample some of the local produce.

Zoe had needed to hold off for as long as possible before unloading some of the cakes because she didn't want the cream and the icing melting in the heat of the day. She'd left some more up at the diner and would have to go back for them later, but she suspected she'd need a brief respite as it was already very warm.

'It does look fabulous.'

Zoe gazed around her. There were around fifteen stalls set up along the beach, from one end to the other, and all were from local businesses in Conwenna and from nearby towns and villages. She knew there would be a similar arrangement at Luna Bay along the coast. That thought gave her a warm feeling, knowing that the inhabitants of this part of Cornwall had willingly taken part in the event to help raise funds for the greyhound sanctuary. Of course, there'd be money in it for them too, and the chance to promote their businesses, but it was still a good thing to do to help out a local charity.

All across the beach, banners rippled in the gentle sea breeze. The blue one for Surf for Sighthounds, featuring the sanctuary's logo of a greyhound silhouette enclosed in a heart folded then straightened out, calling attention to the event. Then there were the different coloured banners for the businesses, a beautiful rainbow that Zoe imagined would look incredible from above. Each stall had designed its own banner, from the greyhound sanctuary's one, to the one for the Conwenna Arms, where they would be selling alcoholic and non-alcoholic beverages, as well as a stall from Truro selling pots of locally grown berries topped with the milky-white ice cream from Foxglove Farm. The event that Nate had organized had brought businesses together and that could only be a good thing for the area.

The weather was perfect – the sky was a flawless blue, and the sun beamed down. That would be good for business too, and Zoe was glad she'd had the foresight to stock up on bottled water to sell.

Every so often, small white boats sailed past the cove, heading from Conwenna harbour to Luna Bay. Zoe knew that a few companies had worked together on this to ensure that tourists and locals could travel easily between the two locations of the event. The surfing would take part in Luna Bay because it was more open, and the cove was too small to accommodate all of the participants, their boards and the news crews that were covering the event.

Just as that thought crossed her mind, a helicopter passed overhead, going in the direction of Luna Bay. She suspected it was a news crew but it could be celebrities or even surfers being brought in for the surfing event.

Her stomach lurched. She was glad she had an excuse not to be over at Luna Bay; the last thing she would want would be to watch as the crowds cheered. Nate wasn't actually taking part because he had to travel between Luna Bay and Conwenna Cove all day, but she knew he'd probably oversee some of the children's bodyboarding lessons that Lucinda from Riding the Wave would offer at the cove.

It was certainly going to be a busy day, and she hoped with all her heart that it went well for Nate, because he'd worked so hard to organize everything.

–

Nate waited for the helicopter to land on the space cleared especially on the beach, then watched as the door opened and three men got out. They ducked as they hurried away from the helicopter and, when they were clear, it rose into the air again before flying away.

'There he is!' Lucinda pointed at the tallest of the surfers heading towards them.

'It's wonderful that you managed to get him to come. It'll be really good publicity for the event, Lucinda.'

'He said he was glad to help out. I know the media sometimes make him out to be an arrogant arsehole, but I think a lot of it's put on for the cameras.'

'He can be as arrogant as he likes as long as he draws the crowds.' Nate chuckled and Lucinda nodded.

'If only I was twenty years younger...'

'Hey, you never know. You could be exactly what he likes in a woman.'

'You think?' She gave a throaty laugh. 'I can't be bothered with all that, these days, Nate. Besides, the chicks who hang around the likes of him are simply too much for me to deal with.'

'The chicks?' He assumed a shocked look.

'I'm allowed to say that, Nate – I used to be one.'

Lucinda looked every bit the seasoned surfer today in her turquoise board shorts and black polo shirt with the Riding the Wave Surf School logo. Her blonde hair was a mass of loose curls and her sparkling green eyes twinkled with excitement. She would be giving lessons to children at the cove later on but had wanted to come with Nate to greet the professional surfers who'd agreed to take part for free.

'Finn!' Lucinda flung herself into the arms of the tallest of the men and he lifted her off her feet.

'Lucy-loo!' He gave her a few noisy kisses on each cheek then lowered her to her feet. 'So good to see you again, babe!'

Lucinda gestured at Nate. 'This is Nate Bryson who's organized the whole event.'

'Good to meet you, pal.' Finn shook Nate's hand firmly.

'Likewise. Thanks so much for agreeing to come.'

'My pleasure! Always happy to help out if I'm in the country and, of course, all publicity is good publicity, right?' He winked, and Nate was sure he'd seen the man's front teeth sparkle like a cartoon character's.

Lucinda introduced the other two surfers to Nate, then they made their way along the beach to where a caravan had been parked for them to be able to change and shower.

Nate had also arranged food for them and for the local press to interview Finn as part of the coverage of the event.

'If you need anything at all, just shout,' Nate said to Finn and his companions before they went into the caravan. 'Before I forget, Lucinda has arranged for your boards to be delivered to the door… seeing as how they couldn't travel with you.'

Finn grinned. 'Didn't want to weigh the helicopter down and risk plunging into the sea.'

'Certainly not.'

Nate smiled. 'See you later.'

Finn gave a quick salute then disappeared into the caravan.

'You think you can tear yourself away to head back to the cove?' Nate nudged Lucinda. 'I'm sure you can catch up with him later… if he hangs around, that is.'

'Ha!' Lucinda shook her head. 'You're so funny, Nate. Now, why don't you get back to your clipboard and your organizing, and I'll go and teach some kids how to ride a wave?'

'Sounds good to me.'

Nate gave her a peck on the cheek then they parted ways, Lucinda heading down to the water where she'd hop on a boat back to the cove and Nate to his base for the morning, a beach hut on the front where a desk and speakers had been set up to allow the commentator to explain to the public what the surfers were doing.

He could understand why Lucinda might fancy Finn Gallagher. He was a good-looking guy with his height, broad shoulders and lean physique, as well as his dark hair and eyes. He also had that air of arrogance that the successful sometimes have, one of extreme self-confidence. Nate had met guys like Finn before and he knew it didn't mean that Finn wasn't a nice person, but he didn't think he'd want to spend a lot of time in the man's company, especially if he was as keen on being in the public eye as his comment about publicity had suggested. If Finn was a jackass, Nate didn't want to find out firsthand; after all, Finn was supporting the event, and that was all that mattered to Nate.

Chapter 20

Nate watched as Finn and his companions paddled out on the water. It was early afternoon and the men had been in the sea for an hour already. On the horizon, bumps appeared on the water's surface and Nate knew exactly how the surfers would be feeling in that moment as their adrenalin started to pump. The surfers turned their boards around and paddled hard, then the wall of water lifted their boards, their speed increased and, after that, everything was lightning fast.

The three of them were upright, riding the great swells of the sea, their boards cutting through the foam as they twisted and turned, harnessing the power of the water before using it to head for the shore.

And Nate was there with them, adapting to become one with the water, riding the line and following it as it slowed once more.

Nate had chosen not to surf today for two reasons. The first being that he wasn't a professional, and although he was good, he wasn't in the same league as Finn and his friends, and the second reason was that he needed to be available to oversee the whole event, not just the surfing. When he surfed, it took over his thoughts and his heart and left little room for anything or anyone else.

That buzz from being in the water, the anticipation and expectation that came with waiting for the wave then the thrill of catching one, was so addictive. It was all about being in the moment because a slip in concentration would mean that you'd be flipped from your board and sent into the cold depths of the sea.

Nate watched as Finn repeated the process of paddling and waiting, knowing how good it felt to have the sun on his face, the breeze against his wet hair and the taste of salt water on his lips. He would always want to surf, but… something else had entered his life that gave him a buzz similar to that of surfing, only it lasted longer. That something was Zoe and how vivid everything was when he was with her, how incredible it was to hold her and kiss her and how painful it was to let her go. The uncertainty of not knowing if she'd ever want to be with him was like waiting for the perfect wave and worrying that he'd miss it if he didn't act at exactly the right moment.

Nate had never thought he'd find a woman who got to him like the sea did; he'd been convinced that the water would always be his first love, but rather than being consumed by a yearning to get into the water right now, he wanted to head back to the cove to see Zoe, to find out how her day was going and to check that she was all right.

He shook his head at the enormity of his realization. Zoe brought the same euphoria, happiness and fulfilment to his life that surfing had done for so long; just like a wave from the blue, Zoe had crashed into his life and changed his focus. Right now, it was as if he was paddling furiously, trying to intuit which direction was the right one to turn, as he waited for his instincts to tell him when the moment would be right to go for it. The moment when Zoe would be ready to let him into her life.

He knew it could go wrong and he could be dashed against the seabed if she refused to let him in, but he also knew that she was worth taking a chance on, because he suspected that he'd never feel this way again.

-

'Hello, Zoe!' Tom ran up to Zoe's stall and smiled at her from under his baseball cap. His skin was tinged blue with sunblock and he had ice cream around his mouth.

'Hiya, Tom. Are you having a good day?'

Tom nodded. 'I've been body boarding and swimming and bowling and had ice cream and Grace said I can have chips for tea!'

'Ooh! From Catch of the Day?'

He nodded. 'She said all the fresh air makes me hungry.'

'Me, too.'

'Can I have a drink, please?' Tom eyed the bottles of water in the open cooler next to her stall.

'Of course you can.' Zoe got one out and handed it to him.

'Chilly!' he squealed. 'Thank you!'

Zoe watched him run back across the beach to Grace, who was standing with Oli, Amy and Paula. Grace pointed at the bottle of water and frowned, then Tom turned and pointed at Zoe, so she gave a wave to show it was fine and she didn't want money from them. Grace gave her a thumbs-up in thanks.

It had been a fantastic day at the beach. She'd almost sold out and only had a few bottles of water left. There had been a lot of people at the cove and she hoped it had been just as busy at Luna Bay. The small white boats had travelled back and forth all day, ferrying people from one place to the other, and the path to the cove had been busy as people walked up and down it before heading into the village or to the harbour. Zoe had served people with all sorts of different accents, from the familiar, to those she had strained to place. It was good, as it meant that the event had brought people from far and wide, as well as from local towns and villages.

'I'll tidy up here, Zoe, if you want to stretch your legs,' Kierney said.

'Oh, thanks, lovely. That would be great.'

'No problem!'

Zoe padded along the sand, down to the sea and kicked off her flip-flops then walked into the water. It was cool and clear and she sighed as it soothed her hot skin and lapped gently at her ankles. She wished she had the confidence to go in deeper but the idea of being immersed made goosebumps rise on her arms. It wasn't something she could imagine doing again. The fear was too strong.

The buzzing of a boat engine caught her attention and a white speedboat rounded the corner and headed into the cove towards the shallows. There was a splash as Nate jumped down then waded towards the shore.

A day of being in the sun, even with suncream on, had darkened his tan. His thick hair was windswept and seemed even lighter than usual. In his board shorts and pale blue T-shirt, he was every bit the surfer and her heart ached. She wanted him, yet she knew wanting him was fraught with risk.

He spotted her and made his way over to her.

'Hello, freckles!'

'What?'

'You've got freckles all over your nose and cheeks.'

'Oh!' She ran her fingers over her nose as if she'd be able to feel them. 'I had factor fifty on.'

'Looks like the sun still got through. It's quite cute.' His blue eyes twinkled.

'How did the surfing go?'

'Extremely well. Luna Bay was packed. The local businesses will have raked in impressive profits today, no doubt.'

Zoe nodded. 'The diner has done well. I'm glad I decided not to open tonight though, as I'm shattered.'

'Me, too. The idea of a cold beer and putting my feet up is very appealing right now.'

Zoe wondered if he'd joined in with the surfing. She knew he'd managed to get some professional surfers to attend but was certain that Nate wouldn't have wanted to miss out on the chance to show off his own skills.

'Did you surf?'

'No. I thought about it but I had so much to do and I wasn't a patch on the likes of those guys.'

'So what happens now?'

'The day winds down, I suppose. I'm all for helping to tidy up here and getting everyone loaded up, then hopefully I can have that chilled bottle of beer in my hand by about eight.'

'Sounds good to me.'

'Well… why don't you join me?'

Zoe's heart fluttered. 'I'd like that.'

What was the harm in agreeing to have a beer with Nate? He'd worked hard to organize the day after all, and she enjoyed his company.

Another boat came into the cove and three tall men hopped off into the water, then jogged up the beach. Zoe's stomach lurched. Was that who she thought it was? It had been a while but… Suddenly, she grabbed at the front of Nate's T-shirt and pulled him closer.

'Hey, what's wrong? You look like you've seen a ghost.'

She raised her face and met his azure eyes as he wound his arms around her and his strong body pressed against hers. She slipped her arms around his neck and let him hold her tight. When he kissed her, she breathed him in, letting him take away the fear, the sadness and the shock at seeing her ex-husband wading towards her.

'Zoe?'

She flinched when he said her name.

'Is that you?'

Zoe gently pulled away from Nate and turned to find Finn standing right next to them.

'I thought it was! God, it's good to see you, woman!'

Finn grabbed her hand and pulled her into a bear hug. When he released her, she took a step backwards and glanced at Nate, who was staring at Finn with a quizzical expression.

'Nate, man, didn't she tell you?'

'Tell me what?'

'Well, I'm assuming the way you were holding each other means you two are an item, so I thought she'd have told you about me.'

'About you?'

Zoe's heart clenched as she looked from Nate to Finn and back again. What was he doing here? Why was he here after all this time?

'Zoe's my wife.'

227

'Ex-wife,' she added.

Finn shrugged. 'Semantics.'

'No, we are divorced.' Zoe stepped closer to Nate. 'We were separated a long time ago.'

Nate rubbed his eyes then pushed a hand though his hair. 'It's a small world.' He gave a laugh but it sounded forced.

'It sure is… Great day, though, Nate! Well done!' Finn slapped Nate on the back. 'Zoe, we need to have a catch up now I know where you're living.'

Zoe sighed inwardly. She hadn't exactly tried to cover her tracks so that Finn would be unable to find her, but had assumed he wouldn't care where she was. She'd hoped she'd never bump into him again but there was always a chance. If only she'd asked Nate what surfers were involved in the event but then… perhaps she'd been afraid to. She was a local business owner and Nate's friend: she could hardly have refused to get involved and she wouldn't have wanted to do so. Why let Finn control what she did now? What they'd shared was over a long time ago.

When fingers entwined with hers, tears pricked her eyes and she had to swallow hard.

'Come on, Zoe. We need to speak to a few people.'

Nate led her away from Finn and his companions and across the beach to a quieter spot behind the stalls.

'Are you okay, Zoe?'

She nodded.

'You sure? I had no idea he was your ex or I'd have…' He bit his lip. 'Well, I couldn't have asked him not to come because Lucinda went to a lot of trouble arranging it, but I could have let you know… if you'd have preferred not to bump into him, that is.'

'It's all right, Nate. It was bound to happen sooner or later. I can't say I'm delighted but I am glad you were with me.'

'Zoe?' He was still holding her hand and his smooth palm was comforting against her own. 'Will you tell me something? Honestly?'

'Of course.'

'When you kissed me just then… was it because you saw him coming?'

She sighed and dropped her gaze to her sandy feet. She'd abandoned her flip-flops in the confusion following Finn's arrival, and hoped they wouldn't be washed away.

'Nate, I panicked. I haven't seen Finn in ages and when I recognized him, my first instinct was to grab you.'

Nate gazed at her, a small line appearing between his fair eyebrows.

'I'm trying to work out if that's a good thing.'

Zoe was, too. Had she grabbed him because she'd wanted to make Finn jealous, or at least to show that she had moved on from his betrayal, or because she'd needed Nate's love and comfort in that moment?

'I think it is,' she said finally, and Nate pulled her close and held her.

'I hope so,' he whispered into her hair.

She stayed in his arms, listening to the powerful beat of his heart as he gently stroked her hair. His scent of fresh air, suncream and salt, mixed with a faint hint of sandalwood, was the best smell Zoe could imagine and she buried her face in him, wanting it to be just them and no one around them to complicate things. Their relationship was complicated enough already.

A shout from the other end of the beach snapped Zoe back to reality and Nate released her to take a look.

'Nate?' Oli was running along the beach. 'Nate?'

'I'm here, Oli.' Nate jogged over to the vet. 'What is it?'

'It's your mother, Nate. Come quickly.'

Nate glanced at Zoe and the fear in his eyes made her stagger. She knew, having lost his father so young, that this was one of his worst fears. And as he hurried back along the beach with Oli, Zoe followed them. Whatever happened, she'd be there for Nate as he had been for her.

Chapter 21

Nate pounded along the beach with Oli at his side, wishing it wasn't so difficult to run on the sand. His heart was in his mouth and fear raced through his veins.

When he reached the crowd that had gathered not far from the path, he pushed through, his manners abandoned as anxiety gripped him. And then he saw her.

'Mum?'

Grace was with Paula, supporting her with an arm around her shoulders, and Eve was offering her sips from a bottle of water.

'Come on, people, let's give Paula some space.' Oli waved his arms at the onlookers and people nodded then moved away, although a few remained at the edges, keen to see what would happen next.

'Mum?' Nate knelt in the sand next to her.

She blinked at him.

'Has anyone called an ambulance?' Nate asked Oli.

'There's a first responder up near the cliffs so Jack's gone to get him.'

'Nate?' Paula's voice was weak and he moved closer.

'I'm here, Mum. What happened?'

'Oh, love, I think I got a bit warm.'

Grace nodded. 'One minute she was chatting away and the next, she sank to the sand. I managed to grab her and helped her down but she turned ashen and definitely blacked out for a few seconds.'

'Well, drink some more water and we'll get you checked out.'

'Nate?' Zoe appeared at his side. 'Is everything okay?'

'I'm all right, Zoe. It was the heat, I think, love.' Paula offered a weak smile.

Zoe knelt next to Nate and, when she touched his arm, he glanced at her. He was grateful for her support. He didn't know how he'd cope if he lost his mum right now. He'd only just come to terms with losing his dad and even then, his grief was sometimes still so raw. And Paula seemed too young to be ill or to… to die. She had so much life ahead of her. Yes, she'd been through such a lot lately but she was a fighter and she deserved to enjoy her time, not to be torn away now when she hadn't even had a chance to experience the beauty of Conwenna Cove.

'Excuse me!'

Nate looked up to see the green and yellow fluorescent clothing of the first responder as he bobbed through the people on the beach. Jack was at his side, encouraging people to move.

'Right, what do we have here?'

The first responder knelt next to Paula.

Nate reeled off his mum's details then Grace explained what had happened.

'Okay, my name's Michael and I'm here to check that you're all right, Paula. I'm going to ask you some questions and run a few tests, then decide what we need to do.'

As Michael took Paula's blood pressure and ran through his questions, Nate watched his mum carefully. She seemed so small and pale and he knew, in that moment, that she really was as mortal as they all were. His mum had always been the strong one, the backbone of the family, the one he could ring or visit when he wanted a good meal or some advice or to know that someone was in his corner. And that was something he could never take for granted. Who knew how long any of them had? His father's early passing was a painful reminder of that. Nate had always striven to be a live-for-the-moment kind of guy. He had ups and downs, and losing his dad had given him more downs than before, but he'd always taken it for granted that his mum would be there.

But no one lived for ever.

He realized that Michael was speaking, so he shook his thoughts away and focused.

'I think Paula fainted because of the heat and perhaps because she hasn't eaten and drunk enough today. You could go to the hospital to be checked out but I don't think there's any need, seeing as how you're feeling a bit better now. What I do recommend is getting home, out of the sun, and having a good meal and plenty of rest. Paula, is that something you can do?'

'Yes, of course. I'm fine, I've just been a bit tired recently.'

'Well, you should go to your GP and have a full check up soon, but it's not an emergency.'

'I will.' Paula smiled at Michael.

'Okay… uh, Nate?' Michael said.

'Yes.' Nate stood up to face the first responder.

'You all right to get your mum home?'

'Definitely. And thank you.'

'I'm simply doing my job!' Michael smiled at him. 'I'll be nearby if you need anything else.'

'Thanks.'

'And if she seems to deteriorate in any way, phone for an ambulance immediately.'

'Of course.'

Michael walked away and Nate returned to Paula's side.

'Right, Mum, time to take you home.'

He helped her to her feet then scooped her up in his arms.

'Nate! Put me down!'

'Absolutely not.'

'This is silly. I'm perfectly capable of walking.'

'Not today, you're not.'

'I'll bring your things,' Zoe said, as she picked up Paula's bag and shoes.

'Don't worry about the stall, Zoe. We'll help Kierney tidy up,' said Grace.

'Thanks so much, Grace.'

Nate made his way carefully up the steep path. His mother was as light as a child and that made his concern for her deepen. He knew she'd lost weight and that it was down to the stress she'd been through, but she needed to start looking after herself. She was far too precious to become ill and he intended to make sure that she got stronger.

In fact, he knew now for certain that he wouldn't be going anywhere until he was confident that she was well again.

–

'Oh my goodness, Nate, it's boiling in here,' Zoe whispered to Nate, as soon as Paula had gone into the bathroom.

Nate looked around his flat. 'It does get warm but I always open up all the windows and the breeze soon blows through.'

'Why don't you bring your mum up to my cottage? I already suggested to her that she could stay with me. I have plenty of space and with the old stone walls, it's much cooler inside. And it's quieter up there, away from the main street.'

Nate nodded. He knew Zoe was right but it was also a lot for her to offer.

'But you don't know Mum that well and while it's really kind of you, what if…' He chewed his lip. He'd seen how well his mum and Zoe got on and even if it didn't work, they could always find another solution.

'Look, Nate, I'd enjoy the company. Your mum is lovely and it would be nice to get to know her better. Besides, with her experience, I'm sure she can teach me a thing or two about the catering business. She's probably got loads of tips and cheats I could use.'

Zoe's pretty brown eyes exuded warmth and kindness and a surge of emotion shot through him. He wanted to speak to her again about what had happened at the beach and about her ex, Finn, but it wasn't the right time.

'Are you sure?'

Zoe nodded. 'It would be a pleasure.'

'Okay, I'll pack her bag.'

When Paula emerged from the bathroom, Nate explained about Zoe's offer and his mum smiled.

'She did ask me, as I told you, but I hadn't made a decision on what was the best thing to do.'

'Well, if Nate's been sleeping on the sofa here, then it would probably be a good thing, Paula. He can have his bed back and you can recover in my nice, cool cottage.'

Paula smiled. 'That's true, and thank you so much, Zoe. But if I get on your nerves at all, you can kick me out right away.'

Nate shook his head. He couldn't imagine his mum getting on anyone's nerves. He would miss having her in his flat but he also knew that she'd be better off in Zoe's cottage.

Besides, it also gave him an excuse to be there too.

-

Zoe carried a tray bearing three mugs of tea into the lounge and placed it on the small coffee table in front of Paula.

'You did say no sugar, didn't you?'

'Yes, I'm sweet enough, or so Richard tells me!' Paula smiled but she looked drained.

Nate came in through the front door.

'Did you get through to him, darling?'

'Yes. He's incredibly worried as would be expected. He is your husband, after all, and he's going to get here as soon as he can.'

'Oh, no, Nate. I don't want him rushing here. Poor Richard has enough to do.'

'He's your husband, Mum, he needs to be at your side.'

'But I'm fine now.'

'Well, I'll call him again later and see what he says.'

'Thank you, darling.'

'Are you warm enough, Paula?' Zoe asked, knowing that even if it was scorching hot outside, within the thick walls of her cottage it could be chilly.

'Oh, yes, plenty warm, thanks, Zoe.'

Nate sat next to his mother on the sofa and Zoe took the chair. It was strange having people in her home, but not in a bad way. She usually pottered around alone, clearing up her own mess and no one else's, but now she had two people here and her lounge seemed brighter. She had popped upstairs to make up the spare bed for Paula when they'd arrived and she'd enjoyed hearing the low murmur of voices below as she'd straightened sheets and shaken pillows. The only other company she'd had at the cottage was Raven, and the gentle greyhound hadn't made much noise at all.

'Ooh! I forgot to ask if you wanted a biscuit.'

Zoe stood up but Paula raised her hand. 'No, I'm fine, lovely.'

'Actually, she will have a biscuit, Zoe, if you don't mind,' Nate said.

'Will I now?' Paula turned to face her son.

'Yes, because you need to put some weight on, Mum. Build yourself up a bit.'

Paula smiled, so Zoe went and fetched the biscuit tin.

'I don't keep anything fancy… just some digestives and Rich Tea fingers. Supermarket own brand. If I bought anything else I'd eat them in one go, you know, sitting here in front of the TV on my own.' Zoe bit her lip. Why had she said that? She sounded like a right sad case. 'Not that I mind being on my own, but there's no one to share the biscuits.'

She caught the glance that Paula exchanged with Nate and lowered her head as her cheeks flushed. Why did she keep digging herself in deeper? She didn't want them feeling sorry for her.

'Zoe, I would be exactly the same.' Paula smiled and Zoe's tension evaporated.

'Well, I am and I do.' Nate grinned. 'I eat all the biscuits and cakes and whatever else I bring home from the cafe. Otherwise it would waste and that would be a terrible shame.'

They drank their tea in silence for a few moments and Zoe had the opportunity to think about what it would be like to have people around, to have a family. She liked how it felt.

'So we need to get you to the doctor soon, Mum, for a check up.'

Paula nodded. 'It's Sunday tomorrow though, so it'll have to be in the week.'

'I'll give them a ring first thing on Monday morning.'

'Are you both hungry?' Zoe asked.

'I could eat,' Nate said. 'I need to pop back down to the beach first though, if that's okay? To check everything's finished and that it's been tidied up. Will you be okay here with Mum, Zoe?'

'Of course. I'll make us some dinner for around six, shall I?'

'That would be great. Mum, will you promise to rest?'

Paula nodded. 'I'll take a nap. I'm struggling to keep my eyes open.'

'Go on upstairs then, Paula. Nate has put your bags in your room for you.'

Paula finished her tea then stood up. She walked over to Zoe and gave her a hug. 'Thank you, sweetheart. You're a lovely person.' Then she hugged Nate. 'And you're a wonderful son. I still think you'd make a great couple.' She gave a giggle then climbed the stairs and, soon, Zoe could hear her moving around above them as she got things out of her bags then climbed into bed.

Nate stood up. 'I'd better go. And Mum's right, Zoe.'

'What, about us making a great couple?' Zoe's stomach did a flip.

'Uh… yeah… I was referring to what she said about you being a sweetheart, but I can see why she'd say the other thing.'

'You know… Finn and I… that was a long time ago, Nate. I was little more than a girl when we got together and he hurt me a lot. He cheated on me, but I think it was already over and the cheating was just confirmation of that.'

Nate nodded. 'You don't need to explain anything to me, Zoe. That's your past and your life and you don't owe me anything.'

But I want to!

'He's a good looking guy, though. He's very successful and must be earning big bucks.'

Zoe chewed her bottom lip. Was Nate feeling jealous or insecure?

'Nate… I would never go back to him. Not even if he wanted me.'

'He looked pretty pleased to see you.'

'He always looks like that. It's his default setting when-ever he sees someone he knows.'

Nate nodded, but Zoe wasn't convinced that it hadn't got to him. She hadn't set out to deceive him by not telling him who her ex was, but she hadn't expected Finn to turn up on her doorstep, either.

'Right, sooner I get down there, sooner I'll be back. You need me to pick anything up?'

'I have plenty in the freezer. Bonus of owning a diner.'

Nate crossed the room and stood right in front of her. 'I'll see you soon.' He pecked her cheek, paused as if he wanted to say more, shook his head then strode to the front door and was gone.

Two hours later, Zoe had pots bubbling on the stove and she'd set the small table in the kitchen with plates and cutlery. She'd popped some frozen bread rolls in the oven and the smell of bread filled the kitchen and lounge. She was humming to the radio, enjoying the opportunity to cook for others in her home, when there was a knock at the door.

Was Nate back already?

She patted her hair, licked her lips then went to answer it, thinking Nate could have let himself in but was probably too polite to just walk into her home, even though his mother was still asleep upstairs.

She swung the door open, hoping to find herself enveloped in Nate's embrace, because that was exactly where she wanted to be, and stopped dead. Because it wasn't Nate. It was Finn, standing there grinning and holding a big bunch of flowers and a bottle of wine.

And Zoe felt as if she'd been catapulted back in time.

Chapter 22

'Zoe!' Finn waved the bottle and the flowers. 'Great to see you again so soon.'

She took a deep breath, closed her eyes, exhaled then opened her eyes. But no, he was still standing there, looking devilishly handsome and confident as ever. The only difference was that his faded jeans were designer, his blue and white checked shirt was freshly ironed and the sunglasses holding his dark hair back from his face cost about a year's salary.

'Finn. How did you find my home?'

'I asked around. It wasn't hard, you know. Everyone knows the lovely Zoe, although I was asking for Zoe Gallagher not Russell at first. When did you change your name back?'

'As soon as I could.' She groaned inwardly at the thought that people in the village might now link her to Finn Gallagher. She had tried to keep her past private.

'Well, aren't you going to invite me in?' He peered behind her.

Zoe leant forwards and scanned the street. She couldn't see anyone she knew, so she ushered him in then closed the door quickly.

'Finn, not to be rude, but why are you here?' She folded her arms across her chest.

'Zoe, your body language is so hostile.' He tucked the wine under his arm then reached out and stroked her cheek. 'Why so angsty, babe? If I remember correctly, you used to get like this when you needed some Finn loving.'

Zoe ground her teeth together as a shudder passed through her.

'Finn... we are not together any more. Obviously! And you are in my home acting as if you still... as if we... oh, shit! You're acting as if the last few years never happened, as if you never screwed my best friend, and as if you have a right to speak to me like this. Which you don't, by the way!'

He flinched at the coldness in her voice but soon regained his smile. Smiling came easily to Finn.

'Zoe, babes, no harm meant. I just saw you earlier and wanted to say hi properly. Nice place you got here, if a bit...'

'A bit what?'

'Well, it's small, hon, isn't it? Not quite what I thought you'd want.'

'I love this cottage and I love that it's all mine.'

He nodded. 'Sure you do, babe.' He held out the wine and flowers. 'Anyway, these are for you.'

She accepted them grudgingly.

'Thank you. There was no need.'

'I don't suppose I could have a glass of something? Thirsty work supporting your local charity.'

'Of course.' Zoe softened a bit. He had come to Conwenna to help out with Surf for Sighthounds, so perhaps he had changed in some ways. The least she could do was offer him a drink.

She took the wine and flowers through to the kitchen, then got a cold bottle of white out of the fridge and poured some into two glasses. She turned to take them through but Finn was there, filling the doorway, a solid male presence, familiar and yet strange.

He cupped her face as she stood there holding the glasses. She tried to shake him off but the wine sloshed up the sides of the glasses and she worried she'd spill it.

'I'm sorry for what I did, Zoe. I never meant to hurt you, babes. Boy, do I miss you.'

Zoe held his gaze, stared deep into his dark eyes and took in the familiar contours of his face, his full lips and his shiny dark hair that she used to run her fingers through. He was as handsome as ever, and yes, she loved him. *Once*. But not any more. That emotion was long gone.

'I don't doubt that you do miss me, Finn. I missed you for a while, but you hurt me a lot and it took me a long time to get over what you did.'

He frowned, his black eyebrows meeting above his straight nose. He was so close she could see the thin white lines at the sides of his eyes from frowning in the sun and his aftershave, exotic and expensive as the clothes he wore, was turning her stomach.

'But you're over me... over us... now?'

'Let's go through to the lounge and I'll explain. You see, I went to see Amelia recently because I wanted to let go of the anger that's been holding me back and stopping me finding happiness with anyone else.'

'You're still angry?'

'No, not really, not any more. This is very strange, being here with you, and my initial gut reaction towards you was anger, but I'm keen to put the past behind us and, seeing as how you've turned up at my home, it's as good a time as any.'

Finn nodded and they went through into the lounge and sat down. Zoe told him what she'd told Amelia when she'd visited her in their hometown. And, for once, Finn listened, and didn't even try to excuse himself for what he'd done to hurt her.

–

Nate reached Zoe's cottage. He'd been back to the beach and to the harbour and everything had been as it should be. All the local business owners had ploughed in and made sure that the day didn't leave any scars on the beautiful landscape. He'd spoken to his contacts in Luna Bay and the council had ensured that a clean up was underway there, too. With it being a bigger place, they'd had more visitors for the surfing event, so had hired contractors to tidy up afterwards. The council employee Nate had spoken to had praised his efforts with the event and said it had been a great success.

So Nate had run the event successfully for a second time. He wasn't sure what the profits would be for the greyhound sanctuary as he'd handed the accounting side of it over to Neil Burton, who had more experience dealing with fundraising. All Nate could hope for now was that it had raised a decent amount to help the rescue dogs.

He paused outside the door and turned around and gazed at the beautiful view. The village stretched out below him, a higgledy-piggledy mix of colourful cottages, shops, restaurants and bars that led down to the harbour where he could see people milling around. The boats were still arriving in turn, bringing people over from Luna Bay as well as taking others back. The sun was sinking on the horizon, bathing everything in a warm golden light, and the sky was swathed in oranges, pinks and purples. It was the perfect end to a perfect day. Apart from his mother's fainting that was, but thank goodness she had only fainted and nothing worse.

Nate had telephoned Richard and he'd said he would ring Paula later on when she woke up. He could tell that Richard was really worried and knew he would have dropped everything immediately and come straight to Conwenna Cove if Nate hadn't reassured him that Paula was, in fact, all right and had fainted because of the heat and because she was in need of some rest. Nate intended on making sure that his mother did rest, which meant that he couldn't leave Conwenna as soon as he'd planned, because right now, he needed to be there for his mum.

He turned back to the door and raised his hand to knock but laughter from inside made him pause. Was his mum already awake? But that had sounded like a man's laughter, and from a man he didn't recognise.

He knocked quietly, so as not to disturb his mother if she was still resting, and Zoe appeared at the door.

'Nate… hi… everything sorted now?'

He nodded. 'All done.'

'Great.' She stood in the doorway as if blocking his path. 'Um, Nate… uh… while you were out, Finn turned up.'

Nate's heart squeezed. 'Oh… right. Do you want me to go?'

Zoe shook her head. 'Definitely not!' She grabbed his arm. 'Please come in. I wanted you to know he was here.'

Nate allowed Zoe to pull him into the hallway.

'He turned up and said he wanted to talk… to clear the air, so to speak. And we have.' She smiled and her whole face softened.

The floor seemed to shift and sway, as if Nate was suddenly on a surfboard, and he put out a hand to steady himself. Did this mean that Zoe and Finn were getting back together then? She looked so happy… so serene.

'Are you okay?' She touched his arm and he stared at her hand, the hand that he had held and that she had run through his hair, the hand that would once have worn Finn's wedding band.

'Yes.' He rubbed his eyes. How could this be happening? He'd thought he would have a chance to speak to Zoe tonight and that they could finally make some sense of what was happening between them but now… it was too late. Finn had arrived and Zoe's heart was already his. He pulled his arm away from her and tried to ignore the flash of hurt in her eyes. 'I just felt a bit surreal there for a moment. Probably need some water.'

Zoe nodded. 'It was a busy day for you. Come on in and I'll get you a cold drink.'

Nate followed her inside even though he wanted to leave. He couldn't walk away because his mum was in there sleeping, and she'd expect him to be there when she woke up. Besides, Zoe had been so kind offering to put her up and Nate didn't want to seem ungrateful. It was an ironic mess because, normally, he'd have been delighted at the prospect of spending an evening with another surfer, talking about prime locations for boarding and the best waves they'd caught. He could even have arranged to meet up with Finn somewhere when he was travelling, but, as it was, the thought of even speaking to the professional surfer brought a sour taste to his mouth. This man had once been married to Zoe and he had hurt her. That was bad enough, but now it seemed that he'd walked into her life and invited himself to her home as if he had the right.

Nate took a steadying breath as he entered the lounge and tried to relax his face. This wasn't like him. Nate never got angry or resentful or… was this jealousy? He didn't do such negative emotions. It wasn't who he was and he didn't like it at all. But he had never been in a situation like this before, and he had no idea how he was going to deal with it.

'Nate! Great to see you again.'

Finn grinned at him from the sofa and Nate assessed the scene that lay before him. There was an open bottle of wine on the table and a huge arrangement of beautiful flowers in a vase on the side that hadn't been there before Nate left. Finn's body language suggested that he owned the room, as he lounged with his knees apart and one arm across the back of the sofa – presumably where Zoe had been sitting, because her glass was on the table next to Finn's.

If this was going to happen then it was going to happen, and Nate realized that he'd have to accept it. He thought the world of Zoe and would be happy for her if this was what she wanted. Of course, Nate knew he could be reading things into the situation, but his nature was to take things at face value and there were so many signs here in Zoe's lounge. Perhaps this was why she had been reluctant about getting involved. She'd known Nate was going away and perhaps, even if she was unaware of it, she'd been nursing feelings for her ex that had never waned.

It happened. It was life. Nate would survive.

Zoe returned with a tall glass of water that clinked with ice cubes and handed it to Nate, then she perched on the sofa. Nate noted that she took the cushion that was as far away from Finn as she could. Was that for Nate's benefit, or how she'd been sitting before he arrived?

'Nate, I was just telling Zoe that love is a wonderful thing and that once you find the person for you, you should never let them go.'

Finn smiled at Zoe and Nate had to fight the anger that surged inside him. An anger he had never experienced before, let alone had to struggle with.

Zoe looked down at her hands where they fidgeted nervously in her lap.

'You know… I was an idiot in the past and I didn't treat Zoe very well, but we've talked it all through, haven't we, babe?'

Zoe nodded and glanced at Nate before leaning forward and grabbing her glass of wine.

'And we've sorted it all out now, so there won't be any more hard feelings.'

'Great.' Nate focused on relaxing his hold on the glass of water so it didn't shatter in his hand. 'That's good news.'

'Yes, we had a good chat and I hope we can put it all behind us now and move on.' Zoe sipped her wine then placed the glass back on the table. 'Because that's what's best for everyone really, isn't it?'

She met Nate's eyes and his heart threatened to shatter into a thousand tiny pieces. Was it best for him? Best for them? It didn't feel like it.

'After all,' Zoe continued, as she stood up and walked over to Nate, before sliding her arm around his shoulders.

'I told Finn that we're very happy together and I don't want any bitterness from my past spoiling that.'

Nate frowned as he looked up at Zoe. Her hand gently caressed the back of his neck above his shirt collar, and her thigh was pressed against his arm.

'We are?' he asked, confused.

'We are, Nate. You and me. Gosh, you must have had too much sun today.' She gave a light tinkling laugh and the pressure of her hand on his neck increased.

He slid his left arm around her waist and held her tight. 'Sorry… I'm not with it at all. Yes, you know I love you, Zoe.'

She leant over and kissed his head. It was akin to being in an American television show from the Eighties. It was all so… forced. Surely Finn would see through it all?

But, no. Finn was pouring himself another glass of wine and smiling. He really was the epitome of a laidback surfer dude.

They sat together for another half an hour while Finn finished his wine. Zoe stayed sitting on the arm of Nate's chair. Then Finn's mobile started playing some loud rock hit and he swiped the screen before shouting into it. Music came from the other end and a voice that sounded female, then Finn ended the call with a, 'See ya soon, babe!'

'I'd better be going.' Finn got up and tucked his mobile into his pocket. 'Thanks for the wine and the chat, Zoe. Hope you two will be happy and that you enjoy your travels.'

He crossed the room and when Zoe stood up, he enveloped her in a bear hug. Nate suppressed the flicker of irritation that sparked in his gut. Finn was leaving and he believed that Zoe was with Nate, so he had no need to be jealous now. When Finn released Zoe, he hugged Nate too, and Nate realized that Finn did this to everyone he encountered; it was just his way.

Zoe walked Finn to the door and Nate stayed where he was to give them a moment alone, but she soon returned to the lounge.

'Well, that's that then.' Zoe sighed, then flopped onto the sofa.

'I guess it is.' Nate nodded.

'Nate, I'm sorry about all that then… you know, the being-in-love stuff, but he saw us on the beach and the kiss and—'

'My goodness!' Paula exclaimed as she descended the stairs. 'How long did I sleep?'

'We'll talk later, yes?' Nate nodded at Zoe, and she smiled in return. 'Hi, Mum, how're you feeling?'

His mum padded towards him wearing a pair of floral silk pyjamas and a matching lightweight robe.

'I am actually rather hungry!' She clapped her hands. 'Again. It's being in Conwenna Cove, I swear!'

'I'll get a move on with dinner,' Zoe said, as she got up. 'I was keeping it warm until you woke.'

'Sounds perfect,' Paula replied. 'Let me lend a hand.'

Nate watched as his mother and Zoe went into the kitchen and he released a long sigh. He knew relationship stuff was complicated and that he'd avoided it for a long time because of that and other reasons, and yet… as he listened to Zoe and his mum chattering away in the next room, he believed that, for Zoe, he would be happy to complicate his life. His reaction to Finn being around had revealed that to him with startling clarity: he hated the thought of Zoe being with anyone else. The question now was whether Zoe would want to be with him.

It was high time he pulled himself together and found out.

Chapter 23

Zoe spent the next three hours laughing with Nate and his mum. They were such good company and Zoe thoroughly enjoyed having them in her home. She'd kept herself to herself in Conwenna Cove but now she was questioning that decision. Sometimes it was better to let people in, surely? Human company was enjoyable and she felt lighter than she'd done in months. Of course, throughout dinner in her small kitchen, she'd been able to snatch glances at Nate, to watch how his cheeks flushed slightly whenever his mother praised him or told Zoe about something he'd done in his childhood. Zoe had also caught him looking at her a few times and, when she'd met his eyes, she'd melted at the intensity of emotion she'd seen within them. Nate was handsome, it was true, but he was so much more. He was bright and funny and sweet and kind. The fact that Zoe found him hot as hell was just the icing on the cake.

But where was this going? Where could it go? She knew that she wanted to hold him and kiss him and wake up next to him, but was it possible? Or would he soon head off to foreign climes leaving her nursing another broken heart and trying to rebuild her life?

'Right, I shall help you with the dishes then I think I'm going to have to go back to bed. I feel so lazy, but I'm really tired again.'

'Mum, it's not lazy, you've been through a difficult time. You need to rest and recover and that will take a while.' Nate squeezed his mother's hand. 'And, anyway, I'll do the dishes seeing as how Zoe made dinner and you helped.'

Paula smiled at her son, then at Zoe. 'Okay then. I know when Nate's not going to let me plead my case.' She got up and kissed Nate on the head, then did the same to Zoe. 'Goodnight, you precious people. Thank you for a delicious dinner, Zoe, and for letting me stay. That bed is amazing.'

'My pleasure, Paula.' Zoe got up and started carrying things to the sink, and Nate did the same.

'Go through to the lounge, Zoe, and sit down. You cooked so this is the least I can do.'

'Absolutely not! You've had a very busy day, Nate. If we do this together, it will be much quicker.'

They worked as a team, washing, drying, then putting things away. Although it took a while, Nate soon seemed to know his way around her kitchen.

'Shall we go and sit outside? Enjoy the last of the light?' Zoe asked. 'I have some wine left in the fridge. And it's not the bottle Finn brought.'

Nate smiled and she knew she'd just read his mind. He wouldn't have wanted to drink the wine Finn brought with him. There'd been an undercurrent of something emanating from Nate when Finn had been there and she wasn't sure, but she thought it could have been bordering on jealousy. Although why would Nate be jealous? He had no reason to be.

They took a fresh bottle of white and two glasses outside and sat on the wooden bench in Zoe's front garden. The light was fading fast and the moon was already visible. The air was heady with the fragrance of honeysuckle from the plant climbing along the trellis fixed to Zoe's fence, and from the roses that grew either side of her front door.

They sat in silence for a while and sipped their ice-cold wine. Zoe enjoyed having Nate sitting next to her, his large frame filling the bench, so close she could touch him if she moved a fraction.

So she did. Because she wanted to feel his heat and to hold his hand.

And he didn't flinch; he just let her take his hand, then he raised hers to his lips and kissed her fingers, one by one, gently, in a way that made her yearn for more.

'Nate...'

He turned to meet her gaze.

'Zoe.'

'When are you leaving? Is it next weekend?'

'It was going to be but I can't leave until I know Mum is all right.'

'Then you'll be around for a while?'

He nodded.

'That makes it more difficult.'

'What?'

'Trying to resist what I feel for you.'

'Then don't.'

'But... it will be even harder letting you go.'

'Then come with me.'

'How can I do that?'

'I have an idea.'

'You do?' Her heart soared but her feet stayed firmly planted on the ground. What possible solution could he have to their dilemma?

'Trust me.'

'But I can't leave the diner. I can't give my business up.'

'I wouldn't ask you to. But what if I could find someone reliable and experienced to run it for you while we're away?'

Zoe scanned his face, wondering who he was thinking about and whether she'd be able to trust them enough to hand over her livelihood so that she could travel with this wonderful man. The glimmer of hope made her belly fizz with excitement.

'Like who?'

'Look… it's not something I've spoken to her about, not yet, because it hadn't occurred to me before, and I might be overstepping the mark here, so please tell me if I am, but I was thinking that my mum could be a possibility.'

'Your mum? To run the diner?'

He nodded.

'Would she want to?'

'Well, that's what I need to check first, but I didn't want to suggest it to her if I hadn't run it past you first. You could hate the idea and that's fine, but I'd prefer to find out before I speak to her about it.'

'She has lots of experience.'

'Bucket loads, and I know she'd do a great job. I mean… I know she's my mum and I'm biased but she does know the catering business inside out. Plus, she's at a loose end now and looking for work.'

'It sounds like a wonderful idea… but I'd hate to get my hopes up then find out that she doesn't want to do it.'

'Well, let me speak to her and see what she says.'

'Of course.'

'Now… can I kiss you, Zoe?'

'I thought you'd never ask.'

He took her wine glass and placed it on the wooden decking next to his then turned to her and gently cupped her face. He ran his thumbs over her chin, her lips, and moved closer until their lips met. The world around Zoe swirled and all she was aware of was Nate's touch, Nate's lips and Nate's intoxicating scent.

When Nate finally pulled away, Zoe knew she never wanted to let him go again.

'You know…' Nate's voice was husky with passion. 'I would offer to show you the rest of my tattoo now but you have company inside.'

Zoe laughed. 'We didn't see foresee that as a problem, did we?'

He shook his head.

'Bit of a passion killer having my mum in the next room.'

'Yes, I wouldn't be able to… relax.'

'Me, neither.'

'Let's just stay out here for a while then, shall we?'

'Please.'

Nate took her hand and pulled her to the grass next to the bench, then he lay down and she lay next to him with her head resting on his arm.

'Let me impress you with my knowledge of the night sky.'

So he did. And Zoe tried to focus on the dark sky with the twinkling stars and the bright arc of the moon and she nodded and agreed and made all the right noises. But in reality, she was only aware of the warmth of Nate's body, and the muscles in his arm beneath her head. She didn't care if anyone walked past and saw them lying on her front lawn. She didn't care if the air grew cooler or if they didn't finish their wine.

All she cared about was being close to Nate and knowing that he wanted her as much as she wanted him. That was all that mattered to her right now and that, for once, Zoe was living entirely in the moment.

–

The next morning, Zoe crept down the stairs, keen to avoid waking her guests. Paula was sleeping in her spare room and Nate had ended up spending the night on the sofa. Zoe would have loved to sleep in his arms but neither of them believed it would be appropriate with his mother under the same roof, and as they were still in flux about their relationship, they didn't want to confuse matters any further.

When she reached the bottom of the stairs, Zoe peered into the grey light of the lounge. She could make out Nate's bulk on the sofa but couldn't see which end his head was, as he was completely covered with the blanket she'd given him. She approached him on her tiptoes, holding her breath, and leant forwards to get a better look. Reaching out, she gently lifted a corner of the blanket then gasped as Nate opened his eyes and smiled at her.

'I thought I heard you coming down.'

'I tried to be quiet.'

He pushed the blanket away and her breath caught as she saw he'd removed his shirt to sleep. His chest was bare except for a dusting of golden hair and his arms were strong and defined. Her eyes moved lower and desire shot through her as she saw the thin line of hair that ran down his belly and disappeared beneath his jeans.

'You looking for more of my tattoo?' he teased, and she blushed at being caught admiring him.

'Sorry!'

'Don't be. I like you looking at me.'

He slid his arm around her waist and pulled her onto his lap so she was pressed against his chest and his chin rested on her head.

His scent overwhelmed her and Zoe's yearning for him stirred again. She turned her head and pressed her lips to his warm skin and breathed him in, filling her lungs with Nate. It was euphoric, the effect that being so close to him had upon her, and she wished she could stay like that all day. She lifted her chin and met his eyes. She knew she could easily surrender to loving this man and that she would be happy being with him, but she didn't know how long that would last or if he would always feel the same way, and that was such a big risk to take.

She curled her arms around his neck and hugged him tight, wanting him yet holding back because she knew if she made love to him then she would be completely lost, and that thought terrified her. Yet it also made her want to get lost, to give herself to him, because she wanted to feel alive again as only Nate would be able to make her feel.

'Zoe?'

'Yes?'

'I think I just heard a car pull up outside.'

'You did?'

He nodded.

'I'm not expecting anyone.' She sighed, hoping it wasn't Finn back again.

'I think it could be Richard. He said he'd come asap and I'd be surprised if it wasn't today.'

'But it's so early.'

'He's worried about Mum.'

'Of course.'

Zoe slid off Nate's lap, then went to the front window and peered out into the hazy morning light.

'There's a black car out there. I can't tell what it is but it looks expensive.'

'Sounds like my stepfather.'

'Wouldn't they have seized his car, too?'

'He might have borrowed it from a friend if his Audi has been taken by the bailiffs.'

Nate came and stood behind her with his hands on her shoulders. His warmth penetrated her pyjamas and dressing gown and she wished they had more time alone. But for now, at least, they had company.

The car door opened and a man in his fifties got out. He looked well groomed in his lightweight pale blue summer suit and white shirt open at the neck, but his face told a different story. The skin that covered his neck was loose, as if the flesh underneath had fallen away in mere weeks. His brown hair, streaked with white, was combed back from a square forehead and, in the early morning sunlight currently burning through the haze, Zoe could see it was thinning at the temples.

'That's Richard.'

Zoe glanced at herself. 'I'd better get dressed.'

Nate nodded. 'You go on up and I'll let him in and put the kettle on.'

Zoe headed upstairs. From her room above the hallway, she heard Nate open the door and greet the older man and take him through to the lounge. She pulled on jeans and a T-shirt then quickly brushed her hair before going to the bathroom.

When she descended the stairs, Nate and Richard were nowhere to be seen so she went through to the kitchen and found them sitting at the table. Both men wore serious expressions.

Nate looked up. 'Ah, here she is. Richard, this is Zoe, the wonderful friend who invited Mum to stay.'

Richard got up and shook Zoe's hand. 'I'm very pleased to meet you, Zoe, and extremely grateful for your hospitality towards my wife. I can't tell you how worried I've been.'

'No problem at all.' Zoe smiled. 'I'm glad I could help.'

'Do you want tea, Zoe?' Nate asked.

'It's all right, I'll get it. You two carry on talking.'

Zoe filled the kettle and while she waited for it to boil, she tried not to listen to the men's conversation. She hummed to herself as she got bread out of the cupboard and put a few slices into the toaster before fetching the butter and marmalade from the fridge. She busied herself with making breakfast and when it was done, she placed it on the table.

'Shall I go and wake Paula?' she asked.

'Actually, would you mind if I went up?' Richard asked. 'I've missed her dreadfully and I'm desperate to see her. I didn't want to disturb her too early but if I take her some tea and toast, I'm sure she won't mind.'

'She'll be delighted to see you.' Nate smiled.

Zoe loaded a tray with two mugs of tea and a plate of toast, then gave it to Richard and he slowly climbed the stairs.

'Come and sit down.' Nate nodded at the chair Richard had just vacated.

Zoe did so, then picked up a piece of toast and took a bite.

'You probably overheard some of that?' Nate asked.

'I tried not to.' Zoe grimaced. 'But I did hear some of what he said. It doesn't sound good, does it?'

Nate shook his head. 'They've lost the house and Richard's business, but at least Mum has got her redundancy that she put aside in her name, and her pension, although she doesn't want to claim for a few more years.'

'Well, that's something.'

'It's just such a shame, though, you know… to get to their time of life and lose everything.'

Zoe nodded. It must be absolutely awful. She'd been in her twenties when her life had been turned upside down, but to be in your fifties must be even worse. Poor Paula… and she was such a lovely person. Her old fear surged inside at the thought of how vulnerable being in love made her. Would she want to risk losing everything again?

'So what will they do?'

'Cause Mum as little stress as possible. Richard agrees on that.' Nate rubbed his face. 'You know… it's like life is going to get you one way or another. There was my dad, dying in his fifties and not getting to enjoy his later years.

My dad had so many things he wanted to do but… he didn't because of his sense of responsibility towards Mum and me. He wanted to travel and swim and…' He shook his head but his words had lodged in Zoe's chest. Nate's father had been tied to his family and not done the things he wanted to do, then died suddenly.

Nate was so lost in his worries that he was oblivious to the fact that he'd shared something with Zoe that instantly concerned her. What if Nate settled down with her then regretted it? All her fears could be realized then: she would be holding him back and she could be hurt if he left her. It was a minefield.

'Then here's my mum and Richard, still alive but they've lost their home, their car, their financial security. I mean, yes, they have Mum's pension but it won't go far, and her redundancy money is, like… what they need as a buffer against poverty.'

'I'm so sorry, Nate. It's a terrible situation and I don't know what to suggest.'

Nate reached across the table and took her hand. 'Me, neither. All they can do really is try to get jobs. If I go away soon, they can always take the flat above the cafe and—'

'They can't live there, Nate. It's far too small for them. Besides, what about your aunt and uncle?'

'I don't think they'd mind. Kevin and June get on well with Mum, and I'm sure they'd be happy to help.'

'But long term it's not a great solution is it?' Zoe stroked Nate's fingers with her thumb. She wanted to comfort him, to make it better for him, but she didn't know how and she was so afraid.

'Thank you.'

'What for?'

'For being here. I'm so used to thinking things through alone but it's nice to be able to talk about this with you, even if it is all so difficult'

He gazed at her and Zoe's heart swelled.

'I'm happy to be here with you, Nate. Look… I can definitely give your mum some hours at the diner once she's feeling better and I'm sure Richard can find something local. That is, if they want to move to this area?'

'Richard said he does. Said they need a clean slate and that he can't face seeing the home they shared everyday knowing someone else is living there.'

'I know this all seems dreadful right now, but they do still have each other. And they have you.'

'You know… you're right. They could have millions in the bank but if they didn't have each other, then what would be the point? Zoe… I'm not going to go away.'

'What?'

'I can't. Not now. I'm going to stay in Conwenna. I need to be here for Mum and I want to be with you.' He bit his lip as the enormity of what he'd said hung in the air between them.

'You want to be with me?'

Zoe's head spun and she held his hand tighter, as if he could stop her drifting away from the table. She ran through how life could be for them if he stayed. They could live together, go out together on walks and exercise the greyhounds; maybe they'd even adopt a dog or two. They could have candlelit picnics under the stars and maybe he would propose. Would she say yes? She smiled at the thought. They could think about having a family a few years down the line and their babies would be beautiful, blond and blue-eyed like Nate and…

263

She stopped the carousel of her thoughts and got off.

What the hell was she thinking?

Nate was a beautiful, free-spirited man. He needed to travel, to open his wings and fly before it was too late. She couldn't bear the thought of him having regrets as his father had. He loved to swim and to surf, and Zoe couldn't join him in those things. Nate was gorgeous and could have any woman he wanted and Zoe would be holding him back. Yes, he would stay a while longer in Conwenna for his mother but then he needed to go and be free, not be tied to someone with her baggage and her insecurities and her scars. She automatically rubbed her forehead under her fringe as if to remind herself of what she was and what she'd never be. In many ways, Nate was like Finn. They were water babies, at one with the sea and that was something Zoe would never, ever be.

'Zoe? What is it? You don't look… happy about that idea.' He frowned at her and she shook her head.

'Nate, I'll help with your mother's situation and always be here for you…' She took a deep breath. 'As a friend.'

He scanned her face and her cheeks burned. This was agony, like jumping off a cliff; it went against everything her heart wanted and yearned for and yet it had to be done because Zoe knew she couldn't let another man hurt her. And she didn't think Nate would knowingly hurt her, but to wake up one day in the future and see him staring at the horizon with longing in his eyes would truly break her in two. She wouldn't survive heartbreak again and she suspected it would be a hundred times worse losing Nate than it was losing Finn. So she had to do this; she had to be brave.

'As a friend? Zoe… what the hell? I thought you wanted to be with me. I thought we had a future together. All the things I've said to you about my parents and travelling and… I've never felt this way before.'

Zoe bit her lip to stop it wobbling. She wouldn't be the reason for Nate's regrets and she couldn't allow him to break her heart, so she was putting an end to this now.

'I can't do this, Nate. I thought I could but I can't. I'm not ready for this kind of… commitment.'

'You're not ready? Are you saying that you don't feel enough for me to take a chance on us?'

She nodded but she couldn't meet his eyes.

'Okay, Zoe.' He pulled his hand away and tucked it into his jeans pocket. 'I understand. If that's how you feel then I won't try to change your mind. And thanks for the kind things you've said about Mum.' He stood up. 'I'd better go. I have to get to the cafe.'

Nate left the kitchen but Zoe stayed where she was, pressing her nails into her palms and swallowing hard. She knew if she followed him to the door and he said one kind thing, that she would weaken and beg him to love her. So she stayed where she was and only let the tears fall when she heard the front door closing and knew that Nate had gone.

Chapter 24

The next four weeks passed in a blur for Zoe. She focused on working at the diner, exercising the greyhounds and trying not to think about Nate. It was hard. Very hard.

Paula stayed on at her cottage and had started working a few shifts at the diner, and Zoe was finding the older woman's help extremely valuable. They talked about everything and anything but never about Nate, unless it was an anecdote about his childhood or Paula praising him for something. Zoe suspected that Nate had told his mother that things would not progress further between him and Zoe and therefore not to make things awkward by trying to talk about them. And Zoe was grateful for that because talking about Nate would bring everything to the surface again and she couldn't let that happen. Suppressing it was all that was keeping her going.

Zoe had also done her best to avoid Nate, checking with Paula when he might visit the cottage and ensuring that she was out. She spent even more time at work just to be sure, and avoided the sanctuary when he would be there. Even though they lived in the same village it was actually easier than she'd thought it would be. After all, before they'd got to know each other, Zoe hadn't seen that much of him at all.

But tonight, Kevin and June were holding a farewell party at the cafe as Nate was leaving the next day. He was heading off into the world and would be gone for about six months. Zoe knew that this would help her to recover. Knowing that she wouldn't risk bumping into him, that he was thousands of miles away, would help her to heal and when he returned, she would be well and truly over him. Then they could go back to being friends.

Of course it would be that easy...

Richard had been back and forth to Conwenna Cove and had even stayed over a few times at Zoe's cottage, but she knew he was keen to find somewhere cheap for him and Paula to rent. Zoe liked having the company and her nightmares had vanished since Paula had been around, but she was realistic enough to know that the husband and wife would need their own space. Paula treated her like a daughter and Zoe would miss her when she'd gone; there was something so comforting about having another human being around.

Zoe blinked at her reflection in the bedroom mirror. She'd gone with jeans and a lemon and navy polka-dot blouse paired with flat, yellow thong sandals with white flowers that sat above her big toes. Her skin was golden from all the walks in the fresh air and the time she'd spent in her garden encouraging plants to grow and thrive, especially the herbs she was growing for use in the diner. There was a definite comfort to be found in gardening and she'd even been up to Mary Miller's cottage to learn how to grow certain herbs and vegetables. Mary had green fingers and was a good teacher.

While there, Zoe had spent time with Eve and baby Iain, and she'd enjoyed watching the baby change over the weeks. It was amazing how quickly he learnt to do things and his small, smiling face always lifted her mood.

'Are you ready, Zoe?' Paula called from downstairs.

'Yes, just coming!'

Zoe could have made an excuse not to go but she owed it to Nate and to his mother. Not turning up would seem petulant and as if she was bitter, and that simply wasn't true. She was happy for Nate and wanted to wish him well.

Downstairs, Paula smiled at her.

'Oh, Zoe, you're such a pretty girl. *Woman*, I mean.' She laughed. 'I just see you as being so much younger than me. I'm the same with Nate.'

Zoe smiled.

'Uh... Zoe... before we go, I need to speak to you about something.'

'Okay...' Zoe's heart sank at the seriousness of Paula's expression.

'Sit with me on the sofa.'

When they were sitting down, Paula took a deep breath then released it slowly.

'Zoe, I've been trying not to say anything but as Nate is leaving tomorrow, I have to. I can't let this moment pass and do nothing.'

'Paula, please, it's better to let it go.'

Paula shook her head. 'I can't, darling. I care about you both far too much for that. Nate is hurting. I see it every day in his eyes and even in how he moves. He's different, sad, damaged.'

'Damaged?' Zoe scanned Paula's face. 'By me?'

'No, love, not you but by the situation. My son loves you, Zoe. He'd give up this whole travelling plan to be with you if you said the word.'

'But I can't do that to him, Paula. He needs to go, to do this and enjoy it. If he stayed, then one day in the future it could emerge as resentment and I couldn't bear that. Imagine if we had children and he suddenly realized that he'd missed out. And, alternatively, if I said I'd wait for him then he'd be tied to me. He's too good a man to cheat and I'd worry that he'd have regrets. I've seen how women are around him and he could find someone far better for him than me.'

Paula placed a cool hand on top of Zoe's and shook her head. 'He won't find anyone better than you, love. You are the one for him. There is no one better. Why do you doubt yourself so deeply? You're beautiful, intelligent and a successful businesswoman. You're kind, funny and sweet. You have so much going for you and I would be delighted to have you in my family. Listen… I haven't told Nate this but I was never impressed with any of his… flings. They were never good enough for my son but… you! You are perfect.'

Zoe allowed Paula's words to sink in. 'That's a huge compliment, Paula, but there are things about our situation that run alongside feelings. Even if I admitted to Nate that I love him too… and went away with him, because that would be the only way I could allow this to happen so he didn't miss out… then I couldn't just up and leave the diner. Who would run it for me? Who could I trust?'

Paula nodded, then she squeezed Zoe's hand. 'I have a proposition for you. Please hear me out, then you can think about it this evening.'

'Okay.' Zoe smiled, hoping with all her heart that Paula had a magical solution to their situation, and then, that there was a chance Nate would still want her after she'd turned him away.

–

Nate smiled at the party guests and checked that everyone had a drink. He was pleased that they'd all turned up to say goodbye but, in spite of the fact that tomorrow he was heading to catch a flight to Australia, his spirits were low. This should be an exciting day and he knew that once he was on that plane, heading towards his destination, then he'd feel better. At least he hoped he would. His mum was feeling much better: she was visiting the greyhound sanctuary regularly and hoped to adopt Monica once they were settled, and Richard had managed to secure several interviews nearby, so hopefully he'd be earning again soon.

Everything was looking more positive.

Except for one thing.

Nate was leaving Zoe Russell behind, and it was the hardest thing he'd ever done.

But she didn't want him and she'd made that quite clear.

He sipped from his bottle of beer then went to the door and stepped out into the late August evening. The balmy air was fragranced with the sweet scents of the flowers in the cafe window boxes and the mouthwatering aroma of fish and chips that drifted along from Catch of the Day, further along the main street. He was going to miss Conwenna Cove while he was away: the familiar sights, familiar faces, his mum, aunt and uncle… and, of course, he was going to miss Zoe. His mum had suggested that he could well meet someone else and that there were plenty more fish in the sea, but he'd known from her tone that she didn't believe it, that she knew Nate didn't give his heart away easily and that Zoe was the first woman he'd fallen for. Another person couldn't easily replace those kinds of feelings and Nate knew he wouldn't want anyone else. Zoe was special, she was unlike any other woman he'd ever met, and he couldn't imagine another woman coming close. He'd have sacrificed the travelling to be with her and had suggested it but she'd turned him down and it had cut him to the core. He was annoyed with himself for being hurt, wanted to shake himself out of this love-sick behaviour but, try as he might, it just wasn't happening. Nate had it bad.

He looked up and spotted his mum and Zoe strolling down the road. In her simple outfit of jeans and a blouse, Zoe looked beautiful and, once again, he wished she cared for him as he did for her. He knew if she asked him to stay this evening that he'd do it, even if he lost the money he'd paid for the trip.

'Mum!' He hugged his mother then kissed her cheek. 'You look fabulous. And hello Monica.' He stroked the greyhound's chin. His mother had been taking the dog out and about with Neil Burton's blessing, so they could get to know each other better, as well as to socialize Monica, and he loved seeing their bond.

'Hi, Nate.' Zoe smiled at him and his heart lifted a fraction.

'Hi, Zoe.' He leant forwards to kiss her cheek and breathed in her vanilla scent laced with the heady tones of her jasmine shampoo.

'Looks like a good turnout,' Zoe said, as she peered through the cafe window.

'All the regulars.' Nate nodded. 'Can I get you both something to drink? Uncle Kevin has a well-stocked bar for the night.'

'Gin and tonic, please, Nate.' His mum smiled.

'I'll have the same, thanks.' Zoe ran a hand through her shiny hair. 'With plenty of ice, please.'

'Coming right up.'

Nate turned and went inside to make their drinks. This evening was going to be challenging but he also wanted to make the most of it. It would be his last in Conwenna for a while and his last in Zoe's company, and he intended on savouring every moment so that he had the comfort – or would it be torment? – of the memories while he was away.

–

Nate returned with two gin and tonics and handed them to his mother and Zoe.

'Thanks.' Zoe sipped her drink and sighed. 'That is so good!'

'It's the extra splash of gin I add in after the tonic.' Nate smiled. 'It gives it a special finish.'

'You can make me more of these...' Zoe winced. Why had she said that? It wasn't as if Nate was going to be hanging around, was it?

'You should come inside and see everyone.' Nate nodded at the cafe, where the sounds of laughter and voices drifted through the open windows and out to the street.

'I think I shall. See you in a moment.' Paula raised her drink to them then went inside.

'That was subtle.' Nate huffed.

'She means well.'

Zoe's heart pounded now that she was alone with Nate. They were separated from their friends by just the glass of the cafe windows but it felt as if they were miles away. Everyone inside had a smile on their face as they ate, drank and chatted to friends and family but outside, the air between Nate and Zoe was tense and filled with things as yet unsaid, with the fear of holding on yet the devastation of what letting go would mean.

'She does.'

'Nate… your mum had an idea.'

'About tonight?'

'No. About us and about… about how I could come away with you.' She took a shaky breath. He could well have changed his mind and she could be making a fool of herself.

'And?'

Zoe met his bright blue eyes and her whole body tingled with love, need and longing for what they could share. She was afraid to say more yet terrified of letting this opportunity pass. *No more regrets* was the mantra she wanted to live by.

'Paula said that if I trust her enough and that if I want to come with you, then she'll run the diner for me.'

Nate nodded slowly. 'After we spoke about it before, I was going to bring it up with Mum but she got there first. There didn't seem much point in me raising it because you… well, you said we couldn't have a future… but Mum

273

told me she's been thinking about it for a while. I told her it was too late and that you'd made your decision.'

'Is it too late?'

He shrugged. 'I can't play this game, Zoe. I can't bear to feel like you want me then you don't. Tell me now, what is it that you want to do?'

Zoe chewed her bottom lip. She'd asked herself this since Paula made the offer. It was a big ask, not of her but of Paula. But now that Richard had a job possibility on the horizon, and they planned to settle in Conwenna, then it was perfect timing. Paula had experience in catering and of running a business and Zoe had seen over recent weeks how good Paula was in the kitchen, at serving and with customer care. In fact, the customers had loved her and she'd been generously tipped. It was almost too good to be true, and Zoe knew she'd never have another similar offer.

'I'm... excited, nervous, nauseous... so many things. I have so many thoughts swirling around in my head and I don't know which one to pick. This is such a big thing for me, Nate. And for you.'

'Zoe...' He took her free hand between both of his. 'I know what I want. I want you to come with me. But only if you are certain that it's what you want.'

She nodded, blinking hard to clear the tears from her eyes. Now was not the time to let emotion consume her.

'Look, Zoe. No pressure, okay?' He leant forwards and pressed a soft kiss to her lips. 'Enjoy this evening, eat, drink, be merry and be my friend. My mother loves you and will do whether you come with me or not.'

'I don't want her to think I don't trust her.'

Nate held up a hand and shook his head. 'She won't think that. Mum has been through enough in her lifetime to know that not all decisions are easy. She's given you an option but I understand that it's a big decision to make. Remember, I'm not leaving a business behind. I work for my uncle and aunt; I can leave knowing that they'll be fine without me. But for you, this is a big deal. I know why you need to think this through. If you come, then you'll make me very happy but if you don't, then I'll see you again.'

'But not for ages.'

He nodded. 'But it's not… the end. It doesn't have to be. Or maybe it does. It's up to you now.'

Zoe tried to smile but her cheeks ached with emotion, because they both knew that if she stayed then it would be the end of them. How could it not be?

'Now come on inside and see everyone.'

He led her inside and she forced a smile to her lips for the sake of their friends who had gathered to wish Nate bon voyage. Tonight was about Nate and the people who cared about him and Zoe would focus her energies on ensuring that he enjoyed the evening.

Chapter 25

The drinks had flowed with the conversation, laughter had bubbled and the atmosphere had been warm at Nate's farewell party. It was a good gathering and Zoe had enjoyed herself thoroughly, listening to stories of Nate's time in Conwenna and his childhood. It was obvious that all who knew him loved him and that he would be missed.

Zoe stepped quietly away from Grace and Oli and slipped out of the cafe door into the cool night air. From outside she watched Nate. He was deep in conversation with Jack and Kevin, with Paula and June looking on, smiling indulgently at the man they'd both helped shape. Nate was lucky to have had a family who loved him. It was so sad that his father wasn't there to see the man he'd become, but at least there were people around him who cared.

Zoe had missed not having a close relationship with her parents and although she'd tried to push the thought away, it did surface at times like this. It was hard to suppress it when she knew how good it would feel to have a family of her own around who loved her. But that was never going to happen: her own parents and grandparents had gone and she was alone in the world, and there was no point wishing otherwise. She had friends now, and although those friendships were in their early days, she felt accepted for who she was. And that was a gift she'd treasure.

She needed to walk. She'd only had two drinks but her head was fuzzy with the weight of her thoughts so a good walk in the evening air would help clear it. She hoped.

She walked down to the harbour, enjoying the sea breeze on her face and as it toyed with her hair. The lights were on around Conwenna and the moon was out, a silver orb that brightened the cloudless sky and gave the harbour an eerie silver glow. She passed the diner, the wine bar where she had spent a pleasant evening with Nate until those two girls had come along, then walked towards the cliffs. She climbed the path to the top and stood gazing down at the beach. So many things happened on that sand; it was a central point in the lives of the locals. It had seen picnics, carols, proposals, homecomings... and been part of the Surf for Sighthounds event. She had developed so much fondness for this place and it was now rooted deep in her heart. The thought of leaving was actually painful and she knew that whatever she decided, she would always come back.

'Zoe!'

She turned to see Nate hurrying towards her. She waved at him, admiring him in spite of her musings.

'I wondered where you'd gone. One minute you were standing there talking to Grace and Oli and the next you'd disappeared.'

'I needed some air.'

He nodded.

'Haven't you still got party guests at the cafe?'

'A few stragglers, but most have gone home now. Oli and Grace needed to get the children home and Jack and

Eve don't like to leave Iain with Mary for too long. They say it's because they don't want to take advantage of Mary's generosity but, to be honest, I think they miss him. Even when they're away from him for a few hours. It's like they don't want to miss a thing.'

'That's understandable.'

'Zoe, I'm not here to pressure you but I wanted to give you something.'

'You did?'

'Then I'll leave and you'll be free to decide on your path.'

'Nate, I need to tell you something before I make any decisions. I need to tell you a bit more about me.'

'I'm listening.'

She took a deep breath then released it. 'Okay. Here goes.'

–

Nate listened to Zoe without taking his eyes from her face for a second. His heart ached for her as she spoke and he longed to pull her into his arms, but he knew she needed the space to tell her story. So he pushed his hands into his pockets and listened.

'Look at me, Nate. Really look at me for a moment.' She pushed her fringe aside and waited. 'Horrendous, right?'

He shook his head. 'You're beautiful, Zoe.'

'With this?' She pointed at the raised scar on her forehead that was silvery in the moonlight.

'Yes, of course. You think a scar would put me off you? It's not ugly, Zoe, it's part of you.'

She shook her head. 'I hate it.'

'Zoe, there's no need. We all have scars.'

'But this one represents all that was wrong in my past. I know I've told you some of the details and spoken to your mum about them—'

'Mum never repeats what she's told in confidence, Zoe.'

'Well… I just want you to understand that I'm afraid. I trusted Finn and that was a mistake and I know you're different but… I couldn't bear to lose everything again. You're lucky in that you have your mum and June and Kevin, but I have no one else to fall back on.'

'Zoe, Finn was an idiot. He made mistakes that I would never make.'

'He made me feel worthless,' she whispered.

Nate's hands curled into fists in his pockets as he watched the pain that crossed Zoe's beautiful face. Even though it was dark, the glow of the moon meant that he could see every nuance of her features and he was fighting the urge to hug her hard. How anyone could fail to love her, he didn't know.

'No one has the right to do that to you and no one ever will do again.'

'Nate… you need to know that because of what happened when I was knocked off my surfboard… I can't even go into the sea up to my waist. What kind of companion would I be to travel with? I can't swim with you, surf with you or any of that. You deserve someone who'll be able to jump off cliffs into the sea, who'll scuba dive and surf and… and…'

'Zoe, do you think this changes how I feel about you?'

'Well, doesn't it? Don't you need things in common to be with someone? I forced myself to like these things for

Finn and look what happened. I tried to be something I wasn't.'

'You're amazing, Zoe. You're so many wonderful things and you don't even know it. I hate that Finn and your parents didn't make you feel like the incredible woman you are but it's their loss. You have so much ahead of you now and I promise you, life will be better.'

'The diner was the first thing I've had in my life that made me start to believe in myself. I'm still not exactly confident about me… but as a businesswoman my confidence is growing.'

'So it should, but so should your belief in yourself as a wonderful human being.'

'Nate, you're too good to be true.'

She smiled and it lit up her whole face.

Nate stepped forwards and opened his arms and she stepped into his embrace. He lifted her and gazed into her pretty eyes then they kissed, softly at first, before the kiss deepened. The weeks of need and passion and doubt and fear emerged in that kiss, leaving them both breathless and longing for more.

'I wish you could come back to the cottage with me.'

Nate gave a husky laugh. 'Me, too. But not with Mum there. I couldn't… you know…'

'Nor me.'

'And besides, you still need to make your decision.'

'As long as you want me I think I already know.'

He shook his head then kissed her softly. 'Sleep on it. Be certain.'

He buried his face in her neck and breathed deeply, savouring her scent and the softness of her skin. Her arms were tight around his neck and her body was pressed against his and he wished they could stay that way for ever.

When he gently released her, she slid down to her feet and he took her hands.

'I'll be leaving at six in the morning to make my flight.'

'Okay.'

He reached around to his back pocket and pulled out a white envelope that he handed to her. 'This is for you. Whatever you decide to do will be for the best. But remember that you're amazing and that you're going to be all right from now on.'

'But, Nate, I—'

'No need to say more. I'm going to go now to give you some space.' He released her hands then turned to go, but there was one more thing he needed to say.

'Zoe…'

'Yes?'

'I love you.'

Then he forced himself to leave her standing there on the cliff top, his white envelope glowing in her hand in the light of the moon and his heart placed in her hands. Whatever she decided to do now, Nate would accept.

But as for his heart, that would always be hers.

—

Zoe watched Nate walk away then turned over the envelope he'd given her in her hands. It was sealed. If she opened it, her life could change right then and there. If not, she'd never know.

Nate loved her. He'd said as much. The way he held her and kissed her made her feel loved. It was up to her now. Was she prepared to take the chance?

She shivered and realized that she was suddenly very tired. Her bones ached and her head throbbed and she wanted to close her eyes and rest, just for a bit. The gin she'd drunk was probably wearing off and leaving her a bit dehydrated and in need of some water. She'd go home and get a drink then open the envelope.

Back at the cottage she opened the door, wondering if she'd need to explain to Paula where she'd been, but the older woman had left her a note on the coffee table. Nate had told her that Zoe had gone for walk so she'd made herself a cup of tea and gone up to bed.

She ran the tap and filled a glass then took it through to the lounge and sat on the sofa. She drank some of the water then she picked up the envelope and pressed it to her chest as she lay back on the soft cushions. She closed her eyes for a moment, waiting for the throbbing in her head to subside, and ran her fingers over the smooth paper of the envelope.

Nate had written her name on the front – she could feel the impression that his pen had made. Whatever was inside could determine her destiny. She'd take a look in a moment.

She simply needed her head to clear so she could better absorb the information…

–

'Zoe?'

Zoe emerged from the dream in which she'd been paddling in the sea, deciding whether to go in further, deeper, or if it was too much of a risk. Nate had been calling her from a boat out on the water, waving her towards him and promising that she'd be safe with him, that he wouldn't let anything hurt her. She'd wanted to go, knowing that he would protect her from harm, but something had been holding her back.

'Zoe?'

She opened her eyes and blinked, then sat bolt upright and stared at Paula.

'What time is it?'

'Ten past five. I just came down to get some water. I thought you might want to go up to bed.'

'Five in the morning?' Zoe gasped as she realized that it was dawn's grey light seeping through the curtains.

'Shit!' She'd fallen asleep. She scrabbled around looking for the envelope from Nate, and found it under a cushion. 'I only closed my eyes to wait for the headache to go. I was going to open this.'

'What is it?'

'It's from Nate.'

'Oh… right. You haven't looked inside then?'

'No.'

'Are you going to?'

'Yes.'

Zoe's heart pounded as she tore the seal then looked inside. There was a brief note and what appeared to be a plane ticket.

'Oh…' She held them out.

'Read it.'

'It says, "Zoe, I didn't want to make you feel obliged to come with me but seeing as how Mum offered to help out at the diner, I thought you might want this. I bought it a while ago when I was hopeful that there was a possibility of you deciding to accompany me."' She gasped. 'This must have cost him a fortune!'

'Never mind that! What else does it say?' Paula's eyes were wide.

'"If you've decided not to come away, then that's fine. As long as you are happy, that's all I want. However, if you want to come, I'll be leaving the cafe at six in the morning.'"

'What are you going to do?' Paula asked.

'I'm going. But I haven't packed. And my passport... I renewed it last year, just in case I needed it, but it's buried in my cupboard upstairs and... and...'

'Jump in the shower and I'll help you pack. Come on! You can make it!'

Zoe paused for a moment, overwhelmed by the emotions flooding through her and making her tremble. 'But the diner?'

'I've got it, love. I'll treat it like it's my own until you come back.'

'But the books and the banking and—'

'You showed me how you do it all, remember? And what I don't know now, I soon will do. You have a competent staff there, you know. And I'm only a phone call, email or video call away, Zoe. The world is much smaller these days.'

'But it would feel huge if I wasn't with Nate.'

'Exactly, so go shower!'

Thirty-five minutes later, Zoe had managed to drink a mug of tea that Paula had made for her and packed everything she thought she might need into her old backpacking rucksack that she'd used when touring the country with Finn. She'd thrown on jeans and a loose grey top over a vest and pulled on her trainers. She didn't exactly look glamorous but was ready to travel.

'Okay, I think I have everything.'

'Except the ticket.' Paula handed her the envelope she'd left on the coffee table.

'Paula, you're an angel. And you'll stay here with Richard when he comes to the village? Look after my cottage?'

'I would love to. I'll treat it as I would my daughter's home. If we find somewhere suitable to move into while you're away, I'll still keep an eye on this place, though, I promise. So don't worry about a thing.'

Zoe blinked hard.

'Come here.' Paula hugged Zoe hard and when she released her, her eyes were glistening. 'Now, let's get you down there.'

They hurried out of the cottage and down the main street with Zoe giggling nervously. She couldn't believe what she was doing, that she was actually leaving to travel with Nate. This was crazy, impulsive and… it felt so good!

They reached the cafe and she saw that the door was open. Inside, June was sitting at a table drinking coffee.

'Hi!' Zoe waved, hopping from one foot to the other.

'Hi, Zoe. Hi, Paula.' June stood up. 'Everything all right?'

'I'm meeting Nate here.'

June frowned.

Zoe turned to Paula and the older woman shook her head in confusion.

'I'm so sorry, Zoe, he's already gone.' June walked towards her. 'He left five minutes ago. Said he had to make a stop first. Kevin's driving him to the airport.'

The cafe seemed to swirl around Zoe and she grabbed the back of the closest chair. He was gone? Already? But his note had said six. He hadn't waited… He was gone.

Her heart shattered into a thousand pieces…

'Zoe!'

She turned to the cafe doorway.

'Nate?'

'You came!'

'I did.'

He crossed the cafe in two strides and she threw herself into his arms. 'I thought you'd gone.' Her cheeks were wet with tears. 'June said you were stopping off on the way so you left early.'

'I was. I stopped at your cottage. I couldn't leave without saying goodbye, in spite of my intention to leave and not look back. Kevin's car was parked at the harbour so we walked down to pick it up then went straight to your cottage. When there was no answer, I guessed you might have come here. I'm so glad you did!'

Zoe couldn't speak. Her throat was tight with emotion and she held on tightly to him, knowing that she'd have been devastated if he'd left without her.

'It's okay. I'm here, and I'm never going to leave you.'

Zoe nodded, keeping her eyes on his handsome face as if she feared he'd disappear if she looked anywhere else.

'I love you, Zoe, and from here on out, it only gets better.'

Epilogue

Life didn't always work out as you planned. Zoe knew that before she left Conwenna Cove to travel with Nate. Plans, hopes and dreams were things you wanted to happen, things you strove for, but nothing was guaranteed. Leaving with Nate had been a risk in that she didn't know how things would develop between them, and she had left her diner in Paula's care. However, the diner had thrived and Paula had done as she'd promised, keeping in touch with regular updates, and even videos and photographs.

Zoe had enjoyed a wonderful few months travelling with Nate. They'd been to Australia, Hawaii and San Francisco, travelling where their mood had taken them, using the open tickets that Nate had bought. It had been magical and they'd laughed a lot, kissed even more and got to know each other very well.

But about nine weeks into the trip, Zoe had started to feel unwell. She'd been queasy and tired and had assumed she'd picked up a bug at one of their stops. When she hadn't improved, Nate had insisted on taking her to see a doctor and what they'd found out had floored them both.

So they'd decided to return to Conwenna Cove earlier than planned. It was, they thought, the best course of action considering the circumstances, and it would be better for Zoe to be at home so she could rest.

'Shall we do this?' Nate asked, as he held out his hand.

'Best way to see in the new year if we can't do it in New York, Paris or Sydney.'

'Not this time, perhaps, but we'll have other chances…'

Zoe nodded, grateful for Nate's warmth and his reassuring presence. Even after fourteen weeks of being constantly together, they hadn't grown tired of each other and were closer than ever. Zoe loved him, she had no doubt in her mind now, and with every day that he cared for her, loved her and treated her so well, her defences lowered a bit more. She knew it would take a while longer for them to completely disappear, as she'd taken a long time building them, but she was convinced that Nate would soon clear them away for ever.

They stood outside the cafe and peered through the glass. Only four months ago, they'd been right there, wondering what their future held.

Now they knew.

'Let's go in.'

Nate pushed open the door and the warmth from inside enveloped them.

'Nate! Zoe!' Paula squealed as she rushed towards them and hugged them both in turn. 'I'm so happy you're home!'

'Good to see you both.' Richard smiled at them from under a golden party crown. 'Can I get you a drink?'

'Please,' Nate said.

Richard went to the counter where Kevin and June were serving drinks and returned with two flutes of champagne.

'Nate!' June spotted them and hurried over, hugging them with as much gusto as Paula had. 'Oh, my darling, I had no idea you were coming home yet!'

'Well, we thought we'd come back and surprise you all, seeing as how… well, we wanted to come home.'

'We were ready,' Zoe added, squeezing his hand.

'Did you know they were coming back?' June asked Paula.

'Only yesterday. They let me know because of the cottage and the diner, but they asked me to keep it quiet so they could surprise everyone.'

'We weren't certain until last weekend, anyway,' Nate explained, 'and we thought it would be a nice surprise.'

'Well, that it is!' June clinked her glass against theirs. 'And just in time to see in the new year.'

An hour later, after many hugs and well wishes from friends and family, Nate and Zoe accompanied everyone who'd been at the cafe down to the beach. They took several coolers filled with bottles of champagne, plastic flutes, battery-powered lanterns and plenty of blankets.

On the way there, they stopped at the new bench on the cliff top. It was in the exact spot where Zoe had sat with Raven and where she'd sat that day when she'd watched Nate surfing and worried that he'd hurt himself when he'd fallen off his board. So much had happened since then and her life was very different now. On the back of the bench was a brass plaque. Zoe leant closer and read the inscription:

This bench is dedicated to the rescue greyhounds of Conwenna Cove. You leave your pawprints on our hearts.

Zoe ran her finger over the words and whispered, 'Love you, Raven.'

'You all right, Zoe?' Nate asked, his arm around her waist.

'I am and this is wonderful. Did you arrange it?'

'What Zoe wants, Zoe gets.' He smiled. 'You said that a bench would be a good idea to remember all the grey-hounds that have passed through Conwenna, so I asked Neil to take care of it while we were away. We can come and sit here anytime we like.'

'Thank you. You really understand me, don't you?'

Down on the beach, Kevin counted down to midnight using his mobile phone and all the locals cheered.

When everyone had hugged and clinked plastic flutes and celebrations were well under way, Nate took Zoe's hand and led her away from the others, to a quieter spot on the sand.

'I'm sorry we had to cut our travels short,' Zoe said, as she gazed into his eyes, their depths illuminated by the moonlight.

'I'm not.'

'Honestly?'

'I had a great time, Zoe, but only because I was with you.'

'But don't you wish you were still out there, seeing all the wonderful sites the world has to offer.'

'I can see everything I've ever wanted right here in front of me. Besides… who are we to deny our destiny.'

Zoe giggled. 'Our destiny?'

'Well, it could be the champagne but I'm feeling pretty happy about what life has thrown our way.'

'Me, too. And I didn't have any champagne.'

Nate wrapped his arms around her and they looked out at the water where the surface sparkled like diamonds as the moonlight caressed the surface.

'When shall we tell them?' Zoe asked.

'When we're ready.'

'Well, we know everything's okay after the tests, so how about now?'

Nate released her, then cradled her face in his hands.

'Are you sure? There's no going back once they know.'

'No going back now, Nate. Only forwards.'

He kissed her gently and she melted against him, her love for him tingling in every part of her body and wrapping itself around the two tiny babies that lay nestled inside her womb.

Nothing was certain in life and their contraceptive method hadn't been, either. But Zoe didn't mind and neither did Nate. In fact, once they'd got over the initial shock at the hospital in San Francisco where Zoe had been examined, suspecting she'd contracted a virus or something equally nasty, they'd been unable to conceal their delight. This was meant to be, Nate had told Zoe, and she'd agreed.

'Before we tell them, Zoe, I wanted to let you know what I've been thinking. Even if we don't go abroad for a few years, we can still use the campervan to travel around the country. It was, after all, something I aimed to do with my dad, so I'd love to do that with you and our twins.'

'There's certainly plenty of room for car seats and changing bags.'

'And possibly even a rescue greyhound.'

'Why not two? I hear they're great with children.'

'Sounds perfect.'

'Let's go and share our happy news.'

'Come on then, but I'm warning you, Mum will be way too excited.'

'I'm banking on it!'

She held Nate's hand and they walked towards the people they cared about, the people who'd been there for them over the years, and those who would be there for them in the future. Conwenna Cove was a community, a sanctuary, a home.

And Zoe was a part of it.

In fact, she knew for certain now that her heart would belong for ever with Nate and their family, and for ever at Conwenna Cove.